6 RM

THE GENIUS OF AFFECTION

Also by Marilyn Sides

The Island of the Mapmaker's Wife
& Other Tales

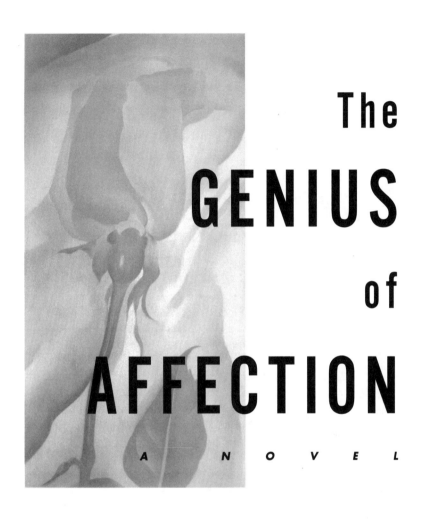

The
GENIUS
of
AFFECTION

A NOVEL

MARILYN SIDES

HARMONY BOOKS · NEW YORK

Published by Harmony Books, 201 East 50th Street, New York, New York 10022. Member of the Crown Publishing Group.

Random House, Inc. New York, Toronto, London, Sydney, Auckland www.randomhouse.com

Harmony Books is a registered trademark and Harmony Books colophon is a trademark of Random House, Inc.

Printed in the United States of America

Library of Congress Cataloging-in-Publication Data
Sides, Marilyn.
The genius of affection : a novel / Marilyn Sides.—1st ed.
I. Title.
PS3569.I4449G46   1999
813'.54—dc21   99–21339
ISBN 0-517-70444-7
10 9 8 7 6 5 4 3 2 1
First Edition

For Marcelle
and
Luc-Léon Clements

I would like to thank my excellent readers: Carolyn Morley, Marcelle Clements, Margaret Cezair-Thompson, and Kathryn Lynch. Gail Hochman and Dina Siciliano have been so helpful and most encouraging. I would like to thank Wellesley College for the faculty award that helped me finish the novel and to give a belated thanks to the Yaddo Corporation for the month in Saratoga Springs that enriched my writing life in so many ways.

THE GENIUS OF AFFECTION

CHAPTER 1

How lucky, how comforting to have a lover on one's fortieth birthday. Lucy Woolhandler had managed, at the last minute, to meet the deadline. The idea of such a deadline she knew to be ridiculous. She wasn't living, was she, in an updated Jane Austen novel, where the problem was to get the pathetic heroine married, not at twenty-two or twenty-five, but at forty? She laughed to herself while driving home from work on this hot, muggy September afternoon. Probably rain. Fortieth-birthday weather.

At thirty-nine, though, dying of loneliness had not been funny, especially not with the prospect of three more deadly lonely decades almost assured her. Lucy had set out to rescue herself, a rescue executed in something like a panic. Six months ago, she had found David Shure. He had been right there under her nose at the Institute where she worked: an unmarried man, an attractive man, a good man. Although he was in his late fifties, the pressing fact of their joint need to be rescued—for she soon persuaded herself that he, too, had to be rescued—made the difference in their ages of little consequence. She had lingered at receptions to talk to him, then she asked him to dinner, and then they fell in love.

As she drove past a garden nursery, its yard forlorn except for a few straggling plants, Lucy—moved still by the spirit of rescue—turned in. As a birthday present to herself, she bought two marked-down perennials, a lavender stunted in its small pot and a coralbells with brown-edged leaves and brown crispy little flowers perched on high thin brown stalks. Packing them into the car, though, she considered her cross purposes. These "second-year perennials," in garden lingo, would take that long to come up with any flourish, yet in two years, maybe she would be living with David, sharing a garden with David. So it was foolish to buy the plants. Still, once she got home, she knelt down and took great pleasure in making room for them in the garden, grown so compact with all her other finds. For one year—two years at the most—the plants would have a home, until she moved and the landlord let the garden go back to weeds, or asphalted it over, as did many of her neighbors in Somerville, one of those small towns edging the city of Boston. The thought of abandoning her garden made her sad. Maybe she wouldn't have to abandon it, though. Maybe she could transplant the flowers, make room for them in David's yard.

Turning the sprinkler on to give the garden a good drink, even though it might rain later, she glanced at her watch. Six o'clock. David would be here at seven. She had to hurry. David didn't like to be kept waiting.

She showered, put on a bit of makeup. Her age showed in her mirror face. Her mother's cheekbones would always give it a strong shape, but already there was a fleshiness around the chin, squaring it off. In her bedroom, pushing back hanger after hanger of silk, linen, velvet, and wool, Lucy was unable to make up her mind what to wear. She should get rid of all these old clothes, except for one or two or three plain cotton things, some sort of monastic habit. A habit would save her time getting dressed. She would save lots of money, too, by not buying any more clothes. At forty the balance of her savings account, three hundred dollars, wasn't much of a safety net. Lucy pictured her safety net as the tiny net used to scoop goldfish from their bowls.

She wouldn't need much money for the rest of her life, would she? In the last twenty years, she had already done everything costly, in terms both of money and of the expense of spirit, that she had once ambitioned to do as a certain kind of novel-reading girl growing up in a quiet middle-class suburb. She had taken so many trips to Europe and Central America. She had worked many boring, ill-paying jobs so she could write and had at last published, not exactly the novels she thought she would write, but two biographies of women artists, *Praise God, Paint Insects, Make Love: Agnes Seitz and Her Painter's Eden 1679–1700* and *Dear Sweetheart: Maria Martin's Artistic Collaboration and Correspondence with John James Audubon 1831–1851,* which read like novels, as many of her reviews, most of which had been quite favorable, pointed out. And she had fallen in love tumultuously three or four times before she fell in love with David, the last time spectacularly and painfully with a married man, Michael Orme—that had cost her almost everything.

For the rest of her life, Lucy could and should and would lead a simple, economical life. She would continue to work at the Institute, where she had landed a teaching job six years ago, a very respectable job with a modest salary. She would continue to write. Already she was launched on her third book, the story of an American woman, a socialite turned collector named Lucy Baldrich, who had traveled to Japan around the turn of the century and brought back rare Japanese antique textiles. The research complete, she could start writing any-time now. She would stay in love and stay at home with David.

Lucy tried on the one very plain black dress she owned. Too tight, she ate too well with David. She peeled the dress off and, as she turned to throw it on her bed, looked in the dresser mirror at this too-round belly. Probably her age showing here, too.

Then Lucy pushed her belly out as far as it would go until it was taut and began to rub her palms in slow circles over the stretched skin, as she had seen pregnant women do lovingly and without thinking. How few times in her life had she tried to imagine herself as pregnant. When she was with Michael, after conversations that hinted at the subject, for they could not allow themselves to think about such happiness. Would she have looked like this if she had ever had a baby? Or if she had a hysterical pregnancy? For Caroline, her sister, that would mean a pregnancy in which she laughed all nine months, for whenever Caroline thought something was funny, she would say, "That's hysterical." Lucy should call Caroline, out in Denver, talk to her nephews, too. She used to call them almost every week, but she had been so busy with David.

Six-forty-five. At last she decided on a short black wool skirt, although it was too hot for wool—already minutes after her shower she was sweating again—and the skirt needed pressing. At least it fit. That decision begat another that would equally force the season. She would wear her black-velvet jacket with its wasp waist and wide shoulders. Lucy, who moments before had been dedicating herself to plainness, began to worry that this outfit was too plain. David liked it when she dressed up. She pulled on a stretch lace top, the lace would show at the neckline of the buttoned-up jacket. The waiters wouldn't see her nipples under the lace. She might let David look.

When she inspected herself in the mirror, though, her nipples didn't show. Her breasts were exposed as merely an expanse of pale skin under a black web, a gently rolling landscape without significant features. Lucy went to the bathroom and brought back a rouge sample from a cosmetic company. Like a character in some silly French erotic novel, she patted the color around the halo of her left nipple, saw how it showed so rosy under the lace, and then did the right nipple. At forty she might as well bring some sort of bravado to the enterprise.

Now that she was almost ready, she began to think about touching David, kissing him after several days of not seeing him. For the last six months, Lucy had been swept up with David, in what he called "the wild time," the time of falling in love, of making love at every possible moment, of neglecting friends and work. The initial excitement having settled down and with school beginning again, David had suggested that they return a bit to their former lives and spend only weekends together. Of course they might see each other at work. Lucy had agreed. She, too, had work to do, she told herself. It would be good to be on a schedule, this was the way this new kind of love, this practical kind of love worked. This week had been the first week of the new regime.

David would be here any minute. She went over to her jewelry box. Two wasps were poised on its raised lid above the spill of silver bracelets and colored glass beads. Better not disturb them, she would go without, though again she didn't want to be too plain for David. Lucy looked up at the wasp nest under the eave outside her window, where hundreds of wasps clung, busy and still at the same moment. The nest was such an attractive mottled gray-white, like an elegant house with its many chambers enclosed by thin paperish walls like Japanese paper walls, though these probably didn't slide back. Did these paper walls let light through, gray-white diffused light? Did the wasplets know whether it was day or night? Do babies in the womb bloom with the daylight diffused through the wall of their mother's belly?

Last weekend David had spotted the nest and told Lucy she had to knock the nest down with a broom handle, douse the nest with gasoline, burn the nest.

Lucy wanted to believe she and the wasps could live peaceably together. Turning into a Buddhist or a Jain in her old age? Next thing she would be wearing a surgical mask in order not to breathe in the tiniest insects or even germs. Maybe she should simply keep her mouth shut, take a vow of silence. David would laugh at that. How many times had he told her to shut up as she rattled on with one of her stories.

A wasp buzzed by her ear and landed on the bed. How did it get in? Looking closely at the window, she saw another wasp threading herself one leg at a time through an unraveling patch in the screen. How shiny were the black jet beads of the wasp body strung on the tiniest wire, its wasp waist. Lucy would be happy to emulate such plain elegance.

She pulled on her jacket, instantly pulled it off again. A wasp had stung her arm inside the velvet sleeve. Oh, that sting hurt, hurt, hurt. And how red the sting was! Redder than the blush on her breasts. Maybe she would die of wasp venom on her birthday. Wouldn't have to worry about being forty. Lucy shook her jacket— the wasp flew out—and pulled it back on. She would have to do something about the nest after all.

Seven o'clock, on the dot. She was ready. David, who didn't like to be kept waiting, was late. Lucy, restless, gently prodding her sting, had to do something. She went to her study. It was a good moment to straighten up her desk. She couldn't really do anything of substance, but poking at the papers relieved a little of her guilt about her lack of work on the new project. She tidied notecards into a neat stack, lined up the books, and cinched them in tight with the bookends. Picking up a stack of folders to file, she looked through them and stopped. Here was a folder she could not file, one she always forgot about but that kept turning up on her desk almost as a surprise. The folder was filled with newspaper articles in various stages of yellowing. The articles were on children, stories on Chinese baby girls abandoned by parents hoping for a son, on baby girls in India who were left at the doors of orphanages already crowded with rows of swinging cradles. Stories on children living on the Guatemala City dump, on African children serving as soldiers who had mutilated, had murdered, been mutilated, been murdered. It was the horror of the world torn out of the newspaper and hidden in this file. What to do about these children? What to do?

The doorbell rang. She closed the file, thrust it under some loose papers on the desk, she would forget it again. Grabbing her purse, she locked her door, hurried down the steps. Hurry away from that sadness, hurry to make someone in the world happy.

David stood under the porch light, his head bent down in a way that was habitual, that made him seem shorter than he was, but that also put on display his luxurious hair, still black, much to David's content, and one of the reasons he was often taken for a man much younger than his fifty-eight years. His face was rather a heavy face, its expression one of frowning, almost troubled repose, like that of an aging crown prince whose father will not abdicate. Although he assumed a casual pose, his hands stuffed in his pockets, his body had the coiled-up tension of a body carefully kept up. His clothes, too, were kept up. That dark green shirt of substantial cotton would rustle it was so freshly washed, his soft cashmere jacket would be just brushed. The fine silk tie with the plum-colored flowers and green leaves spotless, his shoes so solidly made gleaming.

Lucy wanted to ruffle him up, make him smile. "I missed you," she cried out and threw her arms around him, wincing from the sting, but David didn't see. He laughed and his arms pulled her close to him. How comforting were those arms, sure and tight around her. Maybe they would hold her for the rest of her life.

"Like this lacy thing." David's hands edged under her jacket. "Lacy. Racy. What is it?"

Lucy laughed and pushed away his hands. "Your birthday surprise!" Later, after dinner, when she took off her jacket, he would see, of course, the red raised throbbing welt. He would say, "I told you so."

As Lucy carefully opened the porch door, David watched her and said in fond exasperation, "Did you know the door's hinge is missing several screws? That's why it hangs so crazy. But you're so used to opening the door that way, it seems normal."

"I'll call the landlord, or I'll get around to fixing it someday. I won't be living here forever anyway." Lucy waited a moment to see if he would say anything, but he didn't, and she knew, of course, it was too soon to talk about living together. Embarrassed, she wanted to show that she wasn't hinting at anything, that she was happy with her home, that she was still dug in here. She pointed out her folly, the two new plants, as she turned off the sprinkler.

David said, "I thought I could smell lavender on you. It must be on your hands." He picked up one of her hands and sniffed it, gently rubbing her fingers as he did so.

Lucy sniffed the fingers of her other hand. "Once I knew someone who smelled of lavender as if they had eaten it. The smell poured out of the pores of their body, powerful, musky lavender smell." She stopped short. It was Michael who had smelled like that. The memory of Michael still remained such a vivid fact about the world that she would spontaneously and thoughtlessly bring it up as an incidental anecdote on the subject of lavender. David frowned, and Lucy was afraid he guessed it was some other man, although she had heard herself instinctively use the plural *they* instead of *he,* as she used to with her parents, to turn a boyfriend into a more anonymous group of friends. "How hot it is tonight! I hope it rains, to break the heat."

David said, "It's late, we'll miss our reservation," and hurried to his car.

Two hours later, Lucy sat flatbacked against a wall painted with a huge blue-green map of Italy, its different regions, the Veneto, Apulia, Umbria and all the others, outlined in thick black lines. The map was painted over the rough wall of an industrial warehouse. A triangular heating vent had become a lurid threatening Vesuvius with its thick plume of smoke. Tonight was "Tuscan" month at the restaurant. On the table in front of her lay the remains of two of the special "Tuscan" meals, crumbs of the rich sweetbreads, a bone with a bit of duck flesh and a green olive scrap clinging to it. The "Tuscan" wine bottle was empty. Only a short while ago, Lucy had been contemplating the thought of a more monastic life. Now she was so full of rich food and soggy with wine—if she pressed a finger into her skin, wine would seep out. Under the table, she unbuttoned her skirt, as the waitress recited the dessert special.

"Our 'Tuscan' dessert is a fig hazelnut tart. A crust of ground hazelnuts, with a thin layer of fig mousse, hazelnut topping, filigreed with a spangle of caramelized sugar."

David had his elbows on the table, his hands clasped before him, as if he were about to rub his hands in delight. "It's your birthday, you have to have dessert."

"But I'm so full," Lucy protested.

David slapped his hands down on the table. "One tart. We'll split it." Then he turned halfway in his seat, cocked his face at the waitress, and smiled. His teeth gleamed and his eyes narrowed in pleasure and appeal, knowing and not knowing that his smile was so attractive, which ambiguous knowledge gave his smile even more charm. The waitress smiled back at him. "And two decaffeinated coffees."

How young the waitress was. Was this the beginning of old age, to be surprised at how young everyone else was? Lucy used to treat her students like her younger sister—would she now feel more like their mothers?

After the waitress left, Lucy sighed. "I feel a bit decaffeinated myself."

"Hard to be forty? You can tell yourself you don't look your age. Remember when I first met you, I thought you were thirty-five instead of thirty-nine?"

How relieved David had looked when he discovered she was thirty-nine and not thirty-five, which would have been only two years older than his elder daughter.

"Don't you think that priding oneself on looking young is a sure sign of being old?"

David hunched his shoulders. He often prided himself on looking young. "Now that I'm getting closer to sixty, I think I'm accepting the aging process."

Lucy grinned. "Excuse me, *the aging process*? You mean getting old?"

"Well, aging's more than getting old, aging is a developmental process—"

"You don't want to say *old*. *Old*'s the ordinary word."

"Aging's a process of acceptance, acceptance of your age—" David turned red and his eyelids dropped, hooding his eyes.

Lucy was instantly sorry for picking at his words. Smiling, she said, "And yours will be"—she tried to think of a phrase he would like—"a lyrical acceptance!"

"Whatever that means," he snapped, but looked mollified. He brought out a black shiny box. "Time for your birthday present."

"No. No present. This dinner is enough, more than enough." Although David made much more money than Lucy, she tried to keep a kind of equity between them. The present looked alarmingly expensive.

"Come on, take it!" David pushed the box over to her. Lucy edged the gold string over the corner and opened the box. Inside lay a bracelet of burnished silver disks like archaic shields locked into a battle line. She fastened it around her wrist and held it up for inspection, careful not to let the sleeve fall back and reveal the swollen sting. "Thank you, it's wonderful. I was feeling a little bare tonight, a little too plain."

"And—" David handed her an envelope. Lucy opened it and

took out a card in the shape of and printed with an antique fan. On the fan a bucolic picnic was under way in a mannered garden. Women with white powdered hair lolled about in a state of extreme décolletage. Beribboned men laughed and leaned over bosoms. A handwritten note read, "Happy Birthday from a FAN of yours!"

Lucy groaned, as she knew David expected she would, and then laughed. "Someone was telling me that punning is almost always done by men. It's a way of taking over conversations, maybe by reducing them to the lowest common denominator—"

He grinned a child's grin, all lips and sheepish. "Shut up and look inside!" Inside the card was written, *One free trip to Mexico.*

Though she kept smiling, Lucy was embarrassed at and puzzled by the lack of enthusiasm she felt. Traveling with a lover had always been, for her, one of the greatest pleasures of being in love. There was the money, she couldn't let him pay for it all, so she would end up spending too much money, when she should save her money. And she had to get started on her book. That was it, her anxiety over starting her book.

David was talking, leaning over the table, his chin resting on his clasped hands. "How about next summer? I've got an idea for my next book and want to get started now. By summer I'll need a break."

Lucy saw her advantage and turned the conversation away from the trip. "What's your idea?" She tucked the card back in the envelope. "Tell me. Tell me."

David leaned back in his chair and clasped his hands behind his head. He was already settled into the luxury of enough intellectual capital to carry him through the next five years. His last book, *Mao Meets Mohammed: Chinese Muslims in the Twentieth Century,* appeared two years ago, and since then he had been casting about for another topic. "Well, I've said what I wanted to say about my Chinese Muslims, about how they have managed to be Chinese and

Muslim at the same time. I started to think about other people with two cultures, especially those who end up forgetting one of them. Remember that talk at the Institute on the descendants of crypto-Jews in New Mexico? I'm haunted by how the speaker described them as the people who light candles on Friday, who separate milk and meat, circumcise sons, who observe the Sabbath on Saturday, who bury their dead before sundown and put Jewish symbols on their gravestones, all without knowing why they do it. There were once Jews in China, with synagogues and Torah scrolls, but the synagogues fell into ruin, and why rebuild, no one could read the scrolls, which had been stolen or lost anyway. Now none of the descendants of the Jews would know what a synagogue is, what a Torah scroll is. I want to look at what all these communities had in common—how these people tried to hold on to a self and how it slipped through their fingers. I'm going to include the crypto-Christians in Japan. When they were persecuted, the religion went underground for centuries, so hidden under the cover of Buddhism that its practice became hardly recognizable as Christian. I thought about taking us to Japan, since your book has to do with Japan, but Japan's too expensive."

Lucy was startled. No, she would not go to Japan. Even to see the places her Lucy Baldrich had visited eighty years ago. Japan wasn't that small a country and had millions of people, still she couldn't risk running into Michael, who was there on a cultural exchange, and Michael's wife. Lucy had suffered too much shame in her own mind as "the other woman" to venture anywhere near Michael and his wife.

David had stopped talking and was looking at her.

Lucy nodded her head to show she was listening and thinking about what he said. "So your idea is a meditation on forgetting, the slow sure process of forgetting, even while trying not to forget. I have a question—what does it mean to you?"

David barked, "It means my next book! What do you think it means?"

Lucy, as always, flinched as he snapped at her, then, as always, quickly reminded herself that it was only his usual manner. She tried to explain herself. "You know what I mean—why is it interesting to you, personally? Because you were raised by a Jew and a Christian, neither of whom, you once told me, was religious?"

David's blue-green eyes looked at her and at the same time looked inward, as an animal looks inward when caressed. He seemed pleased that Lucy remembered this about him, something he had mentioned in passing but that was important to him. "Of course, it's myself I'm thinking about. I only light candles if the electricity goes off. My parents' history was the history of forgetting. And that forgetting wasn't governed by the tragic glamour of persecution."

Lucy watched David lift up his hands as he spoke. A quality of appeal lay in the gesture, an appeal to contemplate the general sadness of forgetting. She sensed, though, that there was something more. David, himself, felt forgotten, by his parents, someone. The project would be the outward manifestation of his brooding over that loss. This moved her, and she wanted to heal that loss by remembering things about him, by reminding him that someone was paying attention. His hands were also very strong hands, like a sculptor's hands shaping space. Shaping her breasts as he held them up to his lips. Once when they flew to New York together, she who was always afraid to fly held his hand, and he held hers so tightly, so kindly in her moment of need, shaping her fear into comfort. She might die, but at least she would die with someone. Yes, she did love him, she would show him how much she loved him, she would go on the trip to Mexico with him.

The dessert arrived on an enormous plate, a birthday candle stuck in the nougat. Lucy blew out the candle, but after a few seconds, it flamed up again. She had to give it a hard pinch. David shoved a forkful in his mouth, the caramel crystal threads splintering and catching the light like a light frost on his lips. Lucy dipped her spoon in the swimming pool of cream and licked it, too rich and too sweet.

Roughly wiping his mouth with his napkin, David cleared his throat. "I think going to Mexico won't be too expensive."

For all her resolve to take the trip with him, she said a little too flatly, "Yes, Mexico. Though my mother will be angling for me to come to Colorado next summer, because I didn't go this summer. You could come, too."

"Not quite the romantic vacation I had in mind."

"We could do it on our way to Mexico or on the way back. Or I can do it by myself. But I'd like you to meet my family."

In a high-pitched voice that she knew, by now, accompanied his emotion, he said, "I guess I thought we'd do a lot of real traveling together. I didn't travel much when Maureen and Olivia were young. After I got divorced, I didn't like traveling by myself. But you've traveled so much. I thought it would be so much fun to go with you." He stopped for a moment and looked away. "Maybe you've been to Mexico with someone else, one of your other men. We don't have to go there." Before Lucy could say anything, he added, "I won't go to Italy, though. I already went to Italy with Susan."

Lucy *had* been to Mexico with Michael, but before Michael she had traveled to other places with other men. At her age, and at David's age, didn't they both have histories with other people? She herself didn't care what David had done with Susan, a woman he had been seeing several years ago. That wasn't the point. The point really was, and now Lucy had worked it out for herself, the point was, she didn't care if she ever took another trip in her entire life. Traveling was too much about distraction, about running away from home. All she wanted was to concentrate on a few thoughts, at home, with someone close by. However, she had said she would go. She might enjoy it. She should act more grateful for the gift. "I'll start looking at guidebooks."

He looked pleased.

Yet she could not help herself. She added, "Let me warn you. When I travel, I like to take slow buses and slower trains. I don't make reservations, so I often end up staying at pretty cheap hotels or too-expensive hotels, whatever's available. So you see, my plan is usually no plan. Are you sure you want me to plan the trip?"

"Forget that, I'll rent a car and drive. I'll choose the hotels. Your job will be to tell me where to go. Division of labor. You do culture and I do the practical things."

"Sounds like my mother and father." She reflected her parents had been married a long time, maybe marriage worked that way. When she started looking at the guidebooks, she would get excited.

The waitress came around with a coffeepot. "Can I warm you up?"

David turned his smile again on the waitress, and she beamed back. How flirtatious he was, Lucy noticed. As innocently as if he were sitting here by himself. Flirtatious, attractive, why was he alone? She was flirtatious, too, attractive, too. Why was she alone? Now, of course, they were together. She reached across the table for his hand.

Sitting next to a wall, they had tables to the left and behind and before them, but nothing to the right. Lucy looked around. "Want your surprise early?" Disengaging her hand, she unbuttoned her jacket and drew aside a lapel, uncovering her breast until he could see the rosy pink nipple under black lace. "I decided that if I had to be forty—"

Someone called out, "David. David?"

David and Lucy looked up to see two couples coming over to

their table, the men in tweedy suits and with scruffy beards, the women slipcovered in long full cotton dresses.

David stood up, shook hands with the men, kissed the women. "This is Lucy. This is Linda and Greg. And Claire and Ron."

Had they seen her baring her breast? Lucy choked back her laughter and tried to smile. Yet as Linda and Greg, Claire and Ron, and David gave the hurried happy synopses of their children's lives—which child was still in school, who had graduated, who was getting married—Lucy's smile began to make her face muscles hurt.

When the other two couples left, David settled back into his chair and began to laugh. The couples were close friends of Becky, David's ex-wife, and he had known them when he was married to her. "I don't mind that they saw you and me. Especially such a sexy you. I wonder if they saw what you were doing? Maureen and Olivia have been telling me that their mother is curious about you."

Lucy teased him. "Gratifying to know she's still jealous?"

He ignored the question. "Claire looks so old and worn out. She used to be attractive. I heard she's trying to get pregnant—and she's forty-six. Gone through a couple of miscarriages, but she still keeps trying. She should act her age. It's so unnatural, confuses the generations."

Before she could stop herself, Lucy said, "Well, you go out with me, and I'm eighteen years younger than you. That 'confuses the generations,' doesn't it?" She could hear her voice suddenly rising and felt her face burn. "What does it matter to you anyway? It's her business."

"I just think it's unnatural."

"I guess I think what's natural and not natural is more complicated."

David frowned, finished his coffee, and threw his napkin down on the table.

Lucy sat very still. Why was she so mad? Perhaps an old reflex—whenever men passed judgment on what women should or should not do, she couldn't bear it and lashed out.

After a long silent moment, David coughed and then said carefully, "I shouldn't have brought that up about Claire. I guess on your fortieth birthday, you might be sensitive about children. Maybe you regret not having a child, even though you've told me that you're satisfied with being a good aunt to your nephews. Still, it's hard sometimes to live with your choices. I know if I were a woman, I would want to give birth, the very physicality of it is so powerful and attractive. I watched Becky give birth twice, and really envied her."

Now Lucy had to be careful, too, in her answer to this. On their second date, quite casually, David had asked her if she wanted to have children. And Lucy had said, truthfully, that no, she liked children, but she had never felt an overwhelming desire to have a child of her own. She was happy to be a good aunt. Looking back on that moment, Lucy knew his question was anything but a casual question: she had been offered an agreement and she had signed it. Whenever the subject of children came up, David would manage to produce the agreement and she would ratify it, as she did right now, saying once more, "I am happy being a good aunt." She paused and then said quickly, "Though there is something I want to talk to you about, something in the family way. It's that you are always saying you hope your daughters, when they get married, don't have babies too soon, that you're not ready to be a grandfather. But I'd like having children over to play." She had thought it all out, had waited for her moment to say it. Lucy and David's daughters quickly discovered they didn't have much in common, except David and their age, which did make Lucy feel sometimes in their presence like his daughter, not his lover, but the daughters seemed happy that their father was happy, and Lucy had no desire to displace them from his affections. She did like to think about their children, though, about all the nice things she could do for them, take them places, make cookies, things she liked to do with her nephews, but they were so far away. She continued, "If you're really so full of 'lyrical acceptance,' you wouldn't mind." It would be an empty house with only the two of them. Lucy recalled that she didn't even live at David's house and concluded abruptly, "You'll be good with grandchildren, I know. You love your daughters."

David rolled his eyes and leaned back in his chair. "You don't know what it's like to have kids around."

"That's not true. I've taken care of my nephews. And I spend time with Hana and her children—"

David interrupted her. "You do? You haven't seen Hana all summer."

Lucy had, in fact, not been to see her best friend Hana since early in the summer, and they had talked on the telephone only a couple of times. Still she defended herself, "I used to. I've been so busy doing things with you, but I will get back to seeing her." She stopped, for suddenly she felt foolish. "I'm sorry, I don't know why I'm saying all this. Maybe I miss my own family too much, miss having lots of people in the house." Her mother and her sister would call tonight to wish her happy birthday. When she got back home on Sunday night, she would listen to their messages on her answering machine as she stood in the dead air that seemed to fill her apartment when she was away for the weekend. Maybe she should get a cat. Something else alive in her apartment would be nice. She pleasurably reviewed a catalog of cats in her head: maybe she would get a red cat, or a white-and-black tuxedo cat, or a tiger cat. Opening her purse to put the empty bracelet box in it, she said, "Maybe I'll get myself a birthday present. Go to the animal shelter and get a cat."

"What would you do with the cat on the weekends, when you're with me?"

"Maybe I'll get two cats, to keep each other company, a nice cat couple, sitting together, night after night, reading the paper. You liked your last cat, what was her name, Venus?"

"The kids' cat. They stuck her with me when they moved out."

Lucy smiled, her voice was softer. "Oh come on, you told me once that you had long conversations with Venus. That you cried when she died. Sounds, too, as if you spent a small fortune on keeping her alive for years. You cut Venus's little pills, into halves or quarters, remember you told me?" To this tender part of David, belied by the roughness, she loved appealing.

"She was as light as a leaf, at the end." He shook his head, "No, all the feeding and medical bills and chasing the animal back in the house or out of the house—no thanks. No cats. Ever again." David pushed himself back from the table. "I'll be back in a moment."

Lucy, a little hurt, watched him walk away. She tried to recover by telling herself he walked like a cat, low slung, easy, but deliberate too—he could be her cat. Instead she found herself thinking he walked more like a handsome rhinoceros, his gait a kind of graceful dangerous lumbering.

Once David had disappeared, she looked around the restaurant. It was almost empty. The waiters and waitresses loitered near the bar, laughing, waiting for the last customers to leave. Tomorrow night and the night after that, the room would be filled again with nicely dressed old, young couples and not-so-old, not-so-young couples, like David and herself, with waiters and waitresses skimming to and fro, lightly bearing heavy plates of rich food and bottles of wine. Suddenly Lucy saw herself sitting frozen in the position of a surfeited patron of the restaurant. How many excellent meals at excellent restaurants had she eaten with attractive, well-dressed men. In how many different cities and countries.

With Michael it had been different. What kind of fashion disaster was he sporting these days? When she met him, he had been wearing that stiff thick-waled corduroy suit he bragged he had bought cheaply in a French farmer's market. When they went to Mexico, he had been all in khaki—a safari jacket and pants with so many pockets between them, he looked like a character sure to be shot in some movie about a former colonial plantation owner—and those silly silky Indian shirts, almost obscenely transparent and always shredding. With Michael she had eaten well—strips of glistening conch with green lime on paper plates in little towns on the coast of the Yucatán. And she had eaten badly—out of curiosity in Quebec province, as they followed the St. Lawrence on its growing gray vast way to the ocean, they ordered *poutine,* an item they kept seeing on menus, and were served a pile of soggy French fries covered in gravy and melted cheese. They had laughed at these, as he called them, food experiments. The best meal they ever had was that lobster roll with thick chunks of lobster on a white-bread split bun with mayonnaise, in that little dark hole of a diner, in the red-brick town of Rowley, up on the North Shore. As they ate, they watched the universal drama of a love triangle unfold in the next booth between a teenage boy, a pretty teenage girl, and a not-so-pretty sulking teenage girl.

Sitting here tonight, Lucy saw herself as forty going on sixty, heading into early well-padded retirement, sitting across from David on a Friday night or a Saturday night on all the weekends for the rest of her life, in this expensive restaurant or another expensive restaurant, a little drunk, too well fed, richly dressed, wearing rattling silver shield bracelets, David richly dressed in another version of his well-tended-to turnout. Nothing in her life would have changed. She would take trips, she would eat out, she would never truly be at home.

Suddenly Lucy was frightened, and she said to herself, get up, now, run away, now. But she was too afraid to run, too tired to run. And where would she run to?

When David returned, he bent down to kiss her and whispered, "Ready? You can finish showing me my surprise, in private." Lucy grabbed his hand and kissed his wrist. He was a good man, attractive, she was too old to be alone again, it would all work out.

He grasped her hand tightly in return, then let it go when the smiling waitress brought the check.

Outside, it was still hot, sticky, the rain hadn't come. In the car, on the way to David's house, Lucy pushed up the new bracelet and under her jacket sleeve traced the tender area around the wasp sting. If only she had died from the sting and did not have to worry about anything ever again. Since she hadn't died, she would have to do something about the wasp nest, or maybe only the screen, that was it, sew up that unraveled patch.

Michael Orme settled into his seat on the bullet train at Tokyo station. A tall, massive man of forty-five, red hair gone peach colored with sun and age, wearing a polite goofy grin, he stood out among the Japanese in the car like a friendly, bulky albino. He was returning to Kyoto from Hiraizumi, in northern Japan, a small town of weathered wooden farmhouses and fields between two mountain ranges. Here, nine hundred years before, ambitious warriors aspiring to peaceful pursuits built a city of golden palaces and golden temples meant to rival Kyoto, the capital. One hundred years later, even more ambitious warriors sacked the city for harboring the fugitive, Yoshitune, who killed himself and had his wife and children killed rather than be captured by the enemy. Of ancient Hiraizumi, only the famous "paradise garden," an earthly evocation of Amida Buddha's Pure Land, survived. Michael called his trip to see this garden a pilgrimage. Gardens were, for him, sacred sites. Although in his professional capacity as a garden historian (his latest book was *From the Ha-Ha to Spiral Jetty: Earthworks 1765–1972*), he would claim the trip as research and have himself reimbursed by the cultural exchange program sponsoring his year and a half in Japan.

Contemplation of "paradise" had filled him with melancholy. Though it was only mid-October, autumn had turned to winter. Leafless trees fringed the garden's pond where once courtiers boated and floated love poems on the water. The rocky islets, once connected to the shore by bridges, and serving as stages for music and dance, were now solitary and silent. Where once forty pavilions stood, a few foundation stones remained. The only color in the scene was the startling green of pine needles and the red of pine bark.

As much as he enjoyed his melancholic mood, though, Michael had to laugh as Japanese tourists, mostly flocks of men in somber business suits, stood next to the stones and stuck their faces in the painted board cutouts of a warrior and a court lady to have their pictures taken. It pleased Michael that for centuries in Japan pilgrims and tourists were indistinguishable.

He could hear the train engine humming. Soon he would be back in Kyoto, where his wife waited for him. Had he come so far to see the garden or to get away, once more, from a silent house?

From his coat pocket Michael took out a book. His life could be described by the list of writers for whom at certain times he felt the affinity of a brother or a sister. His favorite these last two years, Bashō, had made his own pilgrimage to Hiraizumi five centuries after it burned and three centuries before Michael. Bashō had gazed at the ruined palace and written a poem—something about summer grasses and warriors' dreams. Michael flipped through his book looking for it but was stopped instead by the following passage:

"As I was plodding along the River Fuji, I saw a small child, hardly three years of age, crying pitifully on the bank, obviously abandoned by his parents. They must have thought this child was unable to ride through the stormy waters of life that run as wild as the rapid river itself and that he was destined to have a life even shorter than that of the morning dew. The child looked to me as fragile as the flowers of bush-clover that scatter at the slightest stir of the autumn wind, and it was so pitiful that I gave him what little food I had with me."

The train jerked, and Michael involuntarily glanced up and out the window. A woman resembling Lucy Woolhandler, tall, her dark hair pulled back in the way he loved it, her eyes so dark and shining, seemed to be looking at him and waving to him. Had Lucy come to Japan to find him? He had to get off the train, fold her into his arms, hold her head against his chest. Yet the train was moving now, picking up speed too quickly. He pushed up against the window to look back but could not see her anymore. The station had been left far behind in just moments. He fell back into his seat, gasping. His heart seemed to climb literally up into his throat as if to escape from him, and why shouldn't it? He had abandoned Lucy again. He was such a failure. He could not rescue Lucy, could not rescue his wife, could not rescue himself.

Instead, for many years now Michael had engineered escapes, ever since the day he had come in from a long swim, lay next to his wife on a beach, and was almost asleep with fatigue and the sun's warmth when she leaned over him to say, "You know I'll be there to close your eyes when you're dead." She had divined the divorce of feeling that had come upon him, almost at or even before the moment he did himself, and was giving him fair warning of her refusal to let him go. After that day, whenever the fear of surrendering to a kind of death in life seized him, he would offer to give lectures or apply for visiting teaching positions and leave her at home for weeks or months at a time to set up house in a hotel room or in a small apartment near another school, with plastic plates and the bare minimum of furnishings. He would cook the simplest of meals, darn his socks badly, go about in clean but wrinkled clothes. Still he was on his own. Of course when he was home, he was seemingly on his own—he and his wife hardly met at all in the huge Shaker house, which together they had restored. Yet she had taken over the care of him, his food, his clothes, and his social life, arranging for all their appearances as a couple in the small university community where he taught and she worked in the library. They had drifted along with this arrangement for years.

But while a visiting scholar at the Institute, that lovely green garden world near Boston, he had met Lucy, and within weeks, although neither of them meant to, they had fallen in love. He told his wife immediately and the rest of the year had kept her away from him while he made himself part of Lucy's world. When the academic year was over, he had every intention of changing his life. He and his wife could sell the Shaker house for a huge amount of money, for Shaker style was very fashionable and rich professionals were vying to buy up the Shaker houses in the neighborhood, once a Shaker village. He would split the money with his wife. They could go their separate ways. He would be glad to get rid of the house, and not only for the money. He had begun to be frightened as he drove up the long narrow road past the Shaker cemetery with the celibate brothers and sisters chaste even in death, their graves separated by a grassy no-sex zone, and on through the dark woods to the grim house painted a lichenous gray, a house upright like the lichened granite plinths in front. Inside, there were six gloomy floors, most of them shut off, where Shaker sisters had once spun thread on the skeletal spinning wheels, now dusty and idle in the attic, and had ironed and dyed cloth, where Shaker brothers had measured grain. The house felt like a country that had proclaimed a death sentence on him. Even the large garden into which he had poured so much money and so much time, he would be willing to abandon, in exchange for escape.

When he sold the house, he would buy a home with Lucy. She

should have a home of her own. He admired her for living in that small Somerville apartment, like a little ship with its galley kitchen and its large back porch from which he could see all the peaked roofs of the other houses lined up like ships moored in a harbor, ships that in the morning would be gone. But that apartment could only be temporary. What kept her so unsettled, literally? Why didn't she settle into a house where her family from out west, especially her sister Caroline and those funny nephews she was so fond of, could come to stay with her? And with him?

His wife, though, had not agreed to a divorce. She had waited for his return to his regular job, to his world and her world. That summer, too, she developed a serious eye problem that threatened her sight. She had to have an operation. For months she could not work, could not drive, she could hardly see to cook. He could not abandon her and moved back home but only for a while, he told Lucy and himself. When after a year he brought up divorce, she still said no. Michael could not bring himself to commit the violent act of forcing a divorce on his wife. He had hoped, however, that now that his wife knew there was someone else he really loved, she would acknowledge that the marriage was not a marriage and they could divorce politely. He told Lucy to wait, wait.

Lucy said she understood why he couldn't leave his wife then. They continued to talk on the telephone, and he kept saying wait, wait, until he could hear Lucy become embarrassed and start to painstakingly transform the talk of lovers to the talk of friends. Then the event he feared most happened. She announced that she was "seeing" someone else, a quaint euphemism for kissing someone else, making love with someone else. He told himself she could not love this David, because if she did, he, Michael, would be forgotten, erased by love, he would not have merited this telephone call. He seized upon something else Lucy had said as proof of his conviction: that she might even make an "experiment" with marriage. This told him she had no real love for this man, she simply wanted to be married, blindly and desperately. She might do that. So many people did, as Michael had himself, because they had met a good person. Why not marry and settle down at last in their lives? Lucy was around forty, too, a dangerous moment. What could he say to warn her? What did he have to offer her instead of wait, wait? He knew he would wait out his wife, if he didn't die first of a heart attack. He knew he had the will to do that, he could promise Lucy that. But Lucy could not wait.

As the train hurried him closer to Kyoto, an enormous sense of waste struck him. The waste of his life without Lucy, his wife's life trying to hold on to him, and Lucy's life, for she didn't love this man, so, therefore, even of this David's life. It was his own fault for abandoning her. Since she had announced the fact of David, he had wanted to call often. He was afraid, though, that her lover might be there, and he would have to hear the constraint in her voice. She wouldn't laugh, and he couldn't bear not to hear her laugh. She always laughed when she heard his voice on the telephone, before he said anything funny— touching, her absolute faith that he would make her laugh. He felt, too, that he shouldn't upset her, she might not want him to call, though he knew, he was certain that she loved him.

Living only several hours' drive from Lucy, he felt in exile from her. To make that exile even more complete, he had applied for and received his fellowship in Japan. When his wife told him she was coming to Japan, too, he had agreed politely, almost absentmindedly.

In Kyoto it was still autumn, the maples red and orange and yellow. But Hiraizumi's wintry mood had so suited him that here he noted only all the gray things in Kyoto, the color of winter. There were the gray clouds that rose through the narrow ravines to drift over the hills that surrounded the city, obscuring the sacred mountain, Mount Hiei. The gray cement of Kyoto's modern buildings and the gray roof tiles of older houses and temples. From his bus window, as it crossed the Sanjo Avenue bridge over the Kamo River, Michael looked at the river, only a trickle between gray broken grasses. A few cranes hunched their wings and stood on the worn gray rocks, looking around them, eyes squinted against the cold and damp wind.

The bus let him off on Shirakawa-dōri. He started walking east to his house up the hill. Then, in spite of himself, he looked fondly at the familiar little house gardens along his way and acknowledged at last that it was still autumn. Here were the flowers of autumn, blue balloon flowers nodding on tall thin stalks, the yellow chrysanthemums thick-stalked and strong, the bush clover with the little pink blossoms—that abandoned child! He slid open the wooden gate to his own house and garden, stepped in, and closed the gate back behind him. The white cat who belonged to the rented house, whom he had named Tsushima after the tiny craggy islands in the Japan Sea over which Korea and Japan eternally quarreled, called to him with a raucous yowl. By the dim light in the kitchen window, he knew his wife was home. The dividing line between them seemed only more ancient and fresh, for he had seen Lucy again, if only in a waking dream.

In the small garden he tended as if his own, he walked about touching the bamboo, the persimmon tree, the plum tree, greeting these friends. A branch was broken on the small sweet olive tree in the corner of the garden. He broke it off completely, otherwise the poor tree would bleed herself to death. Fallen leaves lay matted on the paths, matted against the rocks. He had raking to do. Time to get the garden ready for winter. His neighbors, whom he consulted for local gardening advice, had told him he should tie straw matting around his cycad palm, cut the last flowers down to the ground. He had sent a long list of instructions to the couple who had sublet his house about how to ready his garden for winter. They should still be watering it. They should get salt marsh hay to mulch the garden. He was not confident they would do any of these things. When he and his wife went back home, when his research was done, he could put a winter-hardy bamboo brake in his garden. He would write Martin, Lucy's friend and a colleague at the Institute, a fellow garden maniac with whom Michael had become and remained friends, to discuss the matter, for he was sure Martin would know all about these winter-hardy bamboos. He almost laughed at himself. So many new ideas for his garden at home, the garden behind the house he wanted desperately to sell. When he wrote Martin, he would ask about Lucy, if he weren't so ashamed of himself.

If he were living with Lucy, he would make a garden for her, a garden of their own, where they could embower themselves. Oh, the trees he would plant for her! A stewartia, with the lovely mottled bark, and a tree with bark smooth like Lucy's skin—even on the most humid hot days cool and dry to the touch.

He went into the house and removed his shoes. In Japan, even though his wife may have accompanied him with some hope on her part to renew the marriage, they ended up with almost the same life they had at home. Even this little house had a strange resemblance to their Shaker house. Both had long dark halls of cool wooden floors, both paid attention to the simple beauty of ordinary fixtures, doors, built-in cupboards. He did his research and writing. She missed so much the routine of academic life and the company of her coworkers at the university that she found substitutes. She had a little work teaching English to Japanese housewives and volunteered her time doing good deeds through the YMCA, the center of the local American community. The only real difference was that they didn't ever appear outside the house together. He took more and more short trips by himself, and she went her own way every day, whether he was there or not.

The pattern of these homecomings was sadly familiar. He would not kiss her, she would not kiss him. Tonight as always they would sleep in their separate rooms. Terrible not to feel desire for a woman, and even after so many years, he felt his guilt like a heavy weight around his neck, dragging him under water. He and his wife would spend weeks together, quietly, then suddenly she would complain, "We don't fuck, we hardly talk, I may as well be sitting next to a stranger on the plane." Michael would gently plead with her once more to sell the house, divide the money, and divorce. She would turn away to cook a meal for him, or mend and iron his clothes, and talk of other things. The violence of these moments, the quiet violence of every day they lived together, made him feel guilty. He did not want to hurt her, but whatever he did hurt her, for he did not love her.

His wife stood in the small kitchen, slicing chicken, tofu, the ghostly white clumps of enoki mushrooms, and green onions, fanning the slices on a large platter. "We learned to make sort of a winter stew in the cooking class, a *nabemono*. I found a *nabe* dish at the YMCA Saturday exchange. Eight hundred yen." She was not tall but was slender enough to look tall, her face in repose triangular, with the pointed chin, which her short hair made even sharper than it was. She wore the plainest clothes, loose clothes that managed to not look formless but to accommodate the certain quickness she had about her.

At dinner they were, as almost always, courteous with each other. He told her about the inn where he stayed, describing its special dish, *sansui*, wild mountain greens, and the little wiry *obāsan* who ran the inn. He laughed as he told her about the gift his hostess gave him as he checked out—a big rock with a little ceramic frog glued to it, which he left on top of a Coca-Cola vending machine in front of a dark little grocery store on a country road, when no one was looking. He didn't want to offend the innkeeper by throwing it away, but the rock was so heavy, he couldn't carry it around with him, though now of course he realized that the old lady who ran the store would find it, would know where it came from and report back to the inn lady, so all his good intentions were in vain.

His wife said, "You should have brought it back. I could have sold it at the YMCA fund-raiser we're having for the stray animal fund. Oh, those two Americans living up near Mount Hiei found a litter of puppies abandoned outside their house. They gave away two by standing in front of the grocery store, and the rest we'll place—I hope they don't end up being abandoned again. I asked my students why the Japanese abandon their pets, don't take them to the pound or give them away. They told me that it was bad luck to have the animals killed, but they don't mind if nature kills the animal. You should see the nice cage George built from scrap lumber for our cats at the YMCA. The cages all connect with tunnels and inside are these perches he covered with old carpet."

At least, Michael told himself, someone was capable of rescue.

His wife, using the long cooking chopsticks, kept the simmering pot stocked. He chose with his chopsticks pieces of chicken or mushroom, dipped them in the dipping sauce, and drank sake heated by his wife. Terrible, the pity he felt for her. Terrible, the lassitude that that pity bred in him. Lassitude that had become convenient for him. He was like a Japanese salary man, who worked and worked at the office, while she did everything in the house. Michael preferred the sight of the husbands and wives he saw in the small Kyoto shops, working together, the kitchen right there, almost in the shop, the sliding door open, the women and men talking and laughing.

Dinner over, he offered to help with the dishes, but as always he was pushed out of the kitchen. He settled himself on the veranda and looked at his garden.

His vision of Lucy at the station haunted him. His chest still hurt with pain spread across it like a bruise left by the blow of a huge fist. He would telephone her tomorrow—thirteen hours behind, he tried to calculate in his head, but it became a muddle, he would work it out on paper. Did he have a phone card so he could call from a pay phone? Maybe he wouldn't telephone her. He would send her postcards—those wonderful rectangles of cardboard that allow for the least presuming of contacts—to show he was still in the world and loving her, it didn't matter if she was with someone else. It didn't matter.

Opening his wallet, he pulled out the much-worn photo Lucy had once given him of her and two of her nephews. One of the boys he had nicknamed the Bubblegum Friar, for the day before the picture was taken, his mother had had to cut a wad of gum out of his hair, and the result was a rather neat tonsure; and the other the Marine Monk, for he had shaved his big muscular head. Lucy looked as she did in his vision, hair pulled back, black eyes, but smiling, her head slightly ducked in pleasure.

The cat came out, sat in front of him and licked her paws, washed her face, took her time.

Ping. Ping. The cat stopped washing and lifted her head.

Michael knew the old couple walking their dog had come to the shrine down the lane. Every morning at seven they came and opened the Jizō shrine, Jizō, guardian of travelers, women and children, dead children, aborted children. They threw out the dead flowers and rotten fruit offerings and put in the flower holder a few small chrysanthemums and beside it two orange *mikan.* They lit incense, picked up the small baton, and hit the brass bowl-bell, clapped their hands and, putting their palms together gently, bowed to the small, round Jizō statues clustered in the wooden shrine, each one wearing the little aprons and knit hats women in the neighborhood had made to keep them warm. At seven in the evening, the couple came again, *ping ping,* and closed the shrine up for the night. Three striped cats hung around the shrine on sunny days. Michael's cat often joined them, stretching out on the ledge where the shrine sat. In Hiraizumi he had seen a Jizō statue with a bib on it, the bib had a cat face, and the offerings were cans of cat food.

Had his wife heard the prayer bell, too? He and his wife had failed to make a child. His wife was bitter about that. They had talked about adopting, but it never happened. Perhaps even then he had known the marriage was a mistake. He should have had a child with Lucy, but it was too late. Even if Lucy didn't love this David as she had loved him, maybe this man would give her a child, and then she might find that life enough to live on.

Suddenly dizzy, Michael reached out a hand to steady himself. His chest hurt, oh it hurt, as his heart raced raced, raced toward his throat. He should go to the English-speaking clinic. He might die here in Japan.

The spell passed. He went into the house. He passed the closed sliding door to his wife's bedroom. The cat looked at it, too, but kept walking. Michael lay down, the cat crouching at his feet.

His wife had told him once she couldn't imagine living without him. As he lay there, Michael could imagine living without himself. When he was a boy and spent summers with his parents in the South of France, acrobatic acts came to town and performed in the town square. The tightrope walkers tied their line above the square, between the large plane trees. He had watched a tightrope walker vanish into a plane tree, vanishing out of sight with his large pole into the dark cave of leaves. As he lay there on that autumn night in Kyoto, unable to sleep, Michael's despair made him wish he could vanish into the crest of leaves, silently, unobtrusively, above the café-tables.

CHAPTER 3

Late in the afternoon, two weeks after her birthday, Lucy sat in her office, ready to work, but she could not work. Instead, she had turned her chair to the window, propped up her feet on the windowsill, and looked out at the Institute's paradise of lake, forest, lawns, at the great humpback of the Asian Studies building, with its turrets of stone and twinkling leaded windows, where David might be working. A very pretty world, but a solitary world. With the different departments scattered throughout the campus, groves and hills separating them from one another, and then with faculty who appeared briefly only to teach and then disappeared into their offices to work or to answer e-mail, she would hardly see anyone at all unless she made an effort. The few students seemed to melt into the forest.

Today, two students drifted along the path beyond her window, tiny figures among huge trees, maple and fir and beech and birch, and Lucy's favorite tree, the enormous copper beech that massively shaded the paths. Lucy admired the beech bark, folded and gray like elephant skin covering the huge trunk, and the thick branches that towered up into one dense ball of leaves, heart-shaped leaves pale peach and green in spring and in summer deepened to a reddish black. Now she noticed that unlike the other trees, its leaves had exhausted their color, so theirs was an inglorious fall among maples that lit up red and orange for the longest suspended moment, double-firing the lakeshore with their burning red leaves and their burning reflection.

Her eyes followed the faint trace of current flowing from the lake into the stream and washing through the reedy marsh where her friend Hana Matsuo's little wooden house sat. She couldn't work. She shouldn't bother David—instead, she would go see Hana. Hana always said something that made her laugh or—it was hard to put into words—made her see something elemental, something akin to wood or rock. How necessary Lucy had always found that contact with the elemental. How much, she realized, she missed it. She picked up the telephone.

When she heard Hana's shy "Hello?" she said, "It's your long-lost friend. I'm in my office trying to work, but I'd rather see you. Can I drop by?"

"Oh, I've been thinking about you. Yes, it's been a long time. But the children are here, and I know it's hard to talk with them around," Hana apologized.

"I'm coming to see the kids, too," Lucy protested, and that was true, she enjoyed watching Hana's girl and boy chase each other around or jump on the couch, it felt like being with her sister and her boys. "And we'll get to talk. Even if we get interrupted, what's important keeps circling back and everything gets said eventually."

Hana laughed. "If you say so. See you in a couple of minutes, then."

After Lucy arrived, they all sat down at the dining room table. Hana handed Lucy a cup of tea. Sachiko, five, and Tak, three, knelt on their chairs and gloated over the plate of glistening chocolate-iced cookies. "Now, let Lucy have a cookie first, please. She's the guest," Hana admonished them. To Lucy she said, "They like it when we have guests, then we have special cookies."

In a few minutes, Lucy began to stretch out, one arm draped over the back of her chair, her legs turned from the table and crossed.

Hana laughed and said, "Look at you, you sit there drinking your tea, taking a bite of your cookie, thinking of nothing else, I'm sure. I seem to remember that once I did that, too. Now my every thought is of the children. Even in the toilet, I leave the door open, listening for a crash and for crying—that is, when they leave me alone in the bathroom!"

Lucy tried to think of something to show Hana she had her own problems and offered up, "I'm not having such pleasantly empty thoughts. I'm getting old. I just turned forty."

"Think how old that makes me. Oh well, you look young." She glanced sharply at Lucy, "And untouched."

Lucy wanted to know what Hana meant by untouched, for Hana always said odd things about people that were peculiarly right, even if uncomfortable.

But Hana had already said to Sachiko, "We'll have to sing 'Happy Birthday' in Japanese to Lucy." Hana turned to Lucy. "She learned it at Japanese school." They sang. Tak mumbled the words as if he knew them.

Lucy clapped and bowed. The children clapped, and their hands stuck together with chocolate frosting from the cookies, so they laughed and smacked their sticky palms together again and again, until Hana wiped their hands and sent them away from the table to play. They took up positions on the sofa. Sachiko opened up her crayon box and arranged some paper on the nearby coffee table, then announced that she would draw the overstuffed chair across the room. Tak yelled that he would draw the chair, too.

"As long as you do it without making us deaf," Hana said to

them. She poured more tea and asked Lucy, "Did David take you out for your birthday?" Lucy nodded, and Hana continued, "That's another thing I never get to do anymore, have an adult meal. Just Howard and me in a nice restaurant."

It was a conceit of Hana's to protest that she was envious of Lucy's life, when Hana loved the life she led now. Lucy said, "You could hire a babysitter, but you don't want to be away from the children."

Ignoring her, which Lucy didn't mind because now she sensed that her friend needed to talk, Hana went on, "And you can do your work. You're starting on your third book. I'm forty-six, and I'm not doing anything since I finished my last book five years ago." Hana paused, then said in a rush, "A while ago, when the children and I were heading home, we crossed that stone bridge over the stream, and I saw it like a Japanese bridge, the arched bridge that leads to the sacred shrine precincts, the bridge from this world to the other world. As I looked at the maple leaves that had fallen onto the still water, floating on the water, I remembered an old poem; it begins—

'red leaves in profusion
follow the stream'

"I miss so much working on poetry, it is as if I have lost someone I love, someone to whom I've said everything in my heart. I look at the children, and I wonder, where do these children come from? When Howard comes home, I think, Who is this man who comes in my front door every evening without knocking? What do they have to do with me?" Hana stopped.

Lucy wanted to comfort her. "You will get back to work soon. You will. This new person in your department, what is his name, the one who works on Japanese and Chinese poetry, maybe talking to him will get you back to work."

"Arthur Wall. Yes, I do hope I get to meet him soon. I like his work—it's so literary. Not all translators are literary. You feel sorry for the original writer."

"You can think of these last years as a fallow time. You know, too, that when you start translating poems again, I'll be happy to read them for you. It helps to know you've got a reader who loves your work, doesn't it? Of course, who am I to give advice, I'm stuck, too. I've done all the research, too much research, but I can't start writing."

"So tell me about your book. Then it will be like having an idea in my head. And better, because I get to think about it, but you have to write it."

Lucy laughed. "All right. It'll help to tell the story out loud. Make it sound alive." She felt better already. How had she forgotten how much Hana helped her with her work? "Well, my American lady, Lucy Baldrich, around 1920 meets a Japanese collector named Nomura, who specializes in antique kimonos. He patiently searches all over Japan for the fragments of old exquisite robes, which over the decades and even centuries were cut up to make altar cloths and purses. Then he pieces the robes together again, though he can never find all the pieces for many of the robes. Lucy Baldrich becomes fascinated with the robes and buys many of them from him."

"That's nice—both of them looking at the fragments of robes. A kind of love story. A love story in which two people love the same thing."

Lucy hadn't thought of it this way but was intrigued. She leaned forward to see if she understood what Hana was saying. "So they share the reassembling of the fragments, like a big puzzle they're putting together—"

"No, no. I guess I'm more interested in the idea of them looking at the fragments, the pieces themselves, not put back together. They feel themselves to be fragments." In a sudden shift, very Hana-like, she announced, "I'm a kind of fragment."

Tak's hand suddenly was reaching up to get another cookie. "Tak, no more. You won't eat your dinner." Hana pushed the cookie plate out of his reach. Tak started asking, "Why? Why?" and twining around her legs.

Lucy looked over at Sachiko's drawing. The chair was perfectly recognizable, but the perspective wonderfully flattened out, like some very modern drawing. She almost put her hand down on Sachiko's hair yet didn't want to disturb her, or have her shake her hand off, when she was so intent on her drawing. Sachiko's hair was decidedly a black brown, not a black black like Hana's hair. Though Hana's hair had so many white streaks these days. Lucy looked at Hana as she was prying Tak off. Her skin was weathered in an attractive way, like weathered wood. Lucy remembered when she met Hana, six years ago, digging in her garden with a pitchfork behind the apartment block near the Institute where they both had lived then and spreading manure in the upturned dirt. Lucy remembered how Hana had planted her feet so solidly on the ground and at the same time talked poetry to her.

Hana picked up immediately where she had left off. "Yes, I used to be a whole, but now I'm a fragment. I'm being fragmented all the time by the children. Only when I think of them can my mind be whole. But it's a disturbing wholeness, because it means the obliteration of myself."

Lucy said, "You wanted that obliteration."

Hana smiled. "Yes."

Sachiko looked up and grinned. "I finished my picture." Tak took advantage of the moment and knocked her box of colored pencils off the table. Sachiko yelled, "Tak! Mama!"

Hana said, "Enough, enough. I want you two to go upstairs and play, now."

"I don't want to play with him."

"I don't want to play with you."

"Well, play by yourselves, but upstairs, now. I want to talk to my friend."

"They don't bother me," Lucy insisted.

But Hana shooed them upstairs, where they banged shut the door to their room. "Ah, peace and quiet. Let me put some more hot water in the teapot."

It was very quiet. The long scroll hanging on the wall lifted lightly in the breeze and knocked against the wall. On the scroll were painted two crayfish, their antennae so delicate and searching, their claws and back scales light washes of ink. Another wooden knock. Lucy would like to paint as delicately as that. She would paint mountains that seemed like mist.

When Hana returned from the kitchen, Lucy asked, "What's life like as a fragment?"

Hana laughed. "It's such a pleasure to get to talk about these things with you—everyone else thinks I'm a little strange." She sat up very straight, looked directly at Lucy, and carefully followed her thoughts. "Let's see. Fragmenting is a kind of everyday thing, it's pretty ordinary. I think the fragmenting of myself among the children, Howard, meals, even Taro the cat, *is* the everyday, the ordinary. So that I hardly have any sense of myself at all like I used to."

"Yes?"

"At first it was odd. The everydayness of the children, life, made me feel uneasy."

"Well, after all, you were disintegrating." Lucy laughed.

Hana frowned slightly. "No, you don't understand. This uneasiness *is* at first disturbing, because you are being parceled out, you are not wholly yourself. Then it becomes something interesting, rather sexy. Much more interesting than thinking my own thoughts. Forty years of my own thoughts were enough."

"Forty—that's when you said you were going to have a karmic change of destiny. Though you weren't sure how it was going to happen."

"Yes, I remember calling it my karmic change of destiny." Hana's face lit up with a smile. "Sounds so easy, as if the change was one big event, when really it took several years of blindly rushing forward without knowing where I would end up. For years I was lonely and wanted a child, I didn't meet anyone, I started to adopt, I wasn't sure, I hesitated. I was afraid so much of the time. I wanted a child so much I started to see my fear like a big square in my head, that I had to somehow angle out. When I got the square out, I met Howard, I got pregnant, and then married."

"This square sounds like a big brain diaphragm."

They laughed.

Lucy wanted to talk about David. She leaned forward, hugged her knees in self-congratulation and relief. "I think my karmic change of destiny has been David. I kept feeling like I had to change my life. I didn't want to be alone anymore. I wanted to be at home with someone, be close to someone. I felt taken over by this almost violent force to do something, even sometimes when I told myself, wait, you're going too fast. I kept thinking, why waste time, why wait anymore?" Lucy stopped for a moment. Then abruptly she asked, "Why did you say I looked untouched earlier? I don't feel untouched. Losing Michael was like an amputation—a breaking down—"

Hana said quickly, "Oh, you know how I say things, but maybe I think you're still untouched because the breakdown wasn't complete. You had to pull back from the edge, not let yourself fragment."

Lucy sat back and was silent for a moment. "Yet it felt like disintegration, like I was standing on some ice field and he was calling to me from some green continent and the ice began to break up and I had to leap in the water and swim to him. Sometimes I feel the mark of him still on me, like a crack in me I can't repair. Even when I'm not thinking of him at all, something he said or something we did together pops up in my mind. It's like being haunted. The other day I started thinking for no good reason about this plant he called a

Tampax bush. It sounds disgusting, but then he showed me one at a nursery, and the flowers were lovely, long, cylindrical, and very red—lovely, it seemed a pretty revision of a Tampax, a pastoral vision."

Hana was silent for a moment. "I always thought Michael was selfish with you, pursuing you when he was married—even though he seemed to be separated at the time. Yet you loved him—I think that's true." Hana then laughed. "I can't think too badly about Michael. Once he put his huge hand on top of Sachiko's little head and pronounced her exquisite with such sincerity. Did you ever ask him to leave his wife?"

"I can't force someone to change their life. They have to do it themselves. At first I was so in love, I didn't think. I told myself, he'll be here for a year, and then who knows what will happen, and that was it. Then I loved him so much, I wanted to be with him always. He kept saying wait, and I wanted to wait, but waiting made me feel like a vulture waiting for the death of something. And then this great panic came pushing me forward, I had to go out and find someone else to give myself to."

"Do you think you'll get married to David, then?"

Lucy leaned forward again, hugged her knees again. "I think that with David marriage might be possible. I love David in a different way from how I loved Michael—but look where that got me. It is love, I think, I'm sure, because sometimes I look at him, and I'm so attracted, and I care so much—he can be so kind. So maybe I can say that I love David in a more ordinary way, and I tell myself that is what ordinary life is, married life is, the day-in-and-day-out life with someone, sometimes it's fun, sometimes it's boring and rather lonely. These days I would like to try on ordinary life. Everything that seemed exotic and unconventional to me when I was young now seems boring to me. What's exotic to me, unknown territory, is ordinary settled-down life, a life plain yet rich with treasure, like the beauty of a plain landscape, the gorgeousness of plain light!"

Hana laughed. "That's ordinary life?"

Lucy waved her hand. "You know me, I would have to have an ordinary with a halo!"

Hana laughed again. Then she sipped her tea and said without laughing, "I'm trying to imagine David with a halo and can't. I think he's a good man, but too often rather rough, a little bullying—his hands chop in the air whenever he takes offense in our department meetings, and he's quick to take offense. Maybe you like that roughness about him, it's very male and attractive in a way. Funny, the word *rough* seems right for the way David talks. A word that begins with a growl and ends with a bite. *Ruuuu-uff.* Well, you're strong, you can stand up for yourself. I wonder, though, if that means you might have to stay intact, to protect yourself. No chance at all for the breaking open, the fragmenting I'm talking about."

"Oh, he acts rough, I think, to defend himself. He's always afraid someone is taking advantage of him, or criticizing him. I think I see through it."

"When are you going to move in together?"

Lucy took a sip of her tea, put her cup down. "I think it will happen, when we're ready. We've only been together six months. For right now, it's nice at the end of the week to go see him."

"But you said you want to live with someone, day in day out."

Lucy felt a bit pressed. "I'm used to living alone, and I can stand it, I think, for a little longer. Then maybe we will be living together, become one flesh. I always thought that phrase was the perfect description—" She stopped.

Tak came tumbling downstairs chasing Taro the cat, a white cat with big orange spots and a flat pug face. Tak caught up to Taro and pulled his tail. The cat gave Hana a look of aggrieved forbearance. "Now Tak, Tak, don't pull Ta's tail. That's not the way to show Taro you like him." She looked at her watch. "I guess I better start cooking dinner."

Sachiko had followed Tak and now pointed her finger at her brother. "Tak, *Tak*! *Don't* pull Ta Ta's *tail*! Let *me* pet Ta Ta. *I'll* show you how to pet Ta Ta!"

Tak threw himself on Taro. This was too much for Taro—he took a swipe at Tak, leaving parallel scratches on Tak's arm. Hana ran over and picked Tak up. Tak looked at Hana with his wide-open brown eyes, his round face crumpling to a cry. "I love Ta, I want to hold Ta, I want to pull his tail. Why Ta hurt me, why?"

Sachiko told Lucy, "I know how to pet Taro. Come here! Taro!" She stamped her feet. The cat sat there staring at them from under the table.

Lucy stood up to go. She looked out the window. The sun had turned the reeds in the marsh behind Hana's house a dark gold, then the sun sank and the reeds became a black thicket against a whitening sky. In a moment the sky, too, would turn dark, so black out here in the country, unlike in town. Lucy said, "This house is perfect for you."

"I know. I love the bittersweet vines that grow here with their red berries and yellow caps and their angular twining that looks so dangerous in the autumn woods. We've seen a fox, and this summer we saw a mother skunk with her five wiggly kits following her like ducklings, each with a white star chrysanthemum on the tip of the tail. It's getting too expensive to rent, though, we really have to buy a house. But unless I find one like this, I don't think I can move."

Sachiko began to pull on Hana's arm. "Pick me up, too."

Lucy headed for the door. As she pulled on her jacket, Hana stood there with the children clinging to her.

Then Hana suddenly asked Lucy, "Do you think you could ever bear taking care of a child?"

Lucy fumbled for her keys. "David doesn't want any more children."

"You've talked about it, then. Do you?"

"I told him I've never desperately wanted to have children, and that's true. The only time I ever thought about having a child was with Michael, just to have another Michael—I didn't tell David that. I said I was happy being a good aunt to my nephews out in Denver, which is true." She stopped. When, though, had she explicitly, consciously decided the point? "Maybe too much babysitting when I was a teenager—I have no illusions."

Hana kept on. "You don't have to limit yourself to the size of his life. I mean, if you marry David, just think, you'll always be yourself, except he will have pruned you down to fit his life, a little like a bonsai tree, stunted to fit in its dish. Of course then you might have these very interesting things to say. How would a bonsai tree talk?" Hana had gotten carried away, then she seemed to hear herself what a frightening thing she had said. "Don't pay any attention to me, you know I say strange things. Anyway, you've got your work, and that's enough for you."

Lucy had her keys out.

Hana hadn't finished, though. "Of course, the love you feel for the children is so interesting that you don't mind taking care of them. When I get back to work, I know I'll be happy, but still it will be the end of a dream. Sometimes I think how nice it would be to have one more baby, to have that little ball of sticky rice growing inside of me. Especially when the children are growing so fast, leaving me—even the flesh I wrapped myself in when they were born is falling away. But I don't think I could do it again. I guess my karmic change is over, that force is spent. Now I'll become an old crone." Then she added, as if she hadn't been listening to Lucy at all, "If you had a baby, I could hold your baby, smell its hair, play with its little hands, and give the baby back to you! You would come by more often, and we could worry about the children, talk about our work, talk about whether to dye our gray hair and indulge in the luxury of protesting that we were too old to have children, whatever did we do it for? We'd become like the ghosts in the Nō plays who haunt the place where once they spent their passions with such abandon—like the maiden, disappointed in love, who threw herself into a river, and on the riverbanks sprang up the yellow flowers that now bear her name. *Disappointed in love,* I think that's tame phrasing for the despair that would make one leap into the dark water. But we would have the children, and maybe you won't be disappointed in love. You'll marry David, or maybe Michael will finally get divorced and come for you. Maybe you'll meet someone else—you deserve to meet someone funny and nice."

Lucy said quickly, "No, David's it. I can't go through this again. I think it will work out. Anyway, I've got to go." Just then she saw a book lying on the little table by the door, on its cover a photo of a shantytown, the steep dirt road rutted by rain, a barefoot woman in shorts and a dirty blouse walking up the street holding a baby, its big black eyes unsmiling. She picked up the book and flipped quickly through it.

"Oh, my friend Rosemary, I knew her in college, sent me her new book about the poor families in Honduras she's been working with."

Lucy stopped and stared at two photographs on facing pages. On one page a baby lay tucked in a tiny coffin, framed in paper lace. The baby's wide-open staring eyes and its ghastly smile were the result of too-thin flesh stretched too tightly across the bony little face. On the facing page, the baby's mother with mild eyes, weary eyes looked straight at the camera.

Hana looked over her shoulder. "That picture stopped me, too. I had to read about it. Often when a baby is sickly, the mother lets it die of starvation to save food for the others. The mother says, oh, he doesn't want to eat, he wants to be an angel and go back to heaven. I guess it used to be like that here and in Europe just a hundred years ago. In Japan, too. We've forgotten what it's like to have to let children die like that. The poor mothers. What if I could not feed Sachiko or Tak?"

Lucy thought about her file of articles on children. "It's as if they are slipping through our fingers." She asked if she could borrow the book. Children slipping through her fingers, Michael had slipped through her fingers. Would she lead a life in which everything slipped away from her? She had to hold on to David.

Hana said, "Do you want to stay for dinner? I feel that if you go now, you'll be slipping through my fingers."

No, Lucy had to leave this minute. She might cry, she might start to fragment, and the prospect did not seem as pleasant as Hana made it out to be. More like complete dissolution. From her car, though, she looked back at the lighted windows and saw Hana busy in the kitchen, the children standing around her. She felt so lonely and sad. She cried a little in the car.

That evening, at her apartment in Somerville, Lucy listened to David on the telephone recount his day, as he did almost every evening. She listened to him talk about a new restaurant he had been to with an old friend from out of town, but as he talked she could hardly listen, she was leafing through the book and again stared at the face of that baby wide-eyed with death. Lucy had a frightening vision of a huge ditch into which the baby disappeared, *a ravening maw,* she said to herself. What a horrible phrase, a melodramatic phrase. Still she saw a huge mouth opening and gulping down all these children, thousands, hundreds of thousands, millions, or some bloody altar or fiery furnace of a Philistine god demanding sacrifices.

CHAPTER 4

At the end of October, on a Thursday afternoon, Martin, a colleague and friend of Lucy's, slowed down as he passed by Lucy's open office door. Lucy, who had been asleep with her head down on her crossed arms, books piled around her, stirred and raised her head, her face flushed rosy, the outline of her wristwatch face imprinted on her forehead. Looking up at Martin, she said, "I think I had a wonderful dream. Someone royal spoke to me." She paused. "I wish I could remember. Maybe I'll have more dreams, though. When I'm not writing, or I'm stuck in my writing, I dream in series, the best kind of dream, with lots of color and usually needing no interpretation." Her face tightened the slightest bit. "I could use a good dream."

"Need a consultation?" Lucy and Martin sometimes played at being each other's therapist and after a session handed over an imaginary hundred dollars. Martin did have the air of a particularly likable therapist, with his rumpled white shirt, sweater vest, baggy pants, untied shoes, and big canvas beach bag of books. "I've been owing you a session for almost half a year, now."

"What I need is not consultation but consolation. I can't believe

I'm forty. How old do I look? How much gray do I have in my hair?" She tipped her head toward him and felt him carefully part her hair to give it a thorough look. How pleasant it was to have a friend who took hair questions seriously. "You should have been a hairdresser."

"What can I say? I took a vocational wrong turn and became a British eighteenth-century specialist. Of course, I could combine the two: in my office hours I could talk about Burke's theory of the sublime while I do the student's hair." He poked at her hair a little more. "Hm, I'd say you've got a silvery-gold effect going. Sort of a vermeil effect."

"Vermeil! A hairdresser for poets." She raised her head and looked at him. "You've got great hair." His hairline was only slightly receding, and his hair was only a little gray. "Like David."

"Everybody thinks that guys over forty with hair don't have hair problems. But there is the hair-growing-on-your-back problem and the hair-growing-in-your-ears problem. And hair's the least of your worries—there's the pecker problem. Lots less lift. You have to think some to get it up."

"You didn't have to think before?"

"Could say it did the thinking for me! Now I have to have a certain long-drawn-out approach for the take-off. Languor, I've decided, is the key."

Lucy boasted a little on David's behalf. "David's close to sixty, but there's still the old flagpole to salute every morning."

"That's different. The morning erection is a constant."

Lucy ignored him. "Must be funny to have this piece of flesh with a mind and power of its own."

"Hydraulics."

"Women mangofy, swell into ripe, juicy mangoes, as Michael would put it. You should see Michael eat a mango. He cuts it in half, scores the pulpy side into perfect little squares with the knife, as only a surgeon's son would do, turns it inside out so it's a mango skyscraper skyline, then devours it sucking, raking it with his teeth, grinning at me with these little mango strings caught in his teeth, juice dribbling down his flabby jaws." She laughed. "That's what sex with him was like, too. Well, not the knife part!"

"Oh, Mr. Lubricity!"

Lucy hastened to give David equal time. "On the subject of penises—here's something funny. Really I shouldn't tell you this— but the other morning David addressed his penis as 'Diane.' It was 'Diane this' and 'Diane that.' He'd die if he knew I told you this."

"So you're having a lesbian relationship with his penis?"

Lucy laughed.

"I hope the 'Genius of Affection' appreciates the, what should I say, 'colorful' reputation you're giving him. The 'Genius of Affection'—a very eighteenth-century title."

Martin remembered everything. Lucy herself had forgotten the title she had bestowed on David. One night, as she swung into the suburban side road that led to David's house, she saw the house with the interior light softly gleaming through the shades as an emblem of luminous love. She was as excited and happy as if it were the very first time she went to his house, after a month of admiring him from afar and inventing excuses to talk to him. She knocked at the back door, and he answered and pulled her in, held her so close and kissed her. In a sudden burst of feeling she had bestowed the title upon him. Now the language struck her as too abstract. "I've been trying out a new metaphor for David. Silt."

Martin started laughing.

"I know it sounds strange. But, think, when rivers overflow their banks, they spread on the exhausted fields the thick rich silt of decay. I keep picturing flooding waters thick with silt, humble but omnipotent silt, rich and dark. After the flood waters recede, things will grow quickly in the loamy soil."

"A 'Genius of Fecundity' flooding your alluvial plain?"

"Metaphorically, metaphorically." She laughed. "I'm still working out the kinks in this idea." She changed the subject. "So how're Match and Fergus doing? I have to come by and see them. I've neglected you all this summer."

"David sounds like a pretty good excuse. But we have missed you dropping by. Match and the baby are fine, just fine. Every day I go home and I think I am so lucky, even when I have to be errand boy for Match and change the baby's diaper and sit up with him at night. Not getting much work done. Just too hard to work when there's so much to enjoy in the world—the baby, the garden, and, as always, Match."

Lucy became a little sad, with the same sadness she had felt after visiting with Hana. A little sad, a little lonely, a little jealous. She looked at her watch. "I better get back to work. Tell Match hello for me. Maybe I'll schedule a consultation soon."

"Like I said, I've owed you one for a long time. And come on over sometime soon. Bring David." Martin turned to leave.

Lucy called him back. "Michael sent me a postcard of a temple garden lush with foliage. The short funny friendly message made me laugh and made me want to write a little note, in return. But I feel guilty about it."

Martin turned around and came back to the door of her office. "So it's a Dr. Love consultation? Dr. Love is always open for business." Martin enjoyed exercising his special "Dr. Love's Love Ministry," as Lucy had called it, a ministry of love advice for all females, for he had a great capacity to listen to and ponder over the complications of the heart. And of Lucy's friends, he was the one who best knew Michael. He had been the one Lucy talked to when she was falling in love with Michael and when she lost Michael. He had made a virtual fortune that year in the therapeutic profession.

Lucy knew Martin would be most indulgent, still she hurried on, rather embarrassed. "The note would be a short friendly note. I know it's over with Michael, but how often do you meet people who make you laugh, who make you feel alive? And I liked how alive to the world he was, he would touch a cat so knowingly, a tree, and a child and me. Everything was to be touched and loved. I hate being out of touch. It's like having a layer of skin stripped away. Never to get it back seems unbearable. Maybe because I'm getting older, I can't bear to lose that layer." Lucy could hear how this sounded and insisted, "It's not about seeing him, or starting up with him again. It's simply to be in touch with him—because Michael is Michael and I am who I am, it's unnatural, a waste not to be in touch."

"Oh, I see, you're writing in the interests of conserving the rarity of true affinity on the planet. The letter's a kind of ecological gesture." Anyone else would have said this in an ironic tone, but not Martin.

Lucy nodded. "I can't bear to lose my sense of how real the affinity was. More real than almost anything else I've felt. I want to acknowledge that. Otherwise it's like denying a historical fact." She thought for a moment. "I don't need to write the letter, saying it to you out loud is enough. Enough of a memorial, historical marker."

"You know I understand. I know that if I lost Match, I'd probably fall in love, but never again in that way."

Lucy sighed. "Here's my hundred, you've earned it."

"All right, good to talk to you." He put his arm around her and said, "Let me just 'hug your neck,' as my aunts down South all say."

Minutes after Martin left, Lucy looked at all the papers in front of her and couldn't bear to work.

She pushed open the heavy doors to the building and turned into the walled garden adjoining it. Her quick steps scattered the pebbles of the path. She flung herself down on a bench, her shoulders went up, and her head came down in her sweater, like a turtle pulling in her head.

She didn't notice a man sitting on a bench across the garden and watching her. He leaned back against the wall and pulled out a very green apple from his pocket. Wiped off the lint and took a big crunching bite.

Looking up and startled by the two eyes looking at her, Lucy gasped, "Oh, Jesus!" Her hand went to her heart. Then she laughed at herself and said to the man, "Sometimes I get so lost in my own thoughts, I jump when anything comes near me." She didn't recognize him as someone at the university.

"But I didn't come near you." He must have heard how sharp he sounded, for a moment later he smiled to show he didn't mean to be.

Lucy looked at this man with his dark hair ruffled up, dark eyes, a thin man, thin as a runner, long and lanky, in an old jacket huddled against the wall, sitting there in the sun with that too-green apple—a spring green, a livid green jarring on her, it seemed so out of season with the autumnal herb garden of brown and muted greens, the lichens on the stone benches dusty green and black. Why couldn't she be left alone? Lucy stood up to leave. "Yes, that's true."

"Don't go," he said quietly. "I don't want to disturb you. In fact, I'm rather tired, and I don't have anything to say."

Lucy did the polite thing and sat back down, closed her eyes. He was true to his word and didn't talk. Even more, he seemed capable of an utter stillness. After a while she found that it was pleasurable to sit in the sun with someone, even a stranger, and let her mind wander. She looked at the garden, a Tudor-style herb garden of lavender, thyme, sage—silvery broad sage leaves. A garden to match the turrets and crenellation of the Institute's architecture. The sun, hot in this protected garden, warmed up the resinous smells of sage and lavender. Michael had promised her a walled garden. As he declared again and again, walls make a garden. He said it would be a punctuation garden, with a eucalyptus tree, because of its comma leaves that dangled down. *Comma,* he elaborated, was *virgule* in French, and *virgule* came from *verge, petit verge,* "little cock," even though, he pointed out, the eucalyptus made big commas. She reached out, picked a leaf from the sage bush, and studied the long slim dusty-green leaf with a minutely cobbled surface. Then she turned her mind, in compensation for thinking of Michael, to try to work out her silt metaphor for David again and decided it wouldn't be an easy one to explain to him, he would get irritated before she could—

Her companion bit into the apple again—the apple seemed determined to act as a go-between.

She looked up and smiled. "Your apple is awfully loud."

He laughed and leaned forward on his bench. "I'm trying to show some signs of life after reading the lines on the sundial here."

With his feet, he had pushed aside the grasses that had overgrown a verdigrised brass sundial. Lucy had never noticed there were words at its base. She came over to look.

> *My name is die*
> *All. You are mortall Creature.*

He said, "I've been living in California and forgotten about seasons—there you can seem to live outside of time. Here where time flaunts itself I'm worried that I'm becoming a mortal creature. All the leaves turning so red and purple and gold, they shout at you *time time time*! That the world is dying. So I had to take a bite out of my ever-green apple. Good old Granny Smiths!"

Lucy stood up and held out her hand. "Lucy Woolhandler."

"Arthur Wall. Your hand is as cool and dry as the skin of my apple. That's nice."

His directness caught her by surprise. Then she remembered, "Oh so you're Arthur Wall, my friend Hana—"

"Hana Matsuo, of course."

"I'm so glad you're here—for her sake, she needs someone to talk to about poetry."

"I'm more of a prose person these days."

"Yes, that's right, I read the other day in the Institute newsletter that you're translating the diary of a medieval Japanese court lady. What's her life like?"

He looked at her. "You really want to know? I can see already that life here at the university is different from life at Berkeley. There people are only interested in their own work. They inquire politely about one's project, but telling them is bad form."

"Tell me, tell me."

"Her life's rather sad and lively at the same time. Spends the first part of it as a lady of the imperial court at Kyoto, getting into romantic scrapes. Her problem is that she is always in love with two men at the same time. Then she falls from Imperial grace, leaves the court, becomes a Buddhist nun. The final section of the diary records her travels, mostly pilgrimages to various temples."

"The court is the lively part and the nun's life is the sad part?"

"No, just the opposite. At court she cries over all her troubles. Japanese poetry is full of tear-soaked sleeves—hers must be very soggy. The lively part is the travels. She's a born traveler and meets all sorts of people on the road, merchants and prostitutes and poor people. A court lady'd never get to do that."

"Do you like writing in a woman's voice?"

"I suppose I might be making her too much like me, romantic when she is ironic. When you are involved with a subject, you become it, it becomes you. Are women ironic or romantic?"

Lucy reflected a moment and smiled. "I've been too romantic. In my old age, maybe I'll strive for more irony. An affectionate irony, though." She changed the subject. "I'm trying to start something Japanese, too. About an American woman, traveling to Japan, at the turn of the century. She is rich and collects antique Japanese robes."

"Do you have a title?"

Lucy hesitated. "I'm not sure I have a real title, only a working title, for myself. I got it from looking at a lovely Japanese screen. The screen's tall and long, mounted with gold paper, and painted on it, in a trompe l'oeil effect, are those long black lacquered bars used for airing robes, and draped over these bars, or rather flung over them as if someone were in a hurry, are three kimonos. A yellow kimono with iris by a stream, a blue checkered kimono, and a gray with a pattern of falling red leaves—"

"Your title is '*Tagasode*'—the poetic word for those sleeves trailing from behind screens, off verandas, provoking a desire to see the hidden woman who wears that exquisite robe."

Lucy laughed. "Of course, you'd know."

"It's not always the sight of the sleeves, but also the smoky perfume in which the sleeves are steeped:

> '*more than the color*
> *of the flower the fragrance*
> *delights my senses—*
> *whose scented sleeve brushed against*
> *the plum blossoms near my house.*'"

Lucy might cry. "Whose sleeves" was a phrase steeped in longing. She could smell the sage in her hands, the dusky-smelling lavender. She started talking to distract herself. "The problem of my title, 'Whose Sleeves,' is that the reader won't get it."

"I have the same problem. I would like to use for my diary the title translated from the Japanese, *Unsolicited Confessions*. The title is supposed to be self-effacing—that these little things she records are of no interest to anyone, although the author also tells us she hopes to keep alive the family literary tradition. That title will mean nothing to an English reader, so I have to call it something like *The Diary of a Japanese Court Lady*. I do hope to capture the feeling of her literary aspirations, for there's something she achieved beyond merely an account of her life, something that spills over into the reader's life."

"I'm usually pretty good with titles, but I'm stuck on one for this book. I'll end up with an extremely dull title, too. *Lucy Baldrich, American Collector of Japanese Textiles in the Early Twentieth Century,* or something like."

"So the phrase 'whose sleeves' is more about you?"

Again, Lucy was surprised at his directness. "Some days I do feel like an unseen woman. One only sees the trailing robe."

"Who's the poet writing about your sleeves?"

She blushed. "People have better things to do."

Arthur smiled. "How did you get interested in a collector? Do you collect anything?"

"No, no. I'm too unorganized and poor. But I think I know why people collect things like paintings, or furniture, or dishes—it's things that have body." Lucy looked up at Arthur. "We love them, want them within reach. Even when we are dead—thus all the precious objects, literally and figuratively, buried with the dead." Lucy stopped a moment. "In Japan my Lucy meets a collector of textiles who is mad about old robes. Once he even arranges a marriage between two antique robes."

"Arranged marriage or true love?"

Lucy laughed. "Even if it's arranged, I'm sure the robes grow to love one another. See, I'm still a romantic."

"So we have some things in common. Dull titles, women traveling in Japan. Your Lucy doesn't become a Buddhist, does she?"

"Once she said, 'I'd rather be a Buddhist than a Baptist.'"

He laughed and then asked her, "Is this your first book? Forgive me for not knowing."

"Please, it's not your field. It's my third. It will be my third, if I ever get started."

"What is the first one about?"

"Oh, I might be lucky with that book. I'm a frustrated novelist, so I try to make these studies have a story. Someone who makes films wrote me recently and said they thought the book could be a great movie. I might get some money! I haven't heard from her again, but I can fantasize."

"You'd spend the money on—?"

Lucy surprised herself by saying instantly, "I'd spend it on a house. A very small house, with a small garden. The picture is so vivid. I see myself sitting on the front steps and a cat sitting in the bushes. I was always so impressed with my grandmother living alone in her farmhouse, though she had a dog and chickens, no cat. We moved so much, when I was young, that she seemed the only person who I knew was truly home." Lucy stopped. It was rather upsetting to discover in her own mind that she had plans other than living with David. This plan must belong to some part of her brain that predated David, that the new David part hadn't yet colonized.

"I just bought a house."

When she heard Arthur speak again, she was startled, she had almost forgotten he was there. "Where?"

"In Somerville. It was cheaper than Cambridge."

"Oh, people always see Somerville only as a cheaper Cambridge. I think Somerville has its charms. The people yell instead of talking, the houses are the sublime of plainness, the gardens small and funny with their grape arbors of iron piping, and those saints' statues housed in the upturned bathtubs!"

"Not quite a realtor's description of a neighborhood's attraction. You seem to know Somerville quite well."

"Oh, I live there, too." She added, "In a small apartment in a house that's falling apart. I like my apartment, up under the eaves, me and the pigeons and the squirrels, who get in under the roof and scrabble around. It's like a treehouse. And I have a bit of garden in front. But the front door is loose, and the rain leaks into the ceiling when a big storm blows through. I should move."

"So, of course you dream about your own snug house, down on the ground."

"What's it like having a house? Being down on the ground, rooted. Seems so exotic to me."

"Rather unsettling. Meryl, my friend—I mean, my wife, we've been together for years, but decided to get married right before we moved here—and I have always lived in rented apartments, too. Apartments are easy to find, easy to leave behind. But now she's ill. We moved here because only in Boston could we get the latest experimental treatments for her, and I wanted to give her a home at last. That seemed important to me, although I'm not sure if Meryl truly cares."

"I'm sorry your wife is sick."

"I thought that having a house would be more peaceful for her, but so far it's been rather noisy. In order to have a ramp for the wheelchair, our yard and house have been invaded by young carpenters, with their loud saws and their radios. Then the medical decorators came in—from the local hospital supply—dragging in their furnishings: hospital bed, sling, wheelchair." He stopped and looked at Lucy—she felt the look almost too sharp a calculation of her. Then he said, "Today is my first day at work. But I couldn't work, I kept wondering, what had Meryl done today while I was away? I picture her lying in bed, looking out the window at the yellow leaves of that giant larch tree next door. Before I left, I opened the shade so she could look out the window. Put the television remote under her index finger. I keep asking myself, did I tell Bonnie, the daytime nurse, to turn the blinds down a little later when the sun shines too directly in the window? Will Bonnie remember all the signals I've worked out with Meryl? Wiggling the finger means she is thirsty. Blinking twice yes, once no, blinking rapidly means she has an itch."

He stopped, then continued as if speaking to himself. "I think, how long will it be before moving that one finger will be impossible? At least the blinking, the doctor said, will not stop. Bonnie, I keep telling myself, is trained to pay attention to these things, I have to trust her. One thing I've always wanted to ask Bonnie or the doctor is, what to do about those little peculiar habitual gestures Meryl had? As long as I've known her, Meryl twiddled her hair. She'd tease out a lock of her hair and twist it and twist it, without thinking. Now that she can't move her arms anymore, does she feel the impulse to still twist her hair? I want to know, should I twiddle her hair for her?"

Lucy had been looking at his hands as he spoke, hands rather thin but muscular. Those hands lifted, fed, washed the sick woman. Held her firmly, laid her down gently. She suddenly thought, he had been attending to her, too, in the conversation, easing her restlessness.

"I'm sorry to tell you all this. You don't know me. To make amends, please come by if you need any help with Japanese." Then he caught himself and added, "But maybe you know Japanese."

Lucy heard the embarrassment in his voice—so the calculation was simply to know if he could confide all this, he has no one here, no friends, why not her. She could be light, too, give some relief to him. She began to rattle a little, "Oh, I can say about three words: yes, thanks, excuse me—*hai, dōmo arigatō, sumimasen*—no, four—delicious, *oishii*!"

He said quickly, "You can always drop by my office in the Asian Studies department. Number 4."

There didn't seem much else to say. Both of them sat for a moment in parallel ruminations. Then Lucy remarked, almost to herself, "If only I could become a Buddhist nun." She looked straight at him, smiled a little. "Clouds coming in." He smiled back, and she looked for a moment too long at his face. It was a haughty narrow face precisely drawn, finely textured flesh taut over the cheekbones, a large arched nose, large dark eyes, intent and cool and thickly black lashed, quite beautiful eyes pitched under thin raised eyebrows, above them a high forehead framed by the almost-squared-off dark hairline. Suddenly she worried that maybe he thought she had been slightly flirting with him, and she had let him believe she was alone. She hastily added, "Maybe you would come to dinner with my friend David and me. You must have met him. He works—"

"Yes, I know his work. Chinese Muslims."

"I'll invite you, to meet other people, if you want to meet other people. I haven't had people over for a long time, it would be nice to have a dinner party."

Martin and another of Lucy's colleagues, Cappy, were laughing as they walked down the sidewalk outside the garden, and seeing Lucy and Arthur, they waved and turned in to say hello.

After Lucy introduced Arthur, he looked down at Cappy's clogs, high-heeled, green velvet, with big black bows. "Your shoes are very Louis Fourteenth." With her long embroidered jacket, her newly permed hair, and these velvet clogs, Cappy did look like a female impersonator of the Sun King. Lucy and Martin laughed. Cappy beamed, delighted to be the center of attention in a very Sun King manner.

"So what were you two laughing about?" Lucy wanted to know.

Martin grinned and said, "Cappy here's telling me about an article she read in the newspaper. On dolphin sex. She's fantasizing about some young and handsome Flipper towing her back to his lair. Flipper flips Cappy."

"I was telling Martin that dolphin sex is very rough. The males gang up on a single female. I always thought dolphins were sweet and intelligent."

Martin crowed, "Oh, it's a gang of Flippers you're dreaming of."

"Well, if it's a gang, not any one in particular and I can't prevent them, then it's not my fault, my husband can't blame me."

"Cappy, Cappy, Cappy," Martin cried out. "What are we going to do with you? What I want to know is, how has Bill kept a hold of you for twenty-two years, you seething hotbed of sexuality?"

Cappy clicked her clogs together.

Lucy was laughing and said to Arthur, "Sex seems to be the main topic in our department, the Humanities Center. We're interdisciplinary, so at least professionally there's copulation going on. My friend David thinks that we're having sex with each other in our offices."

Martin warmed up even more to his subject. "Oh, Cappy, Cappy, yes, office sex. Someday we'll just have to do it. I'm not a dolphin, but how about this: one day, maybe, you'll be sitting in your desk chair, reading, working so hard, and I'll just get on my hands and knees and just crawl up under your dress, under your desk, and you can go on reading, you won't have to do a thing."

Cappy feigned shock. "Martin!" Yet she was pleased. This flirtation had been going on for years, without consummation, but giving both of them pleasure. Cappy, in her mid-forties and the wife of Bill, an engineer, and mother of three teenagers, liked being Martin's imaginary femme fatale. Dr. Love was happy to service her.

"Aren't you both scared of Match?" Lucy asked. Match was ready to give the Antiguan "cut-eye" to any other female who latched on to Martin, which would be a light punishment compared with what Martin would suffer.

Martin's smile was smug. "It's true that since I met Match, I've had a hard life. Those women from Antigua make a man walk the straight and narrow path. I'm 'under manners,' as Match says. For you, though"—he looked longingly at Cappy—"if I were allowed to worship at the altar of your sacred spheres, the risk might be worth it!"

Lucy said, "Martin, what you need in your garden is a statue of Cappy complete with clogs for your very own Cappy-love-goddess shrine. Make it a real Armida's bower of love flowers, bleeding hearts, forget-me-nots, red roses, Venus flytraps!"

"Oh, please, Jesus, please, just once let me be snapped up in Cappy's trap!"

Arthur leaned the slightest bit back against Lucy.

Cappy looked at her watch and sighed. "I've got to go pick up Luke."

Martin said, "I better go, too—Match is waiting." They left.

Arthur looked at his watch and said, "I have to go, too. I'm late." He hurried away.

Lucy didn't have any particular place to be or anyone particular to see. Tomorrow night, Friday night, when the weekend began, she would see David, but not tonight. They were both sticking to their plan of work-week solitude and weekend togetherness.

Back in the library, Lucy looked at the stacks of books, the scatter of pens and note cards. She brooded over the vision of the little house that she had confessed to Arthur Wall. And again she saw a little house, a little garden, a cat, and herself sitting on a front step. And she would have a fence, not high, not to keep people out, but to give a boundary, a border to play with, to trail her robes over. But she saw herself alone in this picture. Her grandmother at least had had a large family, who visited her almost daily. How had this Arthur Wall provoked her to say such a thing?

Lucy picked up a pen and wrote out "Whose Sleeves" in scrawling letters on an index card. The line excited her, made her sad, seemed the touchstone for her feeling about the project. When would feeling turn into words? She tacked the card on the bulletin board above her desk. Now to work. She had an hour before it was time to go home for dinner.

Instead she found herself writing a letter to Michael. Lucy looked around furtively, even curled her hand around the paper to shield her writing, though of course no one could see she wrote to Michael.

Mon St. Michel, St. Michael and All Saints, or Saint of All Things,
I sat in a walled garden today and thought of you. You must have
a garden in Japan. Is it like the garden on the postcard you sent?
Send me a description of the plants and describe their smells. I often
pass the shrub you said has the smell of perfumy powdered thighs,
the one you said you would put in a garden of vulgar smells. A clero-
dendron, I think you called it. Strange how the leaves smell horribly
and the little purple white flowers so sweetly—you're right, like
drugstore perfume. And tell me the polite name of the Tampax bush
you showed me.

Lucy paused. The rest of the letter she wrote very quickly.

I miss you, I miss laughing. Perhaps I'll make a little shrine to my
St. Michael in my garden. I'll build a little box and put some
Christmas tree lights on it—would you like them to blink? I can
repaint you every summer, after winter peels you down to the
cement, or wrap you in burlap like the old Italian men in my
neighborhood do their trees here, to protect them from the heavy
weight of the snow and ice.
I've met a new person at the university, Arthur Wall, a famous
translator and scholar. You would like him.

Why would Michael like Arthur Wall? Why had Arthur Wall
turned up in her letter—because he turned up in the garden?
Because he seemed kind? Yes, like Martin, he truly seemed to have
some of Michael's imaginative kindness—he could make someone
talk, he would listen carefully, and enter into everything said, in a
kindly manner.

She read over her letter. It was short, choppy, with the middle cut
out, the middle in which she might have asked to see him, to make
a plan for the future. She tore up the letter, appalled that she could

have these thoughts at the same time she knew she loved David, wanted to live with David. Her head hurt with double thoughts, of David, of Michael, of David, of living alone.

Lucy gathered together her books. Her dream suddenly came back to her. Upon a throne, a dusky golden throne, Lucy's grandmother sat in her old shapeless green-and-blue-print farm woman's dress. Her eyes a bright blue, her face regal, like an old empress. Lucy's mother stood next to her grandmother—who was curiously not her mother's mother—but they stood together, and her mother handed Lucy her gold and amethyst bejeweled watch on the heavy gold chain. If she didn't write the dream down, she would lose it, this precious fortieth-birthday-gift dream. The gift was of time, when Lucy felt she had no time to waste, that it might already be too late. Time for what?

Would this be, as she had told Martin, the first of several dreams?

CHAPTER 5

That night Arthur, as usual, fed Meryl, washed her. Using the sling, he hoisted her from the wheelchair and lowered her onto the bed. He slid the bedpan under her. The only actions that would be left to her at the end were, the doctor said, blinking her eyes and contracting her sphincter. Rolling her this way, that way, he got her into her pajama top. He lifted her legs and pulled on the pajama bottoms. He put her hands in his lap to trim her fingernails. Her hands were so contracted, with the fingers tightly curled, they looked like Chinese bound feet. The fingernails if not cut would dig into her flesh. He cut her nails very short. Meryl used to keep her nails long and painted to lengthen her already long elegant fingers. He cut her toenails. Instead of curling, her feet were pointed, too pointed—the doctors called it "posturing," as if she were pretentious or posing. The irony, of course, was that she had been proud of her extension when she was a ballet dancer, years ago, and as the ballet teacher she had been until she fell ill. Now the toes were forever pointed, the legs too straight. "Lead pipe rigidity" was the medical phrase for the symptom. She used to paint her toenails, too.

Arthur at moments could detach himself and see the horror of these hands and feet. Yet taking care of Meryl every day and every night, he couldn't remember if he had ever felt the shock of it. The contraction happened slowly—he had seen only what needed to be done next.

Meryl's bangs needed to be trimmed, he saw. Bonnie could try to cut them. He was so clumsy, he would butcher them. Maybe he could get a hairdresser to come over. He wanted Meryl to look as neat as when she could take care of herself. It might be expensive, but why not a little luxury? Her prescriptions were expensive. That reminded him that he needed two refills. He would call the pharmacy later and pick them up tomorrow.

When she was ready for bed, Arthur sat next to her with the pack of cards in his hand and dealt out the game of solitaire on the ottoman next to her bed. He put the cards down for her, after holding them up and asking her advice, on the "ottoman empire," as he called it. King of diamonds.

Meryl had always played solitaire while she talked to him in that high-pitched piccolo voice of hers about her ballet classes, the rehearsals, anything that came to mind, without waiting for or, he knew, needing a response from him. Now he played the cards for her and made an effort to talk, for it was too easy to be silent around her as if he were alone. He would be thinking his own thoughts until Meryl croaked like some strange bird, and he would recall that she was there, though with her throat muscles stiffening, that croak became more difficult to achieve. He should pay even closer attention. Her only sign would be blinking at him. What if then she blinked so rapidly, the volume of signals blurred into no signal, and he couldn't tell if she were making a practical request, say, to turn down the heat? Or a desperate call for help? Of course, if you couldn't turn down the heat yourself and couldn't make anyone do it for you, that would constitute desperation.

He talked to her with as much liveliness as he could muster. He often pictured them both bobbing in the water, like in an old post-card of the Great Salt Lake that Meryl had found in an antique store and carried from apartment to apartment in her box of little odds and ends. The salty water buoying them, tourists sat up straight and played cards on a floating card table and chatted away, laughed.

Arthur talked of the places he and she had visited and where they had lived. How extraordinarily detailed was his memory now of all those places, as he sat with her day after day, night after night. The trip to China, the Great Wall, broken and grassy. The red-cheeked young Chinese women, in drab pants and padded jackets, staring, their cheeks chapped red by the cold wind. The official who had been their guide, a thin young man who smoked and smoked, his frame racked with coughs, his clothing mended clumsily. Arthur even remembered the mending on his jacket, in pink thread and in washed-out blue thread. The gorge of the Yangtze, sheer cliff walls, and their boat among all the other light craft piled high with crates and chickens. Their boat bobbing through the rapids of yellow water. How frightened Meryl had been, of and for all those light craft. The time they spent in Tokyo, in a tiny apartment in one of those quiet neighborhoods behind the big busy avenues. He had worked in the archives during the day, while Meryl had attended performances of Japanese ritual dance. She must have told him about it in detail, but he did not remember those details. When had he stopped listening to her?

Arthur put an eight of clubs in the wrong place—no, no, he should know better by now. He looked up, expecting Meryl to shake her head and say sharply, "No, not there," her irritation triumphing over her incapacity.

The earliest memories, of their meeting in Taiwan, came back to him, in especial detail. Meryl was then married to another aca-demic. Both Arthur and her husband were there to learn Chinese that summer. Meryl had instantly, busily set out to make Arthur hers. He must have seemed lighter than her husband, as light as she felt herself to be, simply floating across the face of the earth. She must have seen immediately that it didn't matter if she talked and talked, he was quiet, shy, and only cared about his work. In Taiwan, they walked in graveyards hidden in the forests on the hills. Did Meryl remember the noisy markets with ducks hanging from bamboo sticks? The kitchen with a flowing drain running right through it?

Meryl's index finger on her left hand moved. The slight movement caught his eye. He looked up. Her eyes were staring at him. She croaked, and he gave her some water. The water spilled a bit, but he quickly caught it with the towel. The finger moved again, he played another card.

What other details might she remember? Did she remember the faces of the women Arthur had thought he loved? She had met them. Did she remember the blonde with the red lipstick, who wore a rosy silk Chinese jacket and black silky pants? This was the scholar of Chinese poetry, small, slim, with her measured British voice, low and even, who wrote notes in Chinese and put them in his pockets, laughing when he pulled them out at parties and looked at them quizzically. Did Meryl remember the dark-haired poet and her long skirts, her furry sweaters, her black eyebrows like diacritical marks? Did Meryl still see now, as he did, their faces, alert, watchful, as she had talked on and on about her dance research at the various dinner parties they had all attended? Did she recall the timbre of their voices on the telephone, leaving messages for him? Did she remember those gifts, books with their prudent dedications to Arthur, soft ski sweaters for all those cross-country-ski trips he took without her, going away and coming back, not looking like someone who had been lonely? These details flashed like slides. Did these details flash in her mind from other angles? She had an eye for detail. One day Meryl had said to him, after a party, that the poet had a white hair in one eyebrow: she must be older than she said she was, she must dye her hair.

If Meryl remembered all these things, did she dwell upon them during the long days?

"And this card?" The jack of hearts—Arthur held it up. He looked over and saw that Meryl slept. Reaching over, he took her glasses off her face. The heavy lenses demanded thick frames, and made her look, with her thin long body, like a dragonfly with its big goggling eyes. He finished the game of solitaire and lost, as always.

Meryl probably knew about these other women and kept herself busy with the dance classes she taught, the research she did on certain choreographers—she had even published a few entries in an encyclopedia of dance, the finding of a new apartment whenever they moved to a new city. She must have believed that he would never leave her. And even when he thought he was so in love with someone else he could think of only them all day and all night, he had never left Meryl. He never left her alone for long in their small apartments, in each one of which she would set up on a nighttable her old little china Chinese dog with chipped and faded gold trim, the cube of rose-colored glass with several crazings that housed a clock, with its face off center and the faintest phosphorescence still clinging to its hands. Next to these she would lay her large black glasses, thick and opaque, collapsed for the moment.

When Meryl fell ill, he had a chance to make amends for the past, through action, not mere declaration. Her legs began to tremble, and soon she needed a cane, then a walker. Her legs stiffened, so she looked like a wooden puppet, and she took to the wheelchair. She had to depend on him. Arthur arranged several trips together. He had quoted the Chinese poem:

> "As for travel,
> On land there are carrying-chairs,

> *And on the water there are boats;*
> *So, if I can but keep my courage,*
> *What need have I of feet?"*

But courage, his courage and her courage, was not, in the end, enough.

After tucking the covers up to Meryl's shoulders, wiping the spittle from her chin, Arthur turned on the monitor, one of those baby-monitoring devices, turned off the light, turned on the night light, and went to his study.

On the table where he worked he had no little objects, nothing stuck to him, as it did to Meryl. He opened his working journal to the last entry, made seven weeks before, before he and Meryl had moved to Boston.

> *Berkeley, September 5. Fires up in the hills. Smoke rising as from a funeral pyre. Our apartment, in this house of wood and redwood shingle, would burn in seconds if the fire spreads this far. My Lady enters into an affair with the man who has pursued her since she was a girl, a man she knows is a kindred spirit. The affair is highly dangerous—she is the concubine of the emperor, to whom her father promised her on his deathbed and for whom she feels a certain affection, for he is kind and the only connection to the beloved dead father.*
>
> *Have worked three hours, will go home, attend Meryl, pack more boxes.*

Arthur wrote:

> *Boston, October 25. Bright northern light, rich blue sky, black pine trunks outside my office window—black-robed priests. Today my first day back at work. I lined up my dictionaries, my reference*

books, laid out my papers and did a few pages. So I rescue my Lady from her suspended animation, so again she is alive, pursuing her affair and petrified by guilt.

Suspended animation—what other way to describe Meryl, sitting in her wheelchair or lying in her bed, motionless. And he could not with his pen return her to complaining, laughing, crying. Even the stage of the disease when she could not control her laughter (she would literally laugh until she was sick) or tears (they flooded her face, smeared her spectacles) was over. In its place was this terrible, almost complete, silence. Arthur looked at his watch. He got up and turned Meryl on her other side. The little things everyone did and never thought about, like the need to roll over in the middle of the night.

He shut the journal.

Arthur went to bed. Before turning off the light, he looked through Lucy's two books, which he had checked out from the Institute's library right before he left that day.

The biography of Maria Martin did read like a lively novel. Maria Martin, a spinster, living with her sister and brother-in-law on his plantation in North Carolina, takes up the watercolor brush for a ladylike activity—when not helping to supervise the house and tend to her nephews and nieces. She finds her favorite subjects the rare plants in her brother-in-law's garden and the gardens of neighboring plant enthusiasts who have had plants shipped to them from all over the world and their own American frontier. Her brother-in-law invites Audubon, the great naturalist and painter of birds, to rest up from his travels at the plantation. Audubon sees Maria's work, and soon she is one of his several collaborators. She paints the purple bristling thistle, in her clear watercolor, upon which Audubon's goldfinch—done in chalky pastel and oil—perches.

Maria discovers in herself artistic and scientific ambition. She travels to famous gardens to note the plants native to habitats she will never visit. From Audubon she receives in the mail dead insects to study and to draw. Her brother-in-law funds all these activities.

It was almost a love story, too, Arthur said to himself. The brother-in-law and Audubon, both married men, seem in love with their Maria, vying with each other, in the letters they exchange, to praise "our Sweetheart." Perhaps it was the love story of a woman in love with two men as well, first the brother-in-law and then Audubon supplementing or supplanting that love. Lucy was scrupulously historical with her detailed account of plantation life, the role of unmarried relations on a plantation, the learned amateur's life, the famous naturalist's life—but still it felt like a love story, which gave the rest a great charm.

He put the book down and turned to Lucy's first book, the life of a seventeenth-century Dutch naturalist, Agnes Seitz, a woman who had married for love and been widowed, lost her child, and taken off to Surinam to study the nature of the other hemisphere. Here was Lucy's description of one of Seitz's paintings: "A southern swamp tree is host to a pedantic gathering of insects. The tree's leaves are sickly brown and chewed, but the tree is not quite dead—it is still capable of putting out a spray of tiny white flowers. Two different spiders have suspended their webs taut between the leaves. A large spider—golden brown, hairy-legged—broods on a huge yellow egg sac, from which tiny spiders crawl and swing on the web. The other spider—smaller than the first, with a black-and-yellow-striped body—crouches at the center of its web, devouring a large red ant. Or is the ant sucking out the life juices of the spider? Two large tarantulas, furry brown black, also inhabit the tree: one has a tiny ant between its mandibles, the other has forced a hummingbird onto its back along the branch. The bird's red-capped head is bent back, its yellow throat is exposed, its blue-green wings flutter seemingly in the throes of death, pressed down by the heavy spider, who has one of its legs in the nest of hummingbird eggs, claiming that, too. Farther down the trunk of the tree, more ants attack a beetlelike form. Giant termites dawdle close by, not part of the action, only spectators."

As Arthur lay there, waiting for sleep, he pondered the two stories. Like a flower, Maria Martin was pressed and dried between these two married men, dying a spinster. Agnes Seitz learned to give a hard look at birds, insects, disease, death. Lucy didn't strike him as like either of them. She hadn't buried her hope in her work or in service to others. She hadn't yet suffered that inevitable blow that made one so familiar with despair that all thought was devoted to doing whatever task was next, day after day, without hope. Odd that somewhere in her she could find a way to write about these women's lives.

Meryl was dying, and here he was coming to life for a moment or two, thinking about Lucy and her hopefulness. It was tempting to be alive again.

Arthur went to sleep. When he woke up at the first light, he lay in bed and took pleasure in lying still, like a child, in a bed that became a raft, especially on this rainy morning, or a nicely caulked boat, like Moses' basket caulked and let drift down the river until it fetched up into the bulrushes.

Did Meryl imagine anything like this? Did she think that the bed was her coffin in which she was buried alive? Yet the bed wasn't the coffin—her own body was the coffin closed upon her, her body so stiffened that only the last little hardening of the shell was left until she became a coffin in a whirlpool, turning and turning, whirling and whirling faster, until dead center in the whirlpool and then sucked down, sunk, and all the caulking in the world, all the shipshaping, would mean nothing.

He looked at his watch. Seven in the morning. Meryl must be awake by now. His second thought was that Lucy's smile, the way she laughed with her friends, reminded him of how it had always started before, the times he fell in love, when he met a woman who seemed to quicken the air around him.

CHAPTER 6

L ucy and David were invited to Martin's for dinner. Since Martin lived up the street from Lucy, David was to come to her house, and they would walk up together.

As Lucy waited for David to arrive, the telephone rang. Lucy's mother said in her light singsong telephone voice, "Hello, hello, I've just got a few minutes before I have to cook dinner. But I didn't want to let any more time go by before we talked."

Lucy quickly said, "I know, it's my fault. I've been so busy with David and school that I haven't called. In fact he's coming in a minute, so—"

"So let's talk for just a minute then. How is David?"

Lucy invoked that most useful of words, "Fine." She didn't want to get into another conversation like their last one, in which her mother had told her that her friends had reported "things" died off with many of these older men. Lucy had known her mother meant sex and had assured her, in the obscure way they always talked about sex, that she didn't have that kind of trouble with David. She did find it touching and amusing when her mother had assured her, in turn, that she herself did not have that problem with Lucy's father. With her mother on the line now, though, she felt irritated that her mother's opinion that David was too old for her could bother her, and at the same time she felt guilty that she couldn't talk about David in some ideal daughterly way when asked about him so innocently.

Today her mother had some more advice for her. "I was thinking that if you two decide to live together, it would be better if you move into a new place together. I've seen it too often with my friends when they get remarried—sometimes one person ends up moving into the other's place. They don't feel free to move things around, and so they're never really at home themselves."

Lucy was taken aback by her mother's sudden veer in the direction of accepting David. And how unnerving it was to feel as if her mother were speaking to her like someone her own age. Did the decades between forty and seventy count for nothing? "Oh, we're not ready to move in together just yet."

"Oh, yes, I guess there's no rush, it's not like you're planning on having a baby. I was only thinking about you and wanted to tell you that."

Did her mother think her too old to have a child? After a few hints over the years that she should get married and have a baby, now her mother sounded as if she had given up on Lucy. To change the subject, Lucy asked, "How is everyone?"

Oh, everything as always was too too busy. Caroline worked too hard at her two jobs. Her two older boys were getting so tall and big, Lucy couldn't imagine how much they ate, how much milk they drank. Lucy's father spent too much time at the church fixing this and that, this week it had been the water heater. Even as they spoke, her father was out at the hardware store, because Caroline's washing machine needed fixing again. But, of course, her mother said, "Now that he's retired, he is always eager to fix something, to have something useful to do." She herself had this slight sore throat she couldn't shake, but nothing serious. "And let me tell you a cute story. Evan [Caroline's youngest] came over yesterday and was downstairs playing with that old dehumidifier in the basement. He put the big globe beach ball on it, then twisted the dials. 'What are you doing, Evan?' I asked him. 'Weighing the world,' he told me, big as life. 'How much does it weigh?' 'A hundred bazillion pounds,' he said, you know, very matter-of-fact."

The weight of the world, Lucy thought, luckily was not on Evan's shoulders. She thought of the picture of the children in Hana's friend's book: the life crushed out of them by the weight of the world.

Her mother had, yesterday, while organizing her desk, come across an old letter from her Aunt Dora. What a funny detailed letter it was. "I should have tape-recorded her before she died—she loved to tell about her people and about Denver in the old days."

"You know a lot about those people and about Denver, too. Record what you know. I'd be interested."

"Not enough time in the day. Well, I can see by the clock that the gang's going to be coming over any minute. I better get some food on the table."

"Thanks for calling."

Her mother kept her on for one more minute. "By the way, what is your plan for Christmas? It'd be so nice to have you here. Caroline misses you so much, and so do we. You could bring David, too."

"Well, we both have a lot of work of our own to do once school lets out. And David's daughters are here—we'll probably have some sort of holiday celebration with them."

"What about next summer?"

Lucy said quickly, "David and I are thinking about going to Mexico next summer—but I'll try to come." In a few minutes, there would be such a bustle in her mother's kitchen, all her family eating, laughing, talking, rushing in and out the door. The moment she hung up, it would be so silent here. "I miss you all so much." The doorbell rang. "I've got to go."

"Well, let me know about coming this summer. Think about it."

"I will. Love you. Thanks for calling. Good-bye."

As Lucy and David walked up to Martin's, she brooded over the call with her mother. Then she smelled wood smoke in the air. People were lighting the first fires in their fireplaces, settling into their homes for the long winter.

David asked her, "Started writing today?"

Whenever David pressed her about her book, Lucy felt as if a teacher were after her. "I took some more notes."

"Hah, you can take notes until the end of time, you know."

"Someday I'll simply start."

"You can say that until the end of time."

Lucy was silent.

"Who else is coming to this dinner?"

"I don't know, could be the three of them or ten people. Dinners at Martin's are like freight trains, he keeps adding on cars." They turned a corner. "Arthur Wall lives on this street." Lucy looked at each house—which one was it? Then she saw the plain little house with the heavy new ramp built up to the side door. The day she had met him in the garden came back to her. How startled she had been, how warm the sun, how sad the story of his wife, Meryl. And he had asked her so many questions, she had said so much about herself, she was a little embarrassed. Still, his dark eyes looking at her so directly had not been unpleasant. Again she had that sense that he had attended to her in some way that gave her relief.

"Why does he live in Somerville? With what we're paying him, he could live in Hunnewell or Cambridge. I mean, it's all right for you to live here, you're kind of a bohemian in your own way."

"Martin lives in Somerville. He likes Somerville."

"Well, Martin's kind of eccentric."

"But you like eccentrics, don't you?" Lucy relaxed. She laughed and kissed him and held him tight. He held her close for a moment, too. They walked hand in hand the rest of the way.

The instant she saw Martin's house, Lucy was struck by how even more overgrown the garden had become since the last time she stopped by—and how delightful such excess was. The tall, rather plain Victorian house, with its sharpened-pencil tower, foundered among vegetation. In front a wandering pine's languid limbs limply arched up and fell, trailing their branches. Large azaleas and rhododendrons skirted the porch. A stand of thin bamboo rattled in the autumn air. Small trees, dogwood, and dwarf pines lined the driveway, branches reaching to tangle with other branches and form a dark tunnel. Suddenly enormous floodlights came on and turned that tunnel green-gold-red, and there was Martin himself, shovel in hand, standing among new shrubs still tilting on their burlapped root balls.

Martin saw them and said, "Match sent me out here to hold you off a minute. She wants that baby fed, and we'll distract him from the tit, hard as that is to believe. Someday that boy'll regret any second he didn't dig in. If he feeds now, we can play with him a bit and put him to bed. I thought I might start in on making some holes for my new rhodo room—"

Lucy laughed. "Rhodo den!"

"Filled up with my new Caribbean rhododendrons—in Match's honor. This one's called Trinidad, there's Jamaican orange, and St. Lucia—'course you all will have to come back in the spring to see how great these colors are."

"Take us on a little tour. David likes to garden, too."

"All right, the tour's theme will be Lucy's favorites." They walked into the backyard. He pointed out a tree. "Here's what Lucy calls my lipstick tree. It's a pink copper beech, the leaves have this pink edging like lipsticked lips."

Lucy stepped over to another tree. "And here's my first favorite tree of yours, the metasequoia. It looks so ancient, and its little frondy leaves are so soft. How big it is now. I haven't been here for ages." She saw David looking at her, then at Martin and frowning. Lucy wasn't sure what was wrong. Perhaps he was feeling left out, so she contracted her pleasure and said, "Tell Martin about your moon garden," and at that moment she thought that no two gardens were more different than this jungle and David's tidy patch.

David was pleased to detail all the white flowers he had in his garden. Martin became excited and suggested other white flowers, piling white upon white, Latin name upon Latin, until the baby Fergus came to the screen door and called to Martin, "You, you, you."

Match waved to Lucy over Fergus's head. "Hiii." Martin opened the door, picked up Fergus. They all went into the kitchen. What a handsome family: Martin with his longish dark hair, blue eyes, pale skin, spectacles, the big hands and feet, shoelaces as always untied and trailing. Match, dark brown, black eyes, coral lips, shapely body in her simple black dress. She was tiny but stood with a dancer's carriage, so that Lucy and Martin agreed she was the tallest short person they knew. Fergus, in a T-shirt and brightly colored pants, waved his hands, dancing to reggae in the background.

"So what does James Brown say, Fergus?" Martin asked the baby.

"Ye—ow," Fergus shouted.

Match said, "Oh, Martin. Fergus is into reggae now. Don't get the child all mixed up."

The inside of the house was Match's, uncluttered though filled with books, soft chairs, and bleached white shells from the white beaches of her home in Antigua. A huge length of blue African cloth was draped on one wall. Below it on a side table were neat little dishes of olives, nuts, peppery shrimp. The dining room table was set and brilliant with a huge bunch of roses, the last of the season, from Martin's garden. Match grinned at Lucy and David. "You've seen the yard. I'm telling him, he's got to stop planting roses, but then they are so beautiful."

Cappy and Bill arrived. Match poured the drinks. Martin swung Fergus around and talked sports with David and Bill.

Lucy asked Match about her novel, or her "navel," as they had christened it.

"Oh, it's coming along, you know." She worked as much as she could, though it was hard with the baby. Martin helped out, he was wonderful. "But I simply feel, Lucy, that it would mean so much to Martin, to finish his own book. 'Get out of that damn garden,' I tell him, 'put down the baby, and finish your book.' It's like he can't bring himself to face it. I don't know what else to say. So I just put my head down and go ahead with my own work."

Match turned to Cappy. "And when are you going to write your novel? Your kids are almost all grown up, you will have all the time in the world."

"Not a novel—a medieval romance, with a glittery cover, ripped bodices, though they didn't exactly wear bodices in the Middle Ages."

"A wimple-ripper?" Lucy offered, and at the same time glanced over at David. From sports Martin had moved David back onto gardens—Bill had wandered away—and they seemed to be having a nice talk. Again she wondered what had displeased him so during the garden tour. Since he seemed to be pleasantly occupied for the moment, she bent down to grab Fergus, lifting him up, tickling him, enjoying his squeal of pleasure, the feel of his solid little legs. "So he really has blue eyes."

"Must be my Scottish lineage lining up with Martin's vaguely Celtic ancestors," Match said. "He's going to be so much lighter than me. At home, when a baby is born, everyone lines up to come see it, see if it has good features, see if it is light or dark. My grandmother said when she saw me, 'But why is that girl so dark?' I had a friend here the other day, though, who said no one from Antigua would ever think Fergus was white because Fergus's nose was such an Antiguan nose. As we say, the coffee always rises through the cream."

Lucy started laughing, and Cappy asked Match if her family had a clan plaid.

"You mean that they could wear as sarongs to the beach?"

"There could be a clan plaid beach towel—!"

The doorbell rang. It was the Yus, a Chinese couple who also worked in Asian Studies at the university. Martin and the Yus belonged to the New England Bamboo Society. Mrs. Yu had seen his name on the membership list, recognized it from the university, and given him a call. Now they had long long talks about bamboo. Arthur Wall had come with the Yus. It turned out that Mr. Yu, a scholar of Chinese painting, and Arthur had collaborated on several books. Arthur was introduced around.

"We've met," Lucy said, smiling hello, startled once again at his direct look.

Lucy liked the Yus (she could never call the older couple by their first names) and was relieved to see them here because they were also friends of David's—he would not feel left out, alone among her friends. Hovering at David's side, she urged him to talk about his new project with Mr. Yu and Arthur Wall. Once he was launched, she left to help Match in the kitchen. When she returned, though, she found that Martin had joined them and begun a conversation on winter-hardy bamboos. The Yus entered into the discussion with great energy. David and Bill stood there, a bit back, left out, looking bored and sullen, but not bothering to engage each other. Lucy tried to console herself that this was part of the life of couples—they didn't enjoy the company of each other's friends. She herself wasn't particularly attracted to David's daughters and his friends, but she could get through an evening with them. And so would David tonight. Still, she was about to go over to him when Match looked at her watch and said, "Fergus isn't anywhere near being sleepy. Let's go ahead and eat."

They sat down to dinner. Martin kept Fergus on his knee, while Lucy helped Match serve. They laughed in the kitchen and made a most ceremonial presentation of the crown roast, parading it around the table, bowing to each guest. As Match carved it, Lucy arranged the grilled vegetables on a plate. There were yams, too, and a salad of cherry tomatoes, the last off Martin's vines.

The conversation at the table was loud. Lucy kept an eye on David, at first. He started to talk to Cappy about a proposed change in the Institute's overall policy governing the relation of the different satellite departments, like the Asian Studies department and the Humanities Center, insisting upon the proposal's defeat. He gestured with his hands, and looked thoughtful. He had been articulate, so he seemed satisfied. Yet as the dinner went on, the noisier it became, the less he said. He flung himself back in his chair, his hand over his mouth, his eyelids lowered over his eyes, watching Lucy. She, by this time, was enjoying herself so much, it had been such a long time since she saw these friends, that she forgot to pay attention.

Mrs. Yu took Fergus on her lap, bounced him, and sang a little song to him in Chinese. Martin asked her how many grandchildren she had.

"My eldest daughter has two, girl and boy. We're waiting for the second daughter to get *one in the oven.*"

Everyone laughed. Mrs. Yu learned much of her colloquial English from daytime soap operas. She and Match liked the same show and were soon catching each other up on the complicated life of Cricket, supermodel and brilliant lawyer. While everyone else made fun of them, Lucy, who watched soap operas off and on, argued, "But soap operas *are* like real life in a way. They follow the long-drawn-out changes that happen to characters, families over time. Life happens over time, not like in the movies."

"I keep telling my daughters to take their time. I can wait for grandchildren," David grimaced.

Lucy told the others, "I know David will be the first in line to get his hands on any grandchild, and I'll like having a baby around."

"Grandma Luc-y!" Cappy crowed.

David made a face.

"But Lucy's too young!" Match burst out, looking around for assent at everyone. "She should have her own baby."

Lucy willed her smile to stay in place and looked at David, who stared at his plate and shifted slightly in his chair.

Cappy rescued them by telling Martin and Match about a wonderful place to take Fergus this winter. She had taken Luke, her youngest, there just last week—with five of his friends—to a butterfly aviary in Westford, a giant greenhouse filled with plants and butterflies. "I would have enjoyed it more, of course, without six boys to keep from squashing the insects."

Bill, who had gotten up from the table to lie down on the sofa and seemed to be asleep, lifted his head. "Etymologically speaking, aviaries are for the birds."

Cappy groaned, "Oh, Bill!"

Martin started talking about a part-time job he had had in college, working in butterfly research. "We'd hunt for butterflies in the wild, for scrawny wild butterflies who spent their short lives frantically flying from bird beaks, their tattered wings testimony to many near escapes. In the butterfly lab, their children grew up fat, with stained-glass-window wings perfectly intact. They'd flap so slowly through the air—"

Bill from the sofa said, "I've never seen a bird eating a butterfly."

Arthur joined in the general conversation for the first time. "I'm one of the untouched. I've been in the terrarium of academic life all my life."

Lucy knew that perhaps he had been untouched before, but he

was no longer, he was out in the world, he had fluttered his ragged wings in front of her.

Cappy laughed. "All of us at the Institute are rather like lab butterflies. Lazy and fat and probably happy in our climate-controlled jobs."

Lucy stuck out and waved her arms. "I used to be a wild butterfly—my wings still have a few notches. But since meeting David and spending time in his aviary—no, no his *le-pi-dop-ter-a-ry*"—she bowed toward Bill—"I've been transformed into a fat fluffy butterfly." Lucy twitched her long black eyebrows, and for an instant they seemed antennae.

Match was grinning. "Martin had a specialty in this job. Tell them."

"I was gifted, the head of the lab told me, in mating butterflies." He held up his hands to demonstrate, precisely, how he held the male and how he held the female in their breeding position.

In what position, Lucy wondered, would he mate the specialist on early Christian sects, "Miss Yachting," with the classicist whom Lucy and Cappy had nicknamed "Odalecherous," because he struck languishing poses on garden benches?

"A monstrous coupling. If I ever find them doing it in a dark corner I'll take off my clog"—Cappy reached under the table and waved a clog in the air—"and squash them!" She banged the clog, not too hard, on the table.

Martin grabbed Cappy's mustard-yellow clog, held it out of her reach. "Think what these clogs do to—for—shoe fetishists! Bill?"

"Time for the next course," Match called out, and bustled about clearing plates and bringing clean ones, Lucy helping.

When everyone was served, the talk turned to the exhibition Mr. Yu and Arthur were working on for the Institute's exhibition of Chinese paintings.

Lucy became very excited. "I love those paintings, the mountains so eroded down to the humps of rocks. I love the little figures walking up the steep paths, or sitting watching the moon from their viewing pavilions. I love the dragons swirling like mist around mountaintops. I like their cat whiskers, their sexy muscular tails and haunches."

Mr. Yu said to Lucy, "Maybe you would like to come with my tour group to China. We'll see Buddhist cave paintings, what is the word—"

"Fresco?" Arthur prompted.

"Yes, fresco on cave walls, very interesting."

Mrs. Yu added, "Good food, too. My husband knows all the good restaurants in the province. My husband—he 'gets around.'"

While the others laughed, Lucy was still thinking about Chinese painting and turned to Arthur and Mr. Yu. "I have a question. I read somewhere that since the Buddha was born in the foothills of the Himalayas, Indian paintings of him always feature hills or mountains as a small background detail, but that in China those mountains and craggy hills become the painting, so much larger than any human presence."

David cut in, "You don't know anything about those paintings!"

Lucy's mouth was open but immobile. Her face hurt with the sudden hardening of it into a blank stone tablet. She turned to David and almost hissed, "I said I had read it somewhere. I wasn't claiming to know everything." Flushing a deep red, she made an effort to breathe regularly. Then she looked embarrassed and tried to smile.

Everyone started talking, and in a few minutes, when Match said she had to put Fergus to bed, Lucy jumped up and followed her upstairs. Cappy came along, too.

"I apologize for getting mad down there."

Cappy laughed. "Bill puts me down, too, when people are talking about my work. But he makes more of a joke about it."

As she unfolded the diaper, Fergus's legs and bottom up in the air,

Match said, "I like David, but it's like he can't let himself go. You can't let him hold you back. I'm not sorry I said something about a baby. So, when're you going to get yourself one of these?" The diaper on, she put her nose next to Fergus's, who crossed his eyes in pleasure. "Martin and I can't think of you not having a baby. You know what really works is to elevate your womb after sex. Once Martin held me upside down by my ankles to shake the sperm in. 'Martin,' I said, 'you're going to break my neck—'"

Lucy heard herself say, in a flat voice, "David doesn't want another child. And I understand that." She listened to the talk downstairs, she could hear Martin talking, Mrs. Yu laughing, Mr. Yu making a long explanation, Arthur Wall's quiet voice, and she could see David sitting there, silent, angry.

Fergus cried and twisted as Match wrestled him into his pajamas. She said to Lucy, "Well, in that case, when's Michael coming back?"

Lucy said quickly, "I have no idea. That's all over."

"I'm kidding. We'll figure out something. Now go over to the table, get a pen and paper, and write this down. It's the telephone number of my psychic—a session only costs forty dollars. And she's wonderful. She really, really helps. Sometimes I just fax her—she says she can feel the vibrations through the fax! She'll tell you what to do about getting a baby. Really!"

Cappy sighed loudly. "I said this to Match, and I'll say it to you: don't have children. They'll ruin your lives. I mean I love my husband and my children, but you can't do anything. You rush between your job and home. Match, you had it so good. You got to travel, have lots of sex. Besides, here I am about ready to be free again, have fun again, and you're busy changing diapers and soon will be talking about first grade. It's not fair."

Match and Lucy laughed, and Match immediately became her most soothing self. "Oh, Cappy, think how much pleasure you'll get in writing me postcards from foreign places."

Downstairs they sat down to dessert, an apple pie that Cappy announced with great satisfaction that she had made Bill make. As they ate, everyone was silent, then Martin looked curiously at Bill. "I might be wrong, but I think there's a war going on between the sweet and the salt in this pie."

"Yes, yes," everyone cried.

Bill laughed. "I made a mistake in the recipe and put in a little bit more than a pinch—more like half a cup. I didn't think you'd notice."

"Bill!" Cappy cried.

They all laughed and ate the ice cream. Arthur turned to Lucy and said, "I'm reading your book on Maria Martin. It seems to be a love story."

"Yes, Lucy's favorite kind of love story—the platonic but tormented kind. Lucky for me, Lucy doesn't like that in real life." David laughed. He pushed himself up from his chair. "Time to go."

On the way home David said, "I think you had too much to drink."

"Well, we were all drinking—you, too."

"But I can handle my liquor. You get loud and talk too much." He walked in silence for a minute. "Did you ever have an affair with Martin?"

Lucy had strayed to the other side of the street and was shuffling her feet through a large pile of dead leaves to hear their dry papery rustle. She stopped and laughed. "No, never."

David hurried on. "You always seem to be flirting with him. Why shouldn't I think that you've slept with him?"

"I haven't slept with every man I know." Lucy was tired suddenly. A sharp sense of her loneliness filled her and made her afraid. Maybe it was true—maybe she had made a fool of herself, talked too much, drank too much. And it had been a long evening for David. Lucy reached for his hand, so she could walk hand in hand, not alone down the street. David was satisfied and grasped her hand tightly.

In bed, as they lay side by side in the dark, both looking at the ceiling, David seemed to want to make up with her and asked a question that he must have felt had the virtue of being complimentary and therefore safe: "Do you know many people who love their work like you do? I know you're having a hard time starting right now, but you will because you love your work."

She reflected. "Not many, really. Match does." Lucy related Match's complaints about the slowing down of her novel and of Martin's book.

"Well, that's what children do."

Lucy ignored how he underlined the point and went on talking. "Most people at the Institute, I think, find their work interesting, and they work hard at it, because they are smart and disciplined. Martin once said to me how rather sad it was to see good people work so industriously, dedicate their talents and their passion to some subject that was hardly worth that dedication of their lives. I think he must feel that way about his own work. It's not like being in love with your work. Like you—you are in love with your work." Lucy lifted her leg in the air to stretch it. She pointed her toe. "And it's very attractive when people love their work. It's one of the things I liked you for when we first met." She turned her head and smiled at him. They did have important things in common. "I think people don't realize how attractive it is. Someone who loves their work is so absorbed in something alive that you think that rich feeling will spill over onto you."

David looked at her stretching her legs and seemed about to put his hand between them, to lift them and come into her—instead he rolled over on his side.

Lucy kept on talking. "I love my work, of course, when the work works. Right now it isn't so pleasant, that's what makes being between books hard, or when you're beginning a book, and you're not sure it's going to work. It's like being out of love, and you miss it, and—"

"Hush, go to sleep."

Soon Lucy heard his breathing slow and deep. Outside the wind picked up, and the tiny scalelike larch leaves that piled up on her back porch rattled along it, the wind chime clanged. Afraid the chime might wake David up, Lucy slid out of bed, pulled on her bathrobe, went out on the back porch to tie it up. The night smelled of autumn, crisp and mouldy at the same time. The stars were bright, the branches of the larch creaked. The night made her suddenly happy, the smell, the stars, the creak were all so lovely. This kind of happiness—she missed it. When had she lost her touch for it? If she could get it back, she could get back to work. And she would find the feeling she had for David was enough. She should gather it up and hold it close to her.

CHAPTER 7

O n a Friday night, David stepped out of the shower, tow-
eled himself roughly. He checked the back of his calves.
Lately he was worried that the calf muscles had shrunk.
Was old age contracting him? Then he looked up at the mirror over
the sink. Here was much still to admire. His arms were still muscular, his chest not droopy at all. His torso might be a little heavy, but
he didn't have a paunch that would hang over his belt. All in all, he
was not in bad shape for an almost-sixty-year-old guy. Not bad at all.
He should watch his weight, though. With Lucy, he ate more than
when he ate alone.

His penis twitched—must be the thought of Lucy—like a dog
rolling over in its sleep chasing some dream rabbit, then hung there.

Had his penis always hung slanting left? A month ago Lucy had
asked him that. He should know, she said, because he sometimes
went to a tailor to have clothes made, an old indulgence of his, and
she had heard that tailors cut pants for whichever way the customer's
penis slanted, asking their customers, "Do you wear yours to the left
or right?" David said his tailor never asked him about his penis.
Who had she heard this from? he demanded. Oh, someone had told

her, she had heard it somewhere. They were lying in bed, in the morning—David never knew any woman who chattered so in bed. Sometimes right in the middle of making love, Lucy wanted to stop and tell him some story. Spoiled his concentration. Shut up, he would say, and kiss her to stop the talking. Before sex, her head propped up on one elbow, she talked and talked, stroking his cock almost thoughtlessly. An invitation to make love? Or did she see his penis as her pet cat? That morning, though, David had decided he didn't like the feeling that one of Lucy's former lovers was in bed with him, someone she had discussed penises with before him. Twisting away from her, he sat up on the side of the bed, his back to her, paused, then stood up and went to shave. Often when David tried to get out of bed in the morning, Lucy locked her legs around him to keep him there a few minutes longer, but that morning she knew he was annoyed. She slid out of bed and gathered her clothes.

When he went to pick up some pants at the tailor's, David meant to verify whether this penis lore was Lucy nonsense or not, but forgot.

With three swoops David and his mirror double combed their wet hair into place. He was ready.

Ready to enjoy the weekend because, ever since they had agreed to get together only on the weekends, he had accomplished so much. This week he had completed a difficult chunk of research and finished reading a labored dissertation on the Maoist persecution of ethnic minorities. The time he had spent on that piece wasn't wasted, for as he read he held up a paper bag with two cans of chicken broth to strengthen the tendon in his arm, after pulling it at tennis the week before. Next week he would move up to the large cans of tomatoes as he read for his seminar. He had run his two miles every day and done his stretching before *and* after. Plus his football team had played on TV and won for a change, which wasn't technically his own accomplishment but was nonetheless gratifying.

He dressed and, as he strapped on his wristwatch, checked the time. Seven. Lucy should be here at seven-thirty.

She had said she would like to stay home this evening, not go out. So in the kitchen the fresh pink chicken flesh glossy with olive oil and speckled with crushed fennel seed was ready to be cooked. The free-range chicken did seem expensive, yet it was satisfying to know he didn't have to worry about the expense, though he reminded himself it never hurt to be careful. The green-and-white fennel bulb waited to be chopped.

Usually Lucy set the table, but since all was in order in the kitchen, he did it. What a good job Lucy had done mending his placemats—he should put out that old but beloved black sweater, see if she could mend it. Tonight they would use his very old silver, collected several pieces at a time: the knives with the curling blades, the large spoons, the three-pronged forks. Two dinner plates, two salad plates of the old white stoneware, cold and heavy, he loved the finely crackled glaze. His children and his friends had never paid any attention to these dishes, this silver. When Lucy paid attention, he suddenly felt that someone had entered his solitary world. How much he had enjoyed it surprised him. Her very first time at his house, she had stood in his living room and held the small sculpted Cambodian head and admired the fine piece of Spanish gold-threaded altar cloth. If he bought that African bust he saw in the auction house catalog, the bust of a young woman with a long neck, with a face of such pure planes and of an expression so haughty and virginal, Lucy would notice right away. He should show her the catalog, to have the pleasure of talking over the purchase.

Lucy was interested in his work, too. Colleagues at the university sometimes inquired about it; his friends and his children never did, and he didn't expect them to, it was after all specialized work meant for readers in his field. Yet the first time he talked to Lucy—she had come to his office with, she confessed later, some made-up reason and what had she worn? yes, boots and a long skirt and a sweater that caught at her breasts—she asked about his work and truly listened, she leaned forward, she asked questions, asked more questions. It made his work seem so alive. He remembered how she had looked at him with so much interest. She continued her pursuit, and though for weeks he hesitated, falling in love was not what he had expected to do again in his life, especially at his age, and with someone her age, yet he had fallen in love, he had to touch her.

Now, seven months later, David saw how Lucy leaned forward to listen to others, asked them questions in her almost relentless fashion, made them feel their work was so very interesting. He had to ask himself, what was Lucy's interest worth when she spent it so promiscuously? Lately, too, he had begun to suspect her of performing an almost perfect imitation of paying attention to him. He had developed an uncanny sensitivity to her, as if measuring constantly the power of her attention with some sort of a Geiger counter, the readings of which dipped into the red danger zone marked "Not Enough Attention." He couldn't bear the slight.

Or was it that now being in love had settled down into ordinary everyday being in love? Oh, those first weeks, when every morning he had seen her car in the Institute parking lot—Lucy is here! he would tell himself. He had expected her at any moment to knock on the door, knocking loudly, almost a banging knock, too impatient to be anyone else as she pressed up against the door with the fun of the surprise visit welling up in her. He would wait a moment, keep her behind the door like someone frozen under the ice, then call, "Come in!" In she would come with a grin, a bit like a student visiting her professor, but come up to him leaning back in his chair, grasp the arms of his chair, lean over him and kiss him, kiss him, until he pushed her away.

Oh, now the tent pole was up. Not bad for an old guy, of course though he wasn't really old, yet. And she wasn't young, she was forty now—thank God. Tonight they would make love. As long as they still made love, everything would be all right. Her new book was giving her trouble, but once she started writing, she would settle back down. She would look at him again with love. For now, he should go on with his work and his life and let her right herself.

Seven-fifteen and still no sign of Lucy. She had said she would be there, he recalled, between seven-thirty and eight. She used to come early. He picked up a bulb catalog that was still hanging around the kitchen. As he turned the pages, he began to think again about his moon garden. David had a vegetable garden and a perennial garden with various pink and red and yellow flowers in it. Neither of these was as satisfying as his moon garden. How pure a pure white garden was. Was November too late to plant more bulbs in it? The Indian summer had held for a long time, with deep blue skies, the air cool but not cold, and even quite warm in the sun. He could tuck in some white crocus, white daffodil bulbs, white scilla bulbs, white narcissus, for the spring. With pleasure he pictured the fresh snappy regiment of one hundred white tulips he had planted two years ago. He would have to buy the bulbs soon. He should buy mulch to bed the garden down for the winter. Salt marsh hay, the best mulch. Tomorrow he and Lucy could drive up the North Shore to Ipswich—he knew a farm there near Crane's Beach that sold bulbs and marsh hay. Go for a walk on the beach, if the weather held on so bright and blue, even a bit breezy would be nice to whip up the sea. He would hold Lucy's hand, kiss her in the sun.

To be drenched in sunlight while kissing a woman he loved. This was something he thought he would never do again before he met Lucy. He had, by chance, gotten another chance. Maybe eat coral red lobster for lunch at that seafood shack in Essex, the juice spitting out at him when he cracked a claw. A cold beer would make it that much better. But then he would fall asleep on the drive home.

The telephone rang, probably Lucy calling to let him know she was running late. Instead it was Olivia, his elder daughter. He could see her, sitting in her little apartment in Jamaica Plain, short, slim, so pretty with her curly brown hair, her wide blue eyes, like a Christian angel, though an angel who slouched around in black leather like a tough kid. How like a kid she was, still, even at thirty-three. A lonely kid. Before he met Lucy, Olivia and David had been lonely together for a long time and had kept each other company, gone to dinner together, to movies. He wished Liv would find someone, his wish accompanied by the slightly superior feeling of having found someone himself.

"Free to talk for a moment?"

Lucy would arrive at any minute, but Olivia was spending a lonely Friday night at home, so he said yes, he had a few minutes before Lucy arrived. He could hear her eating her dinner while they talked. Sounded like chicken, she crunched the bones to get at the marrow. *Crunch, crunch.* David could picture how, as she crunched the bones, Liv held her head down and almost averted, as if not wanting anyone to watch her when she did this, like an animal hiding its eating. Lucy noticed things like this, noticing in a detached, not critical, but not loving way, a sheer taking-note way. Unpleasant.

She asked him how he was, and he recounted all the things he had gotten done this week. She recounted all the little events at her job, working as a lighting expert for a local theater, and then detailed her latest problems with her mother. Father and daughter often complained to each other about how difficult Becky could be. Then Olivia came to why she had called, to report the latest news on her younger sister Maureen, who lived in West Roxbury. "Maureen told me that if she's married in the Eastern Orthodox Church, she gets to wear a big crown. She'd love that. Queen Maureen."

He frowned. He had read an article recently on the growing numbers of Americans converting to the Eastern Orthodox Church.

Would Maureen convert to marry Bojan, onetime physics teacher in Yugoslavia, now a computer programmer and champion chess player at the bars where Yugoslavians in exile gathered? Like Liv, Maureen was pretty, yet her face had become so oddly lined before she deserved to acquire lines—she was only twenty-eight—lines drawn by her feeling of constant aggrievement, which had always greatly provoked David. Whatever kind of wedding it was, Maureen would want it big, and no matter how much he paid, she would always think he had stinted her.

Olivia said, "And once she's married, I bet she'll have a kid right away." *Crunch. Crunch.*

"She better not. She just got her teaching certificate, which I paid for her to get when she decided that being a librarian was not interesting enough, and that after she decided that being an artist was not stable enough, which I told her when she decided to be an art major in college. She should teach for a couple of years before she has kids." David stopped, waited a moment. Then he allowed himself to sigh.

Olivia did not miss the sigh. "What is it, Dad?"

"I was thinking when Maureen gets pregnant, Lucy will take it badly."

Olivia knew instantly what he meant. "You think Lucy wants to have children? You're not going to do that, are you, Dad?"

He could not resist confiding in Olivia, who he knew would always fiercely take his part. "No, I'm sure she doesn't really want to have children. She's always said she likes being an aunt, that's enough for her. Still, now that she's getting older—she turned forty a while back—I think she's feeling like maybe she missed something by not having children, now that it's too late. So when Maureen gets pregnant, it might make her sad, and I'll have to hear about it. When I know that what she really likes is her work, that's what she's chosen to do. Why can't women feel like a book is a kind of child? I guess they feel they have to have it all."

As he talked, he began to think that however resistant he had felt to the idea of grandchildren, the idea of Lucy spoiling it for him, Lucy standing in the way of his family, irritated him.

"But are you sure she knows you're not interested?"

He could hear Olivia shift around at the other end of the line. She had stopped eating. He realized she was very worried.

David said flatly, "She knows. I made it clear to her from the very first—it wasn't very romantic to say it, I know—that if she did want children, she shouldn't go out with me. She's too old now, anyway." He was silent a moment. Then he said, abruptly, "Do you want kids? It's natural to think about that, especially since—"

"I'm thirty-three?"

"Do you feel your biological clock ticking?" He wanted to say to her, don't turn out like Lucy, sad, maybe even regretful, when it was too late, because she had failed to think about it in time.

"Dad! I might like to get a husband first," Olivia snapped. They talked a little more, made plans to have dinner, just like old times, and then they said good-bye.

Seven-thirty. He pulled down the blinds in the dining room and the living room. On the weekends he enjoyed pulling them down to make the house a private world for himself and for Lucy. And the other five nights of the week, when he was alone, he discovered how delighted he was to pull down the blinds and make the house his private world, all to himself, blessedly silent. In a way, his life right now was perfectly arranged: alone and not alone. Grandchildren would come, but not for several years, and Lucy would get back to writing, and the time they spent together would be an easy pleasure again.

Seven-forty-five. A little angry, he decided to do some work. Sitting down at his desk, he looked at an article on crypto-Christians in Japan, the Kakure Kirishitan. The author detailed what fascinated him the most, the manner in which, like the crypto-Jews, the Japanese Christians, under persecution, had for four hundred years hidden their faith so deeply inside a show of Buddhism that their rituals had almost no relation to Christian rituals, except to remind the believers that they were somehow different. Here was his theme for his book, how the very rituals and signs that were to bind a people together could betray them, by becoming empty ritual and meaningless sign. He studied the photographs of crypto-Christian objects that were so fundamentally Japanese. There were tea bowls painted with crosses. Altars with a Buddha in front but, behind two little doors on the back, a crucifix.

He was most moved by a female figure modeled after the Asian goddess Kannon, the bodhisattva of compassion, with her slightly tilted and inclined mild face, her flowing robes, standing in a box shrine with open doors. The statue was very Kannon-like, except that she held a baby in her arms. The Kannon-Mary smiled gently, her lips slightly pendulous, slightly apart, a haunting smile. Her eyes were hooded, cast down. What was Kannon pondering as she smiled? Something like thought but much deeper. Lucy might find the exact words for it, he could only say something clumsy, like *thought,* or *eternal questions,* or *maternal love.*

He realized that Kannon reminded him of several of his little statues—the Mayan girl's head, the Egyptian figurine, the Cambodian bust, the wooden grave carving from Indonesia—he had collected over the years. Lucy's face fit among them, so modeled with its high cheekbones and strong jaw. Not a beautiful face but a handsome, almost severe face. Yet when she smiled, she was pretty and seemed so young. Yes, Lucy was a bit like the Kannon statue, her face sweet and guileless but, at the same time, concealing an obscure place in her, a place like a hidden music box, deep inside her, that sometimes he or something set off by chance, and a lovely tune played, but then suddenly shut off. Then Lucy seemed so cold, like a stone statue.

The doorbell rang. David would open the door and coolly tell Lucy he had to finish some work in his office upstairs, let her fend for herself for a while. He put down his pen. Slowly and heavily he came down the steps. When he pulled open the back door, she said softly, "Hello, how are you?" and looked so sweet and a little sad, that he pulled her inside, pulled her against him as he leaned back on the counter, holding her tight and kissing her. With a kind of shyness, which he always found exciting, Lucy turned her face and gave him her cheek. "No—lips," he ordered. And she turned her soft and warm mouth to his, grasped him, grasped his arms, his shoulders, his waist. She touched his hair, "Why is your hair so soft?" He would not work anymore tonight.

The rest of the evening they fell into their routine when they ate at home. While David cooked, Lucy sat as always at his kitchen table and watched him, talked to him, too, although he didn't like to be distracted. He chopped up the fennel, tossed it with oil, cracked pepper, and fennel seed, layered it in a casserole, shoved it under the broiler. Turning his attentions to the chicken, he paused, gathering himself up as a pianist does before he attacks a piece, then he threw the big skillet on the burner, heated it up, tossed a hunk of butter in the pan. The butter sputtered, and David slapped the chicken in to brown it. Grease spattered everywhere as he bent over the pan with the spatula, turning the meat over with great satisfying splats of fat.

"Were you ever a magician?" she suddenly asked him. "You hold your hands like magician's hands, the fingers curled in, the hands turning slightly up and down, the wrists exposed, your elbows high. It's a nothing-up-my-sleeves gesture. You're ready to summon up rabbits, scarves all tied in a line, eggs from behind my ear."

He laughed, surprised. "Yes, I was. I took magic lessons from Freddy Wilson. When I was nine, I performed tricks at birthday parties."

She was delighted to have guessed this. "I can see you poring over trick books. Sending away for magic kits. Did you have a black cape and a top hat? A hat for your rabbit?"

"Hat. No rabbit. Now, shut up, I can't think if I'm talking to you." He pretended to be annoyed but was very happy. This was the Lucy he loved.

They ate. He urged her to eat more, even when she said she was full, and was gratified when she did. They drank a bottle of wine. As she cleared the table, he put the dishes in the dishwasher. Back in the living room, they listened to music and read.

David tried not to fall asleep, but with all that food and wine, his head began to nod, and then he would jerk it up, straighten up the newspaper that had dipped down, lick his lips, clear his throat to show he was awake.

He heard Lucy say, rather loudly, "I'm tired, aren't you? Wouldn't you like to go to bed?" He raised his head and saw she was smiling. He knew she was saying this for his sake. If she didn't wake him, when he went to bed he couldn't sleep, and he would worry about not sleeping, and then he really couldn't sleep, and he would be tired the next day. However, annoyed at being caught dozing like an old man, he denied it, "I was awake." He waited a few minutes, then threw the paper down, barked, "I'm going to bed." He stumped his way around the house, locking the doors, shutting off the lights.

Upstairs, as he undressed, she brushed her teeth and got into bed. He went into the bathroom, brushed his teeth, came to bed.

Out of habit, Lucy looked up and reminded him, "Your watch." Lucy's one rule was that he had to take his watch off when he slept with her. "I want you completely naked," she used to say.

David was tired, still he rose up on his elbow, held his left wrist out, and slowly, deliberately took the watch off. She was looking at him, at the way he held his hand up, fingers slightly curved. David turned to her, grinned, and began to touch her, she lay uncovered, her left breast soft and round, pink tipped. He was suddenly eager to have her, his lips closed on her nipple, his hand went between her thighs, her thighs sticky with the contraceptive gel from her diaphragm. It was their routine that she would always come to bed prepared to make love. His finger slipped between her labia to make sure, yes there it was. Then he was in her, and her eyes closed in pleasure, her face went pale, he was moved by her virginal look, and breaking free of her arms, he hooked his arms around her thighs, lifted them up, and drove in deeper.

Afterward David curled up next to her and was instantly asleep. At five, he woke up. For once, he was glad to wake up. He had dreamed that he and Lucy were traveling in some hot rocky land, he looked at her and saw that her face—shadowless in the sun—was like a silvery rock face. A lizard clung to her rock face, motionless. He wanted to reach out and pluck the lizard from her face. But he did not dare. As long as he stayed awake, that sense of not daring stayed with him. It was unpleasant.

At breakfast, when David looked up from the sports section, he saw that Lucy had her head down over her section of the paper, turned away from him, and almost crying. He should reach out to her, but as in the dream, he didn't dare. Her sadness seemed hers alone. And he was afraid to say anything—if she wanted to reveal what was going on, she would. When she excused herself to go to the bathroom, David looked to see what she was crying over. Must have been this article, "Female Infanticide." It detailed the fate of Indian and Chinese girls, who were starved to death at home or somehow "disappeared" in the first four years of their lives. He was moved by the article but, at the same time, that the article was about children made him angry. The subject of children had become a subject, he realized, not often spoken about, but always hovering around the edges of conversation.

When Lucy came back, she drank her coffee and was silent.

David did not want his day spoiled. He would bring her back to things that really mattered, that would be good for her to pay attention to. "Want to drive up with me to the North Shore to get some bulbs? Now's my last chance to plant them."

"I should try to do some work. I brought some with me."

"We'll only be gone a couple of hours." He piled temptation on temptation. "It's a beautiful day, we'll stop and have a lobster lunch, go for a walk on the beach." What a picture of indecision she suddenly was, her mouth slightly open, pushing her hands through her hair, twisting her body a bit, full of desire and misgiving, but at least not so sad and preoccupied. He started laughing. "Make up your mind."

With a sudden explosion of energy, Lucy got up, leaned over and grabbed his ears, put her face right up to his, "Yes, yes. Let's go. Let's go for a *driiive!*"

To David—did he imagine it?—her eyes from a nose-to-nose vantage, so full of desire, looked suddenly hard, almost cold and impersonal, coolly observing some object of curiosity, not loving him. He pulled back. Then her eyelids fell, her hands dropped from his ears, dropped to his shoulders to pull him close to her, she clung to him and began kissing him, his neck, his ear. This cold look, this clinging. How did the two go together? Very uneasy it made him. David had to protect himself.

An hour later, David and Lucy sat lulled by the motion of the car into a peaceable silence. He was happy. On these long stretches of highway, he could take his right hand off the wheel and rest it on Lucy's thigh. Yes, Lucy had cried this morning, but now they were fine. Maybe next year he would get some white violets for his garden. How did violets grow, seeds or bulbs or what? But hadn't he read that violets were inconstant in color, changeable, one year white, the next blue, or purple? He couldn't risk it in his white moon garden, he would have to first try them somewhere else in the yard. Now they were in Ipswich, north of Boston. Maybe in a few years, when he retired, he would sell his house and buy a house in Ipswich.

A house with enough land for a garden. Close enough to the beach to walk or bicycle. Could take the commuter train into Boston, get a little apartment in Cambridge, a pied-à-terre, to stay overnight if he had to be in town late. If he lived in Ipswich, he could work in the morning and in the afternoon ride his bike down this very road, beneath these big trees, past the big farm and the hay fields, to the private beach reserved for citizens of the town. Spread his towel and lie there in the sun and read the paper. When Lucy came up on the weekends, they would go to the beach, she would swim in the cold, cold water, and splash around, come back and shake and drip water on him like a friendly dog. He would pull her down to him, kiss her, in the sun.

Maureen and Olivia could come and go at this country house—though if it was a big house, they would have to agree to help him with the upkeep. When they married and had kids, they could come for a week in the summer. Lucy would find out after having children around for a few days that she couldn't wait for them to go home.

He said to Lucy, "Remind me I want to get salt marsh hay, too, today."

Lucy turned to him and grinned. "*Salt marsh hay!* I remember when I first met you, you talked about mulching your garden with salt marsh hay. I fell in love with you for that—well, among other reasons. Did you know that? Because whenever I went to the beach, I always saw these fields of green hay that grew near the sea, wild green hay stalks standing up stiffly in these inlets of brackish water. They seemed so attractive, arousing." She put her hand on his thigh. "But I didn't know what it was called, until you said *salt marsh hay!* *Salt marsh hay,* I love the sound of the monosyllables. *Salt marsh hay,* two flat *a*'s and a full *a*. Strange how one falls in love. *Salt, marsh, hay* seemed like you, plain words, rich words, words like *silt,* yes marshy places and silt-flooded places. I guess it meant, too, you had a garden, meant you had a home, a garden you planted, watered, mulched—a real householder."

David laughed at her. He put his hand over her hand on his thigh. Again, without warning, he had somehow provoked a real look of such sweet love, by doing or saying something so unremarkable, last night lifting up his hands, and now by simply saying *salt marsh hay.*

They ate lobster in Essex, then stopped at the farm for bulbs and hay. Inside, where they sold the bulbs and produce, David felt the end of autumn too near. The tomatoes looked old, their skins puckered and dusty. The bunches of basil and tarragon herbs were black-edged. Outside the rows of chrysanthemums, purple, maroon, yellow, white, in foiled pots, the stems all stiff, the scent of their serrated leaves bitter in the full autumn sun, signaled the most vivid alarm. All morning, as they drove through the little old towns, mums were standing on porch steps, to hold out as a spot of bright color through forlorn November.

David went over to the bales of salt marsh hay. The bristling stalks of lovely greenish gold, at least, still looked like summer. Lucy slipped her fingers up and down the silky stalks she had pulled out. David paid for two bales of hay and helped the young man put them in the car. When he looked up, he saw Lucy had moved from the barn and stood staring out at the farm field of golden hay stubble. The hay, reaped and rolled into huge wheels, stood up immensely in the farm fields, casting shadows like sundials. At its edge, the wild salt hay still uncut was strangely smoothed down by the breeze, like brushed hair. Beyond the salt hay, a silver edging, water. Salt pond or sea? He watched Lucy begin to pick her way through the hay stubble so stiff and bent. David called to her.

She turned and called back. "Just a minute. Going to take a look at something."

He pointed to his watch. "I thought you wanted to work this afternoon."

Lucy walked farther into the field.

David shouted, "I'll wait for you in the car."

She kept walking.

Instead David followed her. The marsh was much firmer than he had imagined, a little spongy—water pooled up into his footsteps—but firm enough. The water drained into braided streams running through the marsh, streams that then ran in deep ditches that he had to jump across. Then he found himself tipped slightly into a round shallow bowl of silky unmown hay.

He saw Lucy ahead of him. If only she would turn back, Lucy should turn back to him.

Salt marsh hay, salt marsh hay. She had loved that he had named it. That she needed to walk into the marsh was a tribute to him, or he could think of it as a gift he had given her, and in a moment he would come up to her and they would look at the marsh together. It was so sunken, so oozing, like sex, fecund, he felt a terrific desire for her, not tempered by his irritation but driven by it. He was about to call out to her, they could fuck there in the marsh, if he could find a dry spot, though what about those ticks carrying Lyme disease? Then he saw Lucy begin to run through the marsh, racing to its boundary, to the end of the marsh, brush, sand—toward that silver line he saw was the sea. The sea stopped Lucy short. Not the marsh. The ocean wide and vast—she stood there on its margin, alone, staring out to sea. David felt the sun warming his face, and if she had asked him to come to her, maybe he would have gone to stand at the edge of the sea with her and kiss her in the sun. But she didn't look around, and he wouldn't follow her any farther. He turned and trudged back to the car. He didn't want her to see that he saw her so alone, beyond the marsh, beyond him. He waited. The time seemed so long.

When Lucy came to the car, David said nothing, and started the car.

Lucy said, "My feet are soaking wet."

He said nothing.

"I'm sorry, I wanted to see the marsh up close, I wanted to see how the hay grew. I saw that there was sea lavender there, these clouds of the tiniest purple flowers on almost invisible stems with base leaves like long lolling tongues. I have sea lavender in my garden, but I never knew it was a wild flower. Then I saw the lighted edge of the field, a silver edge against the sky not too faraway, and though I thought I should turn back, I had to keep going, and I kept thinking, too, every time my foot sank into the marsh, the words *sea level* were suddenly real to me. Here earth and sea mingle at one level. So I had to see the sea, and I went on, it looked immense after the closeness of the marsh, a vast startling immensity, as if I had never seen it before. And then I felt so excited, the excitement brimmed up, foamed up and spilled over, ran down into the sea, until I felt like I had nothing left."

David could not bear the way she spoke about the sea. He had brought her to the salt marsh, she had loved him for the salt marsh, but it was the ocean she had gone to see, not the marsh, the marsh was only halfway there. He shook his head and put the car in reverse and backed out roughly.

She was silent. Then she asked him, "Did you get your bulbs?"

"No. The season's over."

"But you got the hay?"

"Yes."

"Do you still want to go to the beach?"

He could not bring himself to say anything. He had had to wait alone.

CHAPTER 8

A s he ate breakfast on New Year's Day, Arthur looked out
the window of his second-floor study at the snowy sky.
Almost indistinguishable from that sky was the pitched
roof next door, except for the delicate pitchforks of bird tracks. He
would get out his cross-country skis, go to the Institute, and take a
run around the lake. Disappear into the green pines and escape this
unrelievedly white world.

In California sometimes he drove to the mountains for a few
days, to ski in the granite and pine Sierras. He preferred Alpine ski-
ing—this light slipping across the face of the world. One winter he
went with the poet with the black hair, who crouched over her skis
to bind them, looking like a black mink in the snow, fur fluffed out,
eyes bright and alert. Together they glided along the trails, the heat
of her body glowing in the purple sweater next to him, and when he
took off his gloves and held her red cheeks in his hands, they burned
him. She teased him, made him forget himself, forget that self that
styled itself solitary and eccentric—for once he was flesh and blood.
At home, Meryl would hardly seem to notice he was gone, as if her
thick glasses blinded her. She kept talking on the telephone about

the *Nutcracker*—a *Nutcracker* in California seemed such an odd production, but it made the ballet company, for whom Meryl taught, money for the whole year. When he came back, there would be more of the little objects she kept in their apartment, a child's hoard of stones and shells, ceramic chicken salt and pepper shakers with feathers infinitely detailed, old cigarette cases of chipped enamel.

He went into Meryl's room before he left. He had already cranked up her bed so she could look out the window at the snow. Her wheelchair stood folded in the corner—should he move it out of the room? The doctors had said how important it was to keep her mobile, to take her out for a walk, to make her feel in the world. Yet last week Meryl had begun to have difficulty in swallowing her food, and although Bonnie had helped her learn a different way of swallowing, they all knew that sooner or later the swallowing would again become difficult, the doctor would have to set up a feeding tube. There were no experimental treatments for patients who had reached this stage. Meryl was giving up. The first sign was making him understand that she didn't want to be put in the wheelchair again. For a week, every time she was moved into her wheelchair, Arthur felt her resistance. He had figured out finally that she wanted to stay in bed. When he asked her, Meryl shut her eyes for a long moment. The world outside had become and would remain the world framed by her window, a world reduced to a backyard, a fence, sky, daylight, or night. This would be her world to the end.

Arthur found himself imagining sometimes that Meryl had completely changed in personality. She who had talked to keep silence away, now was completely silent. She who used to twitch her mouth, twiddle her hair, busy herself rearranging her little treasures or shuffling cards was now utterly still. She seemed, sometimes, to him to have become a purified being, white robed by the sheets of her bed, a meditator gazing solemnly at the world, but not of the world. Was something secret about her revealed in this stillness?

Had her talk and busyness always been a cover for a fundamental immobility in the world? At other times he knew that Meryl hadn't changed at all. When he looked at her eyes behind the heavy glasses pressing down on her nose, she still had that myopic look of someone peering at things up close, trying to make them out, almost like a little insect who holds her head close to the fruit she is about to nibble, but without that sense of peripheral watchfulness that sends insects flitting off at any slight movement. That myopia had sometimes seemed a burden to him. He had felt she didn't need to think about him because she trusted him as a child blindly trusts that the mother or father is always going to be there.

Arthur told Meryl that he was going out for several hours. She blinked. While he waited for Bonnie to come, he checked that there was the strong coffee Bonnie liked in the Thermos, that the book he had been reading to Meryl was at hand, that the deck of cards waited on the ottoman. He had to go.

Arthur parked on the road nearest the path around the lake. New year, new snow, no footprints yet. He set out through the grove of pines as green and black as he had imagined them. The snow was perfect, not too deep, not too icy, it slid across his skis as he swept through the trees. He glided one foot at a time, and soon he could hear the slap of his skis behind him, the sound of a good rhythm, an alive sound. Here now were the colors of winter, not only green pine needles and black trunks but the blazing yellow of willow branches, the dark red of the berry bushes, the pale gold of tall grasses bent by the snow. Bright red of wild rose hips. When there was a break in the forest, he looked at the old mansions giving onto the lake, their glass solariums greenish in the snow world. He came around the lake to where he had begun and stopped. He rested, caught his breath. He sat so still, the squirrels freely chattered and chased each other winding around tree trunks.

Now for the first time he saw people. Across the lake, which the wind had cleaned so that the ice reflected the dull gray sky like tarnished silver, was a skater and someone sitting on a bench. Arthur started up again, drawn by the sight of people, companions for the moment. A few running steps to get momentum, and then with long, longer glides he passed the stand of white beeches, trunks long and curving and as white as the snow—even the snow did not make them dingy. Finally he crossed the footbridge over the stream the lake fed, good luck, the snow thick here, too, he could cross on his skis without harming them.

As he came closer, Arthur recognized the skaters to be Lucy and David. He stopped. Since the dinner party over two months before, he had seen Lucy only a few times. The Institute was so large and the offices so scattered, he did not often run into her. Plus he was at the Institute only to teach his seminar—he did his own work at home to be near Meryl. The times he had talked to her, David was with her, and she seemed shy of him in David's presence.

He turned his skis off the lake path and slid closer to the lake to stand behind a blind of mountain laurel. Lucy sat on the wooden bench fussing with the fastenings of what looked like brand-new skates. David, already sprinting back and forth on the ice, called out to her, "Need some help?"

"*No,* I can *do* it."

Arthur was startled—he did not know her that well, but she seemed so different from the Lucy he had talked to. Her voice sounded metallic, as if the words had been banged out on sheet metal. Hunched over the skates, her body seemed shrunken. He wanted to return her to that woman who laughed, who was so penetrable the way she said whatever she was thinking, the way she would answer any of his questions without guile, without flirtation, unprotected. He remembered the dinner party and how Lucy's face had hardened when David spoke so harshly to her. That was it, her whole body had hardened now. And hadn't he hardened up—or was stiffening up—in that house with Meryl? If only he and Lucy could have a moment of talk. He would like to talk again with someone who listened, who responded. What could be a happier thing than two people talking to each other, unbending?

David skated farther away.

At last Lucy clicked her fastenings into place.

She started around the inlet, she wobbled but stayed up, accomplished a few small glides, and seemed to feel a little confident. Took a longer glide, wobbled, caught herself, then went down, hard—the sharpness of her "shit" rang out over the ice.

David turned back and skated over to her to help her up, but she waved him off. She got up and started skating again, so stiffly, ready for a fall. David, in contrast to Lucy, looked emphatically energetic, almost triumphantly so. He remained at her side yet clearly was waiting to be cut loose, to go farther out on the lake. He kept going faster and moving Lucy farther out on the ice, where it started to form ridges crusted with snow. She fell again. David did not see her for a moment, and then he was far away. When he looked around, he called out, "Should I come back and give you a hand?"

She only shook her head. She managed to get up and started back to the shore, red-faced and breathing hard, going too fast and not able to stop herself as she came toward the bench there. At the last moment she managed to turn a bit and missed the bench, ending up in a snowdrift not more than a few yards from where Arthur stood. She was plastered with snow. Her hands went up to her face to wipe away the tears with her gloves. For the first time Arthur felt himself a voyeur.

David had skated far away, he was now only a distant figure bent over and exuberantly exercising itself, all alone. Arthur took advantage of the icy separation to talk to Lucy. He skied out from his hiding place, braced himself with his poles.

Lucy looked up at him in surprise, then embarrassment. She blinked her eyes to clear away the tears and tried to laugh. "I'll get up eventually." With a few more slips, she did and managed to catch hold of the bench and sit down. She was breathing heavily. Finally she began brushing off the snow and said, "The problem is that I have expensive new skates, a Christmas gift from David, but can't skate."

He unlatched his skis and sat down next to her. "Take your time. You'll get the feel for it. Don't be too ambitious."

"I was stupid trying to keep up with David." She stopped. "How is Meryl?"

Lucy was one of the few persons on the East Coast, except for the doctors, who knew how ill Meryl was, Arthur realized. So many of his former students were in the area, as were other people he knew in his field, yet he had not contacted them. He said simply, "She's worse, as is expected."

"I'm sorry. You know, I live so close to you, is there anything I can do? If you need something, telephone me. I could run an errand to the grocery store, the drugstore, whatever."

"Thank you, I have the great nurse Bonnie, who keeps us both alive. But again thank you, if I need you I will call, I promise. The difficulty is, there is so much work to be done with Meryl, but nothing can be done really."

Lucy was silent for a moment and then murmured, "I was looking at the ice closely after I fell out there. It's so black and frozen, underneath, though, you see these silver bubbles of air in the ice. So you know there is life under there."

Arthur thought, that ice would melt, those silver bubbles would resume their motion, rise to the surface and release themselves, fish and turtles and frogs would come out of hibernation, slow at first, then quick and alive. He looked at Lucy—her face, too, seemed frozen, so pale and tired. "How are you? How were your holidays?"

"We didn't do much, celebrated with David's daughters. I should have gone to visit my parents, my sister and her kids, but I keep thinking I'll get some work done, now that the semester's over and papers are graded. I haven't done much at all, though. Today's the new year, and it feels still like the old year. Does any year when one gets older ever feel like a new year again, or only one long continuation of the old old years, nothing changing?"

Arthur could feel a kind of despair brimming in her, threatening to spill over, and said, "Maybe you need a disruption, some abrupt change, something to make you forget about the work and then come back to it."

She shook her head. "That sounds too scary to do in the dead of winter. I'll wait for spring, put off making any big changes until the spring." She said this as if she had deliberated at length. She wasn't, he felt, talking about work.

"Two, three months to go. Can you wait that long?"

"I'm perfecting my stall," she said so abruptly and harshly that she blushed. She tried a lighter tone. "Did you have family here to visit?"

"Neither of us has family, except for the most distant of cousins." How lightly he and Meryl traveled in life.

Several more skaters arrived, put on their skates, and started out onto the lake. They were a Chinese woman—from Taiwan, Arthur identified the dialect that carried over the ice—and her two kids on skates. They trailed behind the mother as she skated around and around the inlet. The children called to the mother, and her voice rang back to them encouraging them or laughing at what they said. Arthur wanted to return Lucy to some sort of life, like these three.

"Try skating, here, close to the bench, slowly, very slowly, don't go fast. Listen to what the mother says."

Lucy looked at him and laughed. "She's speaking Chinese."

"I'll be your mother."

Struggling up from the bench, Lucy began to skate again. Slowly gliding, soon her legs began to work together, and she seemed to be listening to the hiss of the skates with pleasure. She was cautious, but she was skating—even her arms, flailing to catch her balance, described a larger sphere than before, when she held herself so tightly. Arthur kept calling out to her, "Go slowly, slow glides, that's it," and with her eyes almost closed, as if she were lulled by the gliding into sleep she was so relaxed, her skate strokes became longer, she went around and around in a circle. Arthur could hear Lucy humming a meaningless, breathing song, from some deep place in her chest, a stream of almost soundless song of joy, as she took her time, took pleasure in the movements. This was something like the Lucy he had met in the garden. Arthur found himself hungry to touch someone. He was embarrassed to realize how starved he was, how greedy he could be. He would fall upon her greedily if he could. Even now staring at her satisfied some hunger.

She came back to the bench and sat down. "I know it wasn't a pretty sight, but it was fun." She took out a Thermos from the backpack next to the bench, and both she and Arthur drank the black coffee from its lid. "Oh, I wanted to ask about your court lady," she said. "What's happening now?"

"My court lady has entered into an affair with a Buddhist priest. Priests are initiated with these words: 'Caught in the vicissitudes of the three realms of unenlightened men, one cannot break the bonds of affection. To throw away affection and enter the eternal way is to truly repay obligation.' This priest is pressing his affections upon our lady, showing up in her room, every night. She, as always, cannot resist, though, as always, she is afraid to be found out. Afraid of her fate in this world, for if discovered she will lose the favor of the Emperor, and afraid of her fate in the next world, where her father will reproach her. Fear, however, makes her writing even more alive. From despairing, even obsessive confessions of fear, the prose leaps to an exquisite attentiveness to the season, to the peculiar texture of the bark on certain trees. How the child of one of the servingwomen has the smoothest skin and makes graceful gestures in his sleep of picking something, cherries, the lady decides. Just as she protests to her lover that she is going to retire from the court and the world and become a nun herself, the next moment a courtier's beautiful performance of a ritual dance has enchanted her." Arthur looked at Lucy, she seemed to be happily listening to him. This was all it would take for her to fall in love, he saw, describe things, tell stories, he could have her.

Then Lucy looked up. He saw David coming back toward them from across the lake. He didn't want to talk to him. He stood up— "I'd better get going"—and stepped onto his skis. Lucy didn't protest that Arthur should wait for David to return. He saw her visibly stiffen into the woman he had spied upon earlier. It was painful to watch her do violence to herself.

She said to him, "I wish your wife could get better. I guess all I can say is, again, if there is anything I can do, let me know."

Arthur thanked her and left.

From down the path he turned and stopped. Lucy was bent over undoing her skates. David skated up to her, sat next to her, laughing, wiping the sweat off his face in a theatrical gesture. "That was great," he proclaimed. "Who were you talking to?"

Arthur pushed off and circled back to the front stone gate. He had become chilled. Such a cold, cold day.

Back home Meryl lay in exactly the same position he had left her. She would be frozen always into the same position. Bonnie said Meryl seemed all right, as far as she could tell. He went to work again.

Meryl moaned. Arthur got up and went and sat by her side, laid his hand on her fist. Meryl blinked furiously, moaned again—what did she need, water, to be changed, to be turned?—he was here, Bonnie was here. Tears of frustration spilled down her cheeks, and he patted them dry. An evening at her side stretched out before him. Night fell, and as he sat in the dark, next to Meryl's bed, he tried to remember Lucy's cautious yet joyous skating today, but lost sight of her in the darkness.

CHAPTER 9

M ichael elbowed and was elbowed by the crowd pushing through the gate of the Kitano Tenman-gū shrine. The shrine's deity, Sugawara no Michizane, was a scholar and imperial minister of the tenth century who had fallen from favor and been exiled away from the capital, Kyoto, to the southern island of Kyushu, the hinterlands in those days. After Sugawara's death, plagues and fires befell the capital. Its rulers believed Sugawara was exacting his revenge. To appease his spirit, they made him a deity, the god of scholarship, and gave him this important shrine. School-children now crowded the grounds to buy wooden plaques and write on them in black ink their prayers for good grades on exams, then hang the plaques on the special pegs provided. The most desperate students hung their prayers on the neck of the statue of the ox who had collapsed with grief while pulling Sugawara's remains to the cremation grounds. Michael was delighted at the idea of anyone making a scholar a god. From the shrine priests who did a brisk business in prayers and souvenirs, he bought a scroll with a picture of the not-very-vengeful-looking god, only a mild-mannered, melancholic bookworm like himself.

Michael felt even closer to Sugawara when he read, in the booklet that came with the scroll, the legend of his three trees, a pine, a plum, and a cherry. When Sugawara was exiled, his pine stayed in Kyoto. His cherry withered and died. His plum tree so missed its master, it flew to join him in exile. Bookworms in exile. Grieving trees. This would be Michael's favorite temple.

To honor the plum, Kitano shrine had a walled orchard of two thousand plums, and on this February day, for five hundred yen, about five dollars, Michael could stroll among the barely flowering trees. Although the day was very cold, the plum blossom viewers were out in droves, bundled up in coats and scarves and hats and gloves. When they spied a rare blossom or even a half-opened bud, they gave drawn-out gasps of pleasure. Men, old and young, bent by the weight of the enormous cameras suspended around their necks, their arms bristling with tripods, bustled to get the perfect picture of the first white or pink plum blossoms of the season or the perfect picture of their wife or daughter or girlfriend leaning forward on tip-toe to smell the very strong and wonderful perfume of even one plum blossom. All week long as the plums began to open, Michael would be walking through the streets on his visits to gardens, and he would smell the intensely sweet fragrance and look around to find that there, in some sunny protected corner, would be a plum fully blooming, the bark ink black, and the trunk and branches calli-graphically angled.

In the middle of the orchard was a pavilion with women handing out cups of hot plum tea, salty tasting and a light pinkish brown, with floating flecks of gold glinting in the thin spring sun.

Michael held his cup in both hands to warm them. He looked out at the trees, the black trunks a garden of vertical poems, and idly began, out of years of habit, calculating how he could turn one of the fields behind his house into a Japanese plum orchard. As he was debating how much money two thousand plum trees would cost, he suddenly could see himself beginning to dig the first hole for the trees, the house's huge shadow falling upon him and the hole he dug, turning it into a grave, and his wife watching him from a window. He had to sell that house—if only he could sell the house, he and his wife would have more than enough money to start their separate lives. The house was both the tomb and the resurrection. Poor old Shakers, only their ecstatic dreams of paradisiacal golden raiment and golden apples could have lit up that dusky house. He had no such visions.

Then across the orchard he saw his wife, not in a vision, but with her Japanese students, two housewives and a shy young man. He instinctively didn't stand up or wave. Once waiting for Lucy near Harvard Square, he sat on the big granite lintel buried in a little park there, where teenagers and homeless lounged. Two blocks away he spotted Lucy hurrying to meet him, he watched her, and how excited he was, he could stand it no longer, and he sprang up to meet her. That was love, to see her first, from afar, and spring up, run to her. His wife was somewhat taller than her students, but she had begun, he noticed, to resemble them, with her dark subdued dress, her restrained gestures. The small group stopped to look at tree after tree. She must be saying something in English: *tree plum bark blossom white pink green black spring.* The students looked at her, moved their lips, laughed and frowned in embarrassment. They moved on. In a few minutes they would arrive at the tea pavilion. Michael returned his cup and left the pavilion. Not so much to avoid his wife, but because for the first time he saw her in some other world independent of him. At home she had bound herself so tightly to his life, at the university, the life of his friends. Even when he left her at home for a day, a week, a month, months, he still felt himself in tension with her, binding him to her. Here at last she seemed to be living her own life.

As he walked away, he felt elated. Quickly he left the temple grounds to find a pay phone and call Lucy, in his excitement even willing to risk the chance that David might be there. He had to hear her voice.

"Michael!" She instantly recognized his voice and as always said his name in the same way she had so long ago—both as an exclamation of delight and as a laugh. He hoped for her sake that David wasn't there.

He could see Lucy sitting there in the winter twilight: she must be finishing her dinner in the small kitchen where the phone was.

"How are you?" Michael asked, as always with an urgency that must convey to her that he was someone who loved her, no matter what.

She hesitated and then said, "I'm a little tired."

She sounded so sad to him, he could not help but say to her, "My Lucy. I dream of holding you close, holding your skull, such a nicely shaped head, in my hands. I can feel the shape of it in my hands."

Lucy was silent. His unguarded avowal had made her uneasy. He should restrain himself, be polite, not intrude upon her life with this David. After all, he had abandoned her. Yet this scene of his wife leading a life of her own had let him feel like something enormous had been gained. He kept talking. "Remember when we were at that beach restaurant in Puerto Angel, and the waves came in and began to wash away our table and chairs and our shoes and clothes? We had to chase them down into the Pacific, just as the big fish we ordered was paraded past our table, fresh from the boat, poor fish. Then in the evening, while I was pretending to doze, I watched you, lying back in your chair on the beach, slip your hands between your legs, pull back your bathing suit, and begin to clean out the fine sand from your labia, your lips, the 'nymphae' they are called anatomically, and I looked around the beach, and there was another woman and another doing the same thing, in the twilight, all of you sandy nymphs!"

Lucy began laughing, and her next words spilled out as helplessly as his own. "Michael," she broke in, "Michael, if only we could see each other. It wouldn't mean anything, except the pleasure of seeing you."

Michael was stopped short. He still had to make things clear with his wife. He could only, once more, mumble some words about how she should wait, he couldn't leave his wife just now, wait, wait, things would change, he promised her.

On the other end of the telephone line, he heard her become embarrassed. "Oh, I wasn't really thinking that we could see each other. I think sometimes it'd be nice to see you, but I really couldn't, I'm with David." Her retraction was a new wound to him.

Michael saw his phone card was almost used up. "Listen, I'll call again—"

"You don't have to—"

"Good-bye—"

"Good—"

Beep. The card had run out.

His elation had evaporated. He went home and lay down on his bed. Nothing would change. The cat jumped up on his big chest, lost her balance, and rolled off the precarious perch. On the floor, she looked around, as if to dare anyone to say anything. Michael gave her a caress to reassure her of her elegance. At least he could do something for a cat.

He picked up the Peony Society's latest catalog, which the department secretary had forwarded. The telephone rang and rang. His wife must not be back yet. Probably a wrong number, he prepared himself to tell the caller with his memorized lines of Japanese.

"Professor Orme?"

"Yes?"

"Yes, I'm sorry to bother you, I know you are on leave, but I told the secretary it was urgent, and she gave me your number."

The voice of Jane, a graduate student in his department, reminded him again that real life at home was waiting to reclaim him and his wife in seven months.

"I wanted to talk to you about my thesis proposal. I would like to do it on the erotic semiotics of gardening in sixteenth-century France."

This was the kind of study his department encouraged and the kind of study he hated. The writing was always bad. Bad writing made topics on sex so unappetizing.

"Again, I know you are on leave, but I need to get started, and I wanted to work with you, and I thought by the time you came back from leave, I'd have a head start—"

On the other hand, subjects like this turned out to be endlessly amusing in their awfulness. And, perhaps he could get her to write something substantial.

"Could you fax me your proposal?"

"I need a proposal?"

Ah, rescue was at hand. He remembered that Jane was very lazy. "Yes, go to the library and work up a bibliography. What have you read already?"

"Not much, really, I just came up with the project the other day. The title sounded good."

"Do you know what semiotics is?"

"I know what erotic is."

He had almost forgotten being so far away, in this other world, about her campaign to seduce him. Her mind was small and hard as a nut, so neatly packed with its plotting and planning. To take her, push open her thighs, taste her salty cunt would be at best a sharp but very short-lived pleasure. Not like with Lucy, no laughing, no gentleness, no toughness, no intelligence. Beneath the covers of Lucy's bed, in a room cold with early winter, he had caressed her for the first time, she half-lifted from the bed to enfold him in her long arms. Then he alluded to a book they had both read, and they started recalling the book and laughing and talking of so many things, and forgotten what they were about, until suddenly they remembered they were in bed, and she pulled him to her and he buried himself in her.

Michael went to the toilet, taking with him the peony catalog, but he wasn't interested in peonies this year. He stopped and looked everywhere for his bamboo book.

From the toilet he heard the front door open. His wife shuffled her shoes off, then her stockinged feet whispered down the hall.

A few minutes later, he stuck his head in the kitchen. His wife was unpacking the groceries. He tried to help, but she shooed him away. He sat down, and she said, "I got a new student today, I hope he works out with the rest of my group."

They conversed politely over the tea she made. Michael wondered if he, too, were having a conversation lesson with her. He had to get out of the house. As he walked, a spring snow had begun, perfect for snow viewing at a temple garden. He walked north toward Mount Hiei, looking at his street map, winding through this suburb of fields and farmhouses, of villas and Porsches, looking for a temple he had read about in his garden book. Here was the small door, recessed in the line of shops and houses that fronted the street. In the courtyard of the Rengei-ji temple, a very old monk shuffled under the eaves, sweeping the path. He ignored Michael. Inside Michael removed his shoes, paid his fee, and received a lotus-shaped ticket colored with a smiling bodhisattva. He went into the temple, sat down on the *tatami* in the viewing room, and contemplated the garden. The very small garden was set against the hillside, maple trees still bare, azaleas low to the ground, as if crouched down against the cold. The garden was bounded by three elements: a stone lantern near the platform with a sloping mossy-brown mushroom cap and now a smaller cap of snow, a small pond perfectly still, and a bridge of stone on the other side of the pond outlined with a thin layer of snow. After a moment, Michael noticed that line of snow was reflected in, truly floating on the still surface of the pond. The plum season had begun, but in his sector of the city, it was still winter.

The temple was bitterly cold. He envied the attendant the glowing space heater she knelt next to, holding out her hands.

Michael brooded over the telephone conversation. Lucy had made a gesture to see him, and he had hesitated, abandoned her again, lost her again. He should become the brother of that old toothless monk, tending the wintry garden.

Michael watched the line of snow reflected in the pond. The still surface of things could be stirred up only to return to stillness.

What was that sound—faint music—coming closer? Da de da da *dah* da—it was the recycling truck song, "The Last Rose of Summer," that haunted his neighborhood.

An hour later, frozen, Michael left. He would write down notes on winter gardens when he got home, after he warmed his hands at the space heater his wife would have lit for him in his room.

In his garden, the bare persimmon tree's red globes were heavy and wrinkled, like himself, hanging there on the thinnest stems. One good blow, and they would fall and smash on the street, the orange mushy pulp spilling out. But they hung on.

He began to plan in his head a garden he would make for Lucy, a garden whose colors showed in winter, a garden of red berries and reddish branches, shocking-lime-green-stemmed brambles, a shrub of dusky blue. And in the summer, that garden would be shady, gloomy, so secret, he could hide himself there.

CHAPTER 10

As she swung into the street where David lived, Lucy saw that the front windows of his house were dark. They were going to the Yus' for dinner, this Saturday night, so of course the house was dark. Still she wished the windows were lit up.

In the last month, her feeling for David had split into revulsion from him and desire for him. This doubleness frightened and exhausted her. Each weekend she approached his house in horrified disbelief that she was here, again, for yet another weekend, and at the same time with a pleasurable confusion, like the first time she came to visit him and his blinds were softly gleaming with the interior light and the promise of love. The telephone call from Michael had only heightened her sense of the doubleness. She had felt such longing at the sound of his voice yet, at the same time, fear. Michael could not save her from her terrible loneliness. At least with David she had a chance to get out of her solitary apartment, eat with someone, sleep with someone, talk with someone, hold someone close and be held. These actions were of such basic necessity, she couldn't give them up and embrace nothing.

She had resolved, before coming over here tonight, to put away her doubts. It was spring, she had seen a clutch of crocus, purple and yellow. Her resolve found a support, too, in a dream she had, a dream seeming to signal that she still loved David. In her dream, she had entered a shop of Oriental things, idled from glass case to glass case, until she spotted some turquoise, exquisite blue-green Chinese turquoise in flat disks—the stone's beauty came as a shock to her. The owner came over, and Lucy said to him, "The turquoise is so beautiful," but hastened to let him know that she couldn't afford to buy, that she was only looking. The dream was obviously about David, his blue-green eyes. Even though she said in the dream she couldn't afford him, in her waking life, whenever she saw something exquisite, she found a way to buy it. She would find a way to make a life with David. They had moments of such feeling for each other, why couldn't they be happy? If she could get back to work, and the summer's freedom was good for that, then everything would be as it was when they first met, both of them busy working and happy to eat together, to make love.

Sometime in the future, they would become like the cardinal couple who nested in David's yard. Lucy liked the pinkish-dun color of the female's feathers. She would be settled for the rest of her life into her original dream of David's rich ordinariness. She could wait, she had time, that was what the first dream last fall—of her grandmother giving her the watch—had meant. Let her follow the dreams' advice. Her waiting, though, should not be a passive waiting, she would start to enrich their life together, to bring it closer to something livable for her. She would have her sister and nephews out to visit, invite Martin and Match, Hana and Howard, Cappy and Bill over to dinner here.

Today Hana had asked her a favor that fit in nicely with these plans. Hana and Howard had been invited to a wedding. They could take Sachiko, but not Tak, he was too young. At the last moment

Tak's sitter became sick. Could Lucy watch Tak for a few hours the next day? Lucy had said yes. She and David didn't have any plans. The idea that Tak could come be a part of their day seemed to represent the rich, easy domesticity she imagined possible.

She found David standing in the backyard gazing at his moon garden. He kissed Lucy, brushed his palms up over her breasts, and held her shoulders, pulled her close. "Your hair smells of gardenias. Reminds me of prom nights." Then a hair seemed to get stuck on his tongue. He worked his mouth in a variety of grimaces, to spit the hair out. "Look, my tulips are up. It's so warm this spring, they're early. Next will be—" and he listed all the plants he had in this garden. Shasta daisies, white peonies, white rhododendrons, white alyssum, white bellflowers, white bee balm, white zinnias, and at last white chrysanthemums in the fall.

The rows and rows of tall white tulips stood like soldiers three abreast, their heads—petals still closed in a pucker—held high on green straight stems. Next fall, white chrysanthemums would be the only flowers left standing, glowing phosphorescent white, unearthly white, as red, purple, yellow leaves matted against their stems. She couldn't keep herself from saying, "So much whiteness makes me want to plant the most violently colored tulips, parrot tulips with yellow, red, and green stripes, those purple-black tulips, and red red red tulips. A sharp red like, like a bite!"

"Gaudy. Too gaudy," David loftily pronounced.

"Gaudy, gaudy," Lucy teased him.

David began counting the tulips, his finger tapping the air at each number.

"Hana wanted to know . . . "

"*Shush*—" David thrust his other hand toward her, palm out, fingers spread wide. "Eighty-one, eighty-two—"

Lucy saw the white folds of flesh straining between his fingers and the words *Don't fire till you see the whites of their fingers!* popped into her head. She laughed, and stepped over to fondle one of the tulips, such a chill white egg.

"Ninety-eight. Pretty good, almost all of them came up. Ha!" David edged through the ranks to straighten the sagging picket fence behind them.

Lucy began again. "I told Hana we could watch Tak for a couple of hours tomorrow. Sort of an emergency. She will drop him off early in the afternoon and pick him up before dinner. Since we don't have big plans for tomorrow—"

The fence fell back to its familiar dip. Lucy saw David's shoulders go up, his head lower like a boxer. She concentrated on his back, she did like his back. His back was broad, very powerful—she spanned her hands across it when they made love. That was something to hold on to.

David bent down to pull a weed in the tulip bed. "How do you know what my plans are?"

"I'm sorry. I should have checked." Lucy spotted a black cat. "Here, kitty, kitty. Come here, my beautiful Blackie! Or whatever your name is."

"Tak's only what, three or four? Won't he be afraid to stay all day long with strangers?"

"I'm not a total stranger."

"Tak or no Tak, I'm going to watch my baseball game on television." He paused, and his voice quavered. "And I thought you might sit with me for at least part of the game and eat popcorn."

The black cat stretched out her front paws in a curtsy, as Lucy scratched the cat's head. A dog barked, the cat froze, yellow eyes suddenly fixed, then plunged into the tulips, white tulips, white tulips, bobbing their heads.

"Are you ready to go?" David said.

The telephone rang while David was in the house finding his car keys. Lucy waited outside in the car. The call took a while, but just as Lucy was getting cold and about to come in, David was there, locking the door behind him. "Sorry, it was Maureen. I told her we were on our way out. That I'd call her back this weekend."

In the car, David was silent. Lucy, too, didn't say anything, even when she saw a tree all pink with bloom illuminated by a street-lamp, a burst of radiant pink in the dark night. Once she would have pointed it out to David. These days, however, she seemed only able to offer him the slightest surface of herself.

As they pulled into the Yus' driveway, David said carefully, "Maureen's just told me she's pregnant. The baby's due in November. She's starting to plan the wedding."

Lucy said quickly how happy she was for Maureen, and at the same time she felt herself flush and worried she might cry. She was surprised and struggled to control herself. David looked at her and started to say something, but at that moment the other guests, Whitman and Janice, drove up, and the Yus came out to greet everyone.

While Mr. Yu made the final dinner preparations in the kitchen, the rest of the party sat on the sofas in the other half of the large room. Mrs. Yu handed around nuts and poured beer and wine. The Yus had recently moved into this, their new house, and the talk was all about that. Whitman started describing the house he and Janice had bought recently, dwelling especially on the appliances. "We bought a great refrigerator, sort of the BMW of refrigerators. It's so energy efficient, keeps everything the right temperature, but without pumping out the watts. Got this great industrial finish to it, too, a brushed steel."

Janice nodded.

Whitman and Janice both worked on Korean history. Whitman was a friend of David's, from graduate school. Janice, a younger scholar in the field, was not much older than Lucy. They had been married now for two years. Janice, David once told Lucy, didn't seem to want children, she was happy to devote all her time to her career. So, Lucy said to herself, this was the couple she and David were supposed to be, this couple facing them as if a mirrored reflection. There was a difference, Lucy realized. At least Whitman and Janice lived together, had undertaken the adventure, which to Lucy seemed so exotic, the adventure of ordinary life, of living with someone else, day in day out.

Whitman was still talking about refrigerators. "Last time I bought a refrigerator, must have been 1960—bet that thing's still running. You know my wife finally sold our house. Thank God that's over. Oh, she was calling me all the time, about it. Selling the house sent her back to therapy—which I pay for—what I've paid, what I've paid. I tried to get her to call the kids, but she called me every day to talk over the sale. So we talk, we settle something, and the next night she calls to change her mind."

David sighed. "Becky calls now and then, trying to get back something we bought together."

Lucy looked at Janice, seated next to her. Janice had a hand on her forehead.

His ex, Whitman reported, had lately taken up pottery. The kids had stacks of plates and cups by her. Now if she could only make something useful, like tiles. "We're looking at tile for the bathroom."

Janice kept her eyes lowered and both hands were on her forehead.

"Are you all right?" Lucy asked in a low voice.

Janice replied, "I've got a migraine." She held her face very still, as if not to jar her brain. "I don't know what sets it off. The doctors say wine, chocolate, or coffee. I had some decaf this afternoon, maybe somebody mixed in real coffee."

Mrs. Yu said, "We found some tiles on sale at . . . "

Whitman was still talking. "I like these Mexican tiles, the most expensive tiles, that have dog prints in them, chicken feet marks. Makes them authentic."

David said, "Lucy and I are thinking about going to Mexico this summer." He looked at Lucy, and she tried to say something about Mexico, but she couldn't think of a thing. Luckily it was time to eat.

There was more and more food. Dumplings, soup, pickles, a duck cooked in beer for hours, whose flesh came off with the slightest tug of the chopsticks. David ate and ate. "It's all so good I can't stop."

Lucy wasn't very good with her chopsticks, she didn't have the right grip, kept fumbling them, while everyone else was expert. She was tired and her eyes felt scratchy, but she made an effort to look like she was enjoying herself. She asked Mrs. Yu about her soap opera.

Mrs. Yu said, "The strangest thing is that the characters keep changing all the time. There's Jack, for a long time he was the guy who seduced all the women but never married them. Now he's the guy who is always doing the right thing, so understanding—he's a sensible guy."

Lucy was puzzled. "You mean sensitive guy?"

Everyone laughed.

Dessert was a white flan, like the white of a boiled egg but sweet and light. Coffee or tea. As they began to eat, Mrs. Yu announced that she was going to be a grandmother again, her youngest daughter was pregnant—about time, she said. Everyone congratulated her and Mr. Yu. Lucy felt she had to say something, so David wouldn't take her silence as sulking. "I bet your daughter can't wait to get her hands on that baby. You get so curious the last month." She stopped, embarrassed. She didn't want people to think she acted like she had had children. She added, "That's what my sister Caroline always says. That the last month, the suspense nearly kills you!"

Then David announced, "I'm going to be a grandfather, too, Maureen just called this evening to say she was pregnant. I guess she'll have a wedding soon. You're all invited." David, too, was roundly congratulated. Lucy said again how happy she was for him and for Maureen.

"It had to happen sooner or later," David said, and made a face.

Lucy could tell he was very happy. She breathed deeply, blinked hard. She had to be so careful, to sit up straight and stay still, as if she were balancing a heavy container of water on her head that might tip and drench them all.

After dinner they moved back to the sofas. David sprawled to ease the pain of his belly. Lucy excused herself and went upstairs to the bathroom. As soon as she had shut the door, she burst into tears and whispered to herself, *I have nothing, nothing.* How could she go back down the stairs, sit with all of them? She waited until she stopped crying. In the mirror, though, her face was pale and her eyes red. She turned off the light and came back down the stairs.

Instead of going back to the room where everyone was, she found her purse in the living room and took out the little notebook she always kept with her. For suddenly she had an idea, for her book—to include the story of Baldrich's traveling companion, Eileen, an Irish girl whose father, a skilled factory worker, took his family to Japan. Eileen had learned Japanese and wanted to return to Japan. It wasn't only rich Americans who went to Japan in the early years of the century. Now she had three characters of interest, Nomura, Baldrich, and Eileen—what was her last name? Riley, yes that was it. Lucy wrote swiftly. If she didn't write all this down, she knew she would lose it. Sitting on the edge of the chair, taking notes, she soon saw she had opened up a new aspect to her book—this was good, she felt better, even excited. And when she looked up, there was the scroll of a mountain before her, a mountain outlined with thick ink strokes in a modern style, but it was still a craggy mountain. At first she was startled and frightened by these rocky shapes, eroded down to the bare bones, no silt here, no fecundity, but then she began to feel for a moment the energy of the mountains, the crags like scales on an old dragon's back, the mountain alive, powerful. She would like to be a dragon, an old dragon lady, coiled up on a craggy mountain.

From the other room, Lucy heard Mrs. Yu ask, "Is Lucy all right?" Lucy couldn't move or call out.

David went into the hall, caught sight of her in the living room, in the dark. Lucy murmured, "I'll be there in a moment."

David hesitated, then left without saying a word.

When Lucy joined the others, she said, "Oh, I was making some notes for my book, sorry. Lately I forget everything if I don't write it down." She began asking Mr. Yu about the scrolls and the inscriptions.

Finally, the evening was over.

As Lucy and David got ready for bed, they were silent. In all her movements, Lucy was very careful. Something could explode here. In bed, at last, David turned over to look at her. "Do you want to talk about what happened tonight? I think you're upset about Maureen's baby. Do you think I like hiding my feelings about how excited I am to be a grandfather, because of you? You have feelings, well I do, too."

"I'm happy for you and for Maureen, but I can't help it if it makes me sad. I have to say that it surprised me, too, that I would feel so sad. That doesn't mean, though, I'm not happy for her and for you. If you remember, I was the one who said it'd be great to have your grandchildren around here."

"You went off and cried. Everyone could see that you cried. You ruined the evening."

"I don't think I ruined the evening. I'm sure no one thought anything of it, but I'm sorry. Like I said, I was surprised by my feeling. I'm really sorry."

David said nothing. He turned back over and didn't stir again.

Lucy lay there and cried silently. He should be happy about the baby, of course. She was sorry, so sorry, to have become so upset. She would get through this, her pain would pass. What else was there to do? Her tears ran into her ears. She rhymed to herself, *ears filled with tears, I can hear only tears.*

Lucy dreamed that it was still winter, and she was kneeling on the frozen lake. *It's so black,* she said out loud in the dream. Then not far from her a little boy fell through the ice. Lucy skated over to help him, but she fell through the ice, too, she couldn't save him, she couldn't save herself. Looking up, she saw the gray white ice above her, she was slipping away under the ice. *I'm going to die, I'm going to die,* she told herself, then made one last effort, one enormous effort. She pushed up and got her hand above water, holding on to the edge of the ice. In real life that ice would have broken, but it didn't. Then a hand grasped her own and slowly pulled her out. The boy was lost.

Lucy woke up terrified. She had almost died, she was going to die, the child had died. She had been saved, by whom? But the child had died.

David woke up, reached for her breasts. Afraid, she clung to him and they made love. The moment he fell back asleep, she was sick with disgust. Lucy knew she was in grave danger and should flee, put her clothes on and go home. Instead she kept whispering, "I have nothing, I have nothing."

The next day, at one, Lucy saw Tak trudging up the walk in his purple shirt, blue pants, deliberately placing every step of those small green high-top tennis shoes. She opened the door. Tak stopped. "But—"

Lucy was puzzled. Oh, the doorbell. Lucy shut the door. The bell rang and rang and rang. From upstairs, David yelled, "What's going on?"

Quickly opening the door again, Lucy found Tak on tiptoe still pressing the bell. Hana ran up. "Okay, Tak, enough!" She handed Lucy a silver plastic sword. "Tak can't go anywhere without his sword." Lucy admired Hana's jacket of yellow silk. "Howard's mother sent it, you don't think it's too yellow?" Howard honked the horn.

"No, no. It's primrose yellow, it's a spring yellow. By the way, David says hello, he's busy," she lied.

Hana hugged Tak once more, thanked Lucy again. "I hope he's not too much trouble—" She paused. "Maybe I should stay home—"

Howard called, "Let's go." He waved to Lucy, shook a finger at Tak, and said something in Japanese. Hana whispered to Tak, "Be a good boy." She hurried to the car, and they drove off.

While David read the Sunday paper, Lucy and Tak went for a walk. Tak dragged along his sword. He showed Lucy his entire repertoire of thrusts and parries, complete with a complicated story of a hero who saves someone from something. They were heading back to the house when Lucy stopped short at the rows and rows of tall white tulips holding perfectly still. "Guess what? There're almost one hundred tulips here. My friend David planted them all by himself." She tapped the head of the nearest tulip, its tip where the petals had opened an inch.

Tak stared at the tulips.

"He calls it a moon garden. Because all the flowers are white like the moon."

"My mama says there's a rabbit in the moon."

"Really? The moon's a white rabbit?"

"The rabbit at school, Ruby, is white, but she's got big black spots."

"Tulips have a black spot at their center." Lucy tipped a tulip over and pried open the white petals. "See the black smudge at the bottom? Like soot."

Tak touched a tulip. "Feels cold." Reaching out both hands, fingers spread out wide, he began brushing his palms lightly over the tips of the tulips. They swayed back and forth, whole rows bumping heads.

Lucy looked up at the house, saw David in the window reading a magazine. Before Tak's arrival, they had silently and coolly gone about the business of Sunday morning: late, big breakfast, the Sunday paper. He was probably reading the recipes in the Sunday paper magazine, and if she were in the room, he would exclaim, "I can't believe how complicated these recipes are!"

Turning back to Tak, she saw he had his sword raised to whack the tulips.

"No, no, Tak. We better not."

"I want to cut off their heads."

Lucy laughed. "You're right. They are like heads, aren't they? 'Off with their heads!'"

Lucy and Tak were in the kitchen eating chocolate chip cookies, when David came in.

Lucy held up a plate. "Want a cookie?"

"Where'd these come from?"

"I made them. I know what Tak likes. *Oishii?*"

Tak had a cookie in each hand. He laughed. *"Oishii!"*

Lucy translated for David. "It's Japanese for 'delicious.'"

"*Oishii*, huh?" David grabbed a cookie.

Lucy leaned on her elbow, looking at Tak. He sat up straight in his chair, his chin just above the table. He wore his black hair buzzed, a burr of glittering black jet splinters.

On the counter, David had a rabbit defrosting that he was going to cook for dinner that night, a new recipe. Tak fixed his eyes on the rabbit carcass curled up in the plastic sack. "What's that?"

Lucy thought, *I should have put it in the refrigerator.*

"It's a rabbit. It *was* a rabbit," David said.

Tak blinked.

Lucy stood up. "Tak? More milk?"

He looked at Lucy. "And can I have one more cookie, Mama—I mean, Lucy?"

Lucy beamed. She said to David, "Sometimes that happens at home, my nephews get my sister and my mother mixed up, so Mom is Grandma and Grandma is Mom, and when I'm there sometimes I'm Mom and Grandma, too."

David spit out, "But he knows the difference."

"I know," Lucy said quickly.

She began to clear the table. Tak was watching David eat the last cookie. Square teeth, with spaces between them, strong teeth, big mouth opened wide, taking a big bite, the last cookie was gone. Tak kicked the chair legs with his green shoes.

Scrubbing his lips with his napkin, David flung it down. He slapped his palms on the table and pushed himself up. "My game's on." He left.

Tak saw Lucy's purse sitting at the end of the table. "Can I count your money?" He began going through her wallet. Lucy finished putting everything away and sat next to him.

After counting the bills and the change, Tak went through her wallet. "Who's this?" He pointed to a photograph of a little Dracula.

"My nephew, Evan. On Halloween. What were you on Halloween?"

"I was a pirate. I had a patch over my eye, and I carried my sword. I had a big belt, boots, a hook!"

"A hook?"

"My poppa made me a hook, and we taped it on my arm so it didn't fall off. And it didn't fall off at all. Was kind of hard to get candy *and* hold my bag at the same time."

"Do you want to do some drawing? We could draw a pirate. With a hook, a black patch, black mustache, and—a sword!" Lucy took out the paper and crayons she had brought over.

Tak drew a little pirate, with red red blood on his sword and wearing green high-tops. Lucy asked, "Why do you suppose our pirate has green high-tops on?"

Tak stuck his legs out.

"Look at those long legs."

Tak gazed down at his green sneakers. "My feet are getting very far away."

Lucy had to check on David. She went down the hall, stuck her head in the television room. "You winning or losing?"

"Terrible, just terrible."

She walked over to give him a kiss, to say, she was still here, she hadn't forgotten him.

The batter came up to the plate. "He's my guy, come on, whack it out of the park."

Lucy politely waited until the batter hit the ball for a double.

David finally looked up and grinned. "Want to go out for dinner tonight? I can cook the rabbit tomorrow."

"Sure." She could make up the day to him, then, make up the night before. She probably had made a scene at the Yus.

The game came back on. David turned to the screen. "We'll talk about it later."

Tak was not in the kitchen.

Lucy looked in the bathroom, she looked upstairs. He must have slipped out of the house. How could she forget you had to watch kids like a hawk? He could be in the street, he could be run over—

She ran out the front door, circled the house. Around the corner, she caught sight of Tak, thank God, oh thank God Tak was all right.

Then she saw him moving down the row of tulips, popping off the blossoms with his hands. He said, "Off with your heads! Off with your heads!" with such obvious delight. Lucy felt that pure delight so strongly. Several tulips lay flat on the ground. He must have whacked them with his sword, then discovered that popping them off was more efficient and more fun.

David would throw a fit, he would shout at her. He might shout at Tak. Her heart beat hard, her hands felt very cold, but she didn't stop the child. Tak seemed so proud of his systematic decapitation. And so what if he beheaded every single one of those cold tulips, sooty-hearted white tulips?

Then Lucy was accusing herself, it was her fault, she had put the idea in Tak's head. What had she done? She was criminal, criminal. She went over to him. He stared up at her, eyes wide open, afraid. His teeth began to chatter. "I'm kind of cold. Is my mama coming soon?"

"I was looking for you. Let's make some hot chocolate to warm you up, and I've got some marshmallows to put in it, too." She took his hand—how cold and sticky with sap were his fingers. "Let's wash your hands first." In the kitchen, she sat Tak up on the sink's edge. She ran the water very warm, almost hot.

When David came to the kitchen, Tak had a chocolate mustache. "You look like your pirate," Lucy was telling Tak. David took a jar of popcorn from the cupboard. He looked at his watch. Lucy looked up at the kitchen clock. It was three. Hana would be back around four.

Lucy said, "Can I talk to you a minute?"

Tak sat at the table sipping his chocolate. Lucy and David went into the dining room.

Lucy told David that Tak had picked all of his tulips.

"You're kidding?"

"It's my fault. When I was talking to you, he slipped out and picked them all. I'm sorry, I'm so sorry."

David turned and walked out the front door.

Lucy watched him out the window. In the back of the house, he stood in front of the mounds of bruised petals turning a dark tea-stain brown and the rows of tall spindly green stems.

David swung his leg back and kicked the tulips. They flew up in the air.

He walked back in the front door and pounded up the stairs to his study, slammed his study door. Lucy could hear him fiddle with the radio to pick up the final innings of his ball game there.

Lucy and Tak sat quietly at the kitchen table and looked at a book she had bought for Tak and wrapped up like a gift.

At three-forty, Lucy said, "Your mom will be here soon." They packed up Tak's sword and his book, rolled up the drawing. She found a shopping bag to put everything in. "I have a bag, too, that I bring when I come to visit here. I don't really live here, I live in a tiny place on a top floor, way up in the trees. And it's in the city, where there're lots more people."

"What do you have in your bag?"

"What do you think I would need?"

Tak rolled his eyes, this seemed to indicate deep thought. "Toothbrush, pajamas—"

Lucy didn't wear pajamas at David's, so it was only a toothbrush. "And I always have to have a book. And now you have a book." Toothbrush and book and diaphragm, all she had here at David's. She could quickly disappear without leaving a trace.

They put Tak's bags on the front porch. Holding his hands up, his feet on her feet, she walked Tak in giant steps around the front yard and the backyard and the side of the house. She stopped at the rows of green stems and the white tulips scattered over the grass. Tak looked up at Lucy. He wrinkled his forehead, he turned dark red.

She knelt down and drew him close. "Shh. I know. Okay?"

"Okay," he whispered, his breath warm on her ear, his fingers cold on her arm. She almost couldn't bear it.

Lucy said, "Let's pile them up into one big pile."

With the tulips in a chill damp heap, suddenly Lucy looked around, then fell to her knees and buried her face in the tulips. "Tulips smell like no smell."

Tak stuck his face in the tulips. "Smells like nosmell."

"Nosmell, nosmell," they chanted, until *nosmell* did seem like one word, the exact word for the smell of white tulips. They laughed and laughed.

Hana and Howard drove up. David may have heard their car, but he didn't come down.

Hana hugged Tak. Sachiko told Tak, "I ate a big piece of cake with a white rose on it, and look at what I got." She dangled a little packet of rice done up in white netting and ribbon. Tak showed Hana the book Lucy gave him. And he told Sachiko that he had drunk two cups of hot chocolate with marshmallows on top.

Howard made jokes about the wedding and at the same time picked up Tak and held him close, ran his hand over his hair so gently. Tak laid his head on Howard's shoulder, his eyes wonderfully mild. Hana asked, "He wasn't too much trouble, was he? David didn't mind, I hope?" She picked up Tak's bag. After a few minutes they were gone.

Lucy went upstairs and knocked at David's door.

She told him, again, that she was so sorry about the tulips. "I should have watched him more closely."

David sighed, his lips almost trembled. "Well, the tulips are already gone. Nothing to be done. At least the kid didn't pull the bulbs up. It's a lot of work to dig one hundred holes, fill each hole with fertilizer, sit each bulb straight up in its hole, pull the earth back over each bulb, pat the earth down. He's gone, isn't he?"

She still had her hand on the doorknob of his study. She twisted it slightly back and forth. She heard herself say, "Yes. You know, maybe I'll go home. I'm tired."

David looked at her, angry, she thought at first. Then, however, he stood up, came over, and pulled her close. She could feel his cock lift. He said, "We didn't get to spend much time together today. Why don't you stay tonight?" For an instant she wanted to give in to those arms holding her. At the same time she found herself wildly calculating how many years she would have to be with him before he died and she was free. Horrified, she pulled away. "I better go home."

"Go, then." He turned his back on her and started arranging papers on his desk.

There had to be some explanation. She didn't know how to

explain but tried. "I think there's not enough between us. I think I want a home with someone—"

He turned around but looked off to one side of her. "Well, of course, I used to think that maybe later on, we'd live together."

But that wasn't it, Lucy said to herself. "It's more than that, I want some sort of family feeling—"

His face was dark and hard as he faced her at last. "Is this about having a baby? You knew from the very beginning, I didn't want to have any more children, you can't say I misled you."

Lucy almost said to him, in her despair, something that she had not, before this moment, ever put into words for herself: that she had never even considered having his child. That was the truth of things. She couldn't say that to him. She said instead, "This isn't exactly about children, it's about—"

David kept talking. "I've had my children, and if you had a child, you'd pay too much attention to the baby. Not to me anymore." He quickly justified his point. "Some women go crazy, get all wrapped up in the child, you'd be like that. Even now, you don't pay attention to me. You used to pay attention to me, but now you don't, not like at first." David's hand had covered his mouth, but the words came out in a high, almost falsetto voice, that trembled. "Do what you need to do. In fact, I knew this wouldn't work out a while ago. I knew it was over. I don't mind being alone."

"But I don't want to be alone." Yet as she gathered up her things to go, how lonely she felt, how frightened. He followed her out to her car. This was happening quickly. Lucy knew that if she didn't move quickly, get away quickly, she would reach out to touch him, cling to him, and all would be lost. For if she were to touch him now—and he was offering her this temptation, standing so close to her at her car door—they would go upstairs and make love. That would be like death to her. "Good-bye." She got into her car.

David turned and stumped back into his house. Lucy put her

head down on the steering wheel for a moment. Could she be hoping, even now, he would come back out? She quickly drove home.

One afternoon several weeks later, Lucy was at work in her office. The late afternoon sun played through the bright leaves like green skin, so tender. Outside her window, a sleek orange cat jumped up on the stone wall of the terrace that ran along the back of the building. Lucy, since she wasn't getting any work done anyway, jumped up to follow her. The cat looked peculiarly secretive, and Lucy was curious. She hurried out of the building. There was the cat with a small mole in her mouth, the little star of the mole's nose delicate and pink. Lucy could almost feel the shape of the little body, its beating heart, its soft fur, its fear making the poor mole hold still, maybe even in a faint from fear. The cat was so proud. She padded along the top of the wall, back spine a straight line, intent, head down, taut tail swinging back and forth. Lucy made no move to save the little mole. The cat leaped off the wall to the slope below. Lucy bent over the wall to watch her. Under the rhododendrons, their leaves upright for the sun and the buds pink-tipped, ready to burst open, the cat lay down, holding the mole still in her mouth. Why was she waiting? The cat in the green shade, a green cat in a green shade thinking a green thought. Or a green cat in a green shade thinking a bloody red thought. Lucy held as still as the cat. After a minute, the cat got up, slunk away through the bushes, and then with sudden leaps and bounds vanished.

This is what she had come to—following a cat. Yet, what a pleasure, to do one thing so simple. She felt as weightless as light and shadow. The next moment, though, this was an uneasy feeling.

She should go back to work, but she hesitated. She was right under David's window. All those months with him had come to nothing. She looked up at his office window. It was empty.

CHAPTER 11

O n the first day of June, a Saturday, Lucy woke up late, ate breakfast, read every bit of news in the newspaper, and threw it aside. She should do her usual Saturday tasks: vacuum, hang up the piles of clothing suspended on doorknobs and on doors, go shopping. But now that school was out, the papers graded, the committee meetings and the graduation ceremonies over, every day was a Saturday, and she could easily do these things any day of the week. Instead, she told herself, looking at her study, she should sort out these piles of notes and papers, as a way of beginning work on her book. How hard, though, it was to accomplish anything when at the end of the day there was no one to offer relief from accomplishment by touching her or desiring to be touched by her.

The clock said ten. So eight o'clock mountain time. Her parents were eating breakfast. Her mother would be reading her paper, the *Rocky Mountain News,* and her father his paper, the *Denver Post,* or as she and her sister called them, the *Rocky Mountain Snooze* and the *Denver Ghost.* Lucy knew their routine. Up earlier than her mother, her father in his ghostly white pajamas made the coffee and his own "gruel," some sort of instant oatmeal, then dressed to read the paper.

He always waited for his second cup of coffee until her mother slippered in, wearing her pale blue robe, hair fluffy on the sides and flat at the back from sleeping, face a little shiny from the cream she put on it at night. Holding up his cup, he would say, "Hey, while you're on your feets." Her mother always marveled, "He'll wait and wait, no matter how long it takes for me to get out here. I want to say to him what he says to Caroline's boys, 'Are your legs painted on?' But I never do."

This was a good time to call them. The last time, though, Lucy had spoken to her mother, her mother asked her about David and said, after Lucy told her it was over, "I admire you for being able to live alone. I don't think I could do it." Instead, she called her sister.

When Caroline picked up, in the background Lucy could hear her boys talking, a baby crying—whose baby? "Hel-lo! I keep thinking I should call you. Here, Evan, you can feed him now." To Lucy she explained, "We've got the next-door neighbor's baby for the morning. Wouldn't you know, my luck, I can't even get a little girl on a temporary basis. Always boys, boys, boys."

Lucy heard Evan's clear high voice. "This milk, Mom?"

"No, that milk, first squeeze the air out like this—"

"I know, Mom. Let me. Let me."

"It's hysterical. The Evan-guy wants to do everything, feed him, hold him, change his diaper, give him a bath. He thinks we should all get out of his way and let him do it right." Caroline laughed. "Ben and Dan of course want to do the same thing, though they won't admit it. You should see this baby, very very pretty, and what a chunk, big rolls of fat. He's like Dan at that age, fat and hungry."

In the background Lucy could hear a growled "Thanks, Mom."

She could see them all crowded into the small kitchen in the house Caroline had miraculously managed to buy after her divorce. Dan, fourteen, and Ben, twelve, were so tall, probably much taller than the last time she had seen them. Evan, six, yelled, making up for lack of height with volume. Caroline, blond and gray hair, the long long legs sticking out of shorts, circled around her kitchen, whose counters were spattered with pancake batter, cluttered with maple syrup and orange juice and, today, baby bottles.

Lucy said, "Sounds like you literally have your hands full. I won't keep you—"

"No, we're all right. What's new with you?"

"Nothing much. School's out, but I have my own work to do this summer—" She interrupted herself. "I wish I was there, I miss you all so much."

"Are you coming out this summer?"

"I'll try—"

"You have to come and see what I've done to the backyard. We moved the dog pen, put a big flower bed around that tree toward the back, I've got an arbor with grapevines starting to grow on it, big vegetable garden, and a hammock. You know what else I'm going to do? Dad and Mom will think I've lost my mind, but what's new?"

"Knock down a wall in the house?"

"No, but I should, and then invite Dad over. When he sees the wall half gone, he won't be able to help himself, he'll jump in to finish it. He needs a project bad to get out of Mom's clutches. She's trying to get him to do stuff around the yard and to paint the house, so that she can have a big barbecue on July fourth, and of course it has to be perfect—"

Lucy intoned in her mother's voice, "'If it's not perfect, no one will have a good time.' Translation: 'If it's perfect, no one will have a good time.'"

"This year she's even worse, in some sort of cleaning frenzy. Something's up with them. I tried to get it out of Dad, but you know those two, they can clam up pretty tight. Hold on, Evan, no, no, you can't take the baby down the street to show your friends. So, guess what? I'm thinking about getting some chickens."

"Tell me why you want chickens."

"Reminds me of Grandma's, remember all those chickens she had, remember chasing the chickens around? And it's practical. They lay eggs and eat the bugs out of my garden."

"Do chickens eat bugs?"

"Sure they do."

"How do you know?"

"I know."

Caroline already had a menagerie: two dogs, a fat cat terrorized at dusk by a huge owl that swooped down talons extended, two parakeets, a hamster, a ferret, two ducks that nipped at Evan's legs. Now there would be chickens pecking at the ground, strutting, beaky and beady-eyed through the flowers.

The baby started to cry, and Caroline said, "Here Evan, give me the baby."

Evan yelled, "It's still my turn, my turn!"

Caroline laughed. "I better go. *I wish you were here!*"

"Me, too, I miss you all."

Her house was so silent. Fifteen hundred miles away, kids and animals, a baby being passed around, played with, flowers, vegetables, grapevines, enormous blue sky, mountain air that smelled of sage and cut grass. The telephone call made Lucy feel even less like sitting in her apartment all day and working.

The phone rang. Hana said without letting Lucy even say hello, "My mother's here to take care of the kids. Howard's off at a conference. Would you like to go look at houses with me in Jamaica Plain? Someone told me that Jamaica Plain might be an interesting place to live, cheaper than Hunnewell. Howard would like living closer to the city. There's the Jamaica Pond and the Arboretum, a bit of nature for me. I can't bear to leave this house, but we better move."

Lucy was glad to have something to do—vicarious house hunting would gratify her own restlessness. Yet after seeing house after house, they shook off the realtor and sat down in a café. Hana didn't like Jamaica Plain. The houses she could afford stood too close to other houses on weedy, littered, busy, noisy streets, and they weren't that close to the Pond or the Arboretum. Lucy didn't see any possibilities for herself. The houses were all too big. Their yards were dusty and weedy—a garden would take years to flourish.

Hana said, "I can't bear to be so far away from something wild. Sometimes I imagine that out there in the marsh, among the reeds, are these Japanese spirit foxes with foxfire playing over their heads. They've been watching over my babies. Perhaps I'm a spirit fox myself, like in the old Japanese tale, transformed into a human wife until her husband discovers her fox ears when she passes between a light and a thin paper screen. Then she has to leave him, leave her children. They tug at her kimono, her bushy tail showing now under her robe, as she goes back to the forest. But I couldn't leave my children." She smiled. "The good thing about Howard is that even if he noticed my fox ears and fox tail, he wouldn't care. He wouldn't say a thing to break the spell."

Lucy said, "I don't think I can bear to move again, start over in a new neighborhood, alone, one in which I don't know anyone, don't know the streets. I think I better stay put, wait until I'm feeling stronger."

They were both silent a moment.

Hana asked Lucy, "Have you heard from David?"

"No, he wouldn't ever call. I started it, I ended it, I would have to start it again. The thing I most regret was not ending it sooner. I should have known it was over months ago, but I couldn't bear to let it go. There's where the harm was, I forced myself and David, too." Lucy paused, then smiled a little. "I thought I had made a karmic change into some sort of new life with someone, and it turned out to be worse than the old life, which I ended up in again. So much for karmic change."

Hana said, "I think he couldn't change. He wants to be solitary. He thought he could change when he met you, but he couldn't. It's a fatality of character, like in a Nō play, he has to be the way he is."

"Maybe I'm solitary, too. I'll stay untouched, as you said, all my life."

"You shouldn't remember everything I say. No, I don't think so. You do things, you try. Something will happen."

Lucy laughed. "Thanks for the prophecy. The vagueness of it is worthy of an oracle."

Hana insisted. "I know something will happen. I don't have an image for it right now, but I feel it."

"I do feel my state vague, colorless, unworthy of description." Lucy could feel herself about to cry. "We should go."

Hana and Lucy said good-bye at the subway station near Jamaica Plain. That evening, after dinner, Lucy sat on her porch steps and looked at her garden. The tomatoes should be staked up. The basil seedlings should be thinned. Bindweed twined with the oregano and thyme, she should pull it out now before it choked them completely. So many things to do, but Lucy could not, would not lift a hand to put the garden to rights. Something more urgent had to be done. If only she knew what it was, she would do this something, and then everything else would happen. Though it was only the beginning of June, in her mind the summer days suddenly flew by, and it was fall again, the light began to fail, and she would have failed to do something. Could her life go on this way forever, never changing?

Shouting came from down the street. Lucy looked up. Three boys were beating another boy with a hockey stick, another boy held his hand to his face, shouting, "I know your faces." The boy being beaten started running. The three boys chased him, yelling and swinging the hockey stick. Lucy's heart started pounding, and she yelled at them to stop. They looked at her and headed off in the opposite direction. The hurt boy and his friend kept running, too.

A policeman came by. Someone must have called. She flagged him down. To describe the incident, she had to say, what scared her the most, that the boys being beaten were black, the boys beating were white. Three little boys who had seen everything from across the street told the policeman that they were playing roller hockey in the driveway when these black boys ran into these white boys and a fight had started. The kids clung to the porch railings, and one of them kept saying, "I was so scared." The policeman got back in his car, radioed something, and drove off.

Lucy stood on the sidewalk, worked up and helpless. She saw a pair of headphones in the street. The little boys said they belonged to one of the black boys. The headphones were broken but not crushed. The pieces could be fitted back together. Lucy thought about the child's fear and anguish. To lose the headphones, one's little possession, would make it worse. She knew how her nephews treasured their "stuff" beyond any actual worth.

Lucy took off immediately in the direction of the headphones owner to try to return them. That might be a small comfort. She had never walked down this street. It was not on her way to the subway stop or the grocery store. She asked two little girls playing hopscotch if they had seen a boy holding a hand to his face go by. "Was he a white or a black kid?" She had to say black. "Lots of black kids live over there on Murdoch Street." Lucy turned in the direction they pointed. Murdoch Street was lined with the usual Somerville double and triple deckers. Who knew who was inside, she couldn't tell if they were black people, or white, or yellow or blue. No one on the street to ask. She finally turned to go home. She would make a sign about the headphones and put it on her gate, so the boy would see it if he came back to look for them.

As she made her way back with the boy's headphones dangling from her hand, her heart still beating hard after the violence of the incident, she suddenly had a sharp sense of the horror and loveliness of the world occurring so pointedly at the same moment that it was vertiginous. For along the sidewalk were roses lifting red and white faces, clumps of fringed iris yellow and purple, and heavy pink peony heads bending over fences.

Lucy stopped, leaned upon an unpainted splintering fence—maybe a house where white kids lived, maybe a house where black kids lived—and lifted one of the peonies to smell its superb perfume. She brushed her palm over the top of the globe of petals, of densely furled pink petals, pushed back the petals, yet it was impossible to get to the hidden secret core of the flower. Only the little black ants that hurried in and out of the peony, opening up that core with their ministrations, would ever see or know the core. She envied the ants, these spiritual emissaries, missionaries from the hidden center, from the peony's heart, the heart of a deep pink peony world. She could purchase a peony from the florist's, but there would be no ants. Someday, if she had her own garden, in a place where she was certain to live a long time—well, as long as anyone could plan to live in a certain place—she would plant peonies. Peonies were a strange bush, they disappear in the winter, but right away in spring, the reddish spikes cluster, shoot up fast, then come the balls of dark brownish green buds, and the ants get busy helping to unfurl this world of pink translucence and perfume. If only she had ants to open her up?

Lucy pictured David lying down this evening to go to sleep, a bit drunk and sleepy. Would he even think about her, as he undressed, of course not taking off his watch? Did he remember that she called him "The Genius of Affection"? Empty title. Lucy was embarrassed and angry at her own pompous language. All come to nothing.

At least her love for Michael had been real. She had once been opened up. Yet he had left her, and she closed again. In a pitched state of feeling, feeling that since she had nothing and since nothing she tried to do legitimately would work, she asked herself why not be opened up again, one more time? Why not see Michael again?

Lucy hung up the headphones on the fence where the fight had occurred and hoped the child would come back to find them. The moment she was inside her house, she telephoned Michael's number at his university. Standing in the kitchen, looking out the back at the steeply pitched roofs, she heard Michael's voice-mail message. The sound of his voice startled her, she hesitated. Then, happy and afraid, she let the words spill out of her, inviting him to meet her, where, anywhere, why not Mexico again, repeat the past, since there was no future. Maybe he didn't check his messages from Japan, or the message would disappear by the time he checked it. It was like a message in a bottle, thrown off her lonely island into the waves.

In a week, Lucy received the telegram from Michael telling her to meet him in Mexico City on June 23, at five o'clock, in the Casa des Azuelas, the House of Tiles, a huge colonial palace covered in blue and white tiles, now a famous tourist restaurant. There could be no mistake about the meeting place. She hurriedly bought her ticket to Mexico and back through Denver to see her family. After she parted from Michael, her opened, revealed self that Michael always called forth like Lazarus from the grave would be in such a tender state, vulnerable to the greatest sadness. She would need a safe place to convalesce.

The night before she left, she dreamed that she had five children and had to leave them with her sister, for she couldn't take care of them. Another child dream. But she could not afford to pay it any attention. She had to hurtle forward. She fled Somerville, as if a city on fire, bed unmade, dishes in the sink, clothes still hung over the arms of chairs and on doorknobs, the garden turning brown.

CHAPTER 12

When Michael heard Lucy's voice, summoning him to Mexico, she seemed so terribly in need, he could not deny her. In full knowledge of the violent act he was committing, the very one he kept trying to avoid, he told his wife he had to see Lucy. On the day he had to leave she invited her new friends and her students, daring him to go. Moments before they came, he left. She cried, she shouted that she would not be there this time when he returned. He knew she would be. He would come back, and she would keep cooking, talking, ironing his shirts. At least for two weeks, he could feel alive again.

He arrived in Mexico at noon, five hours before he would meet with Lucy. Unable to sleep, he walked from the city's central plaza to the Cathedral of Guadalupe, miles and miles, but that was perfect, he had to walk and walk swiftly to feel he was journeying toward Lucy. Up the broad stairs to the Plaza of Our Lady of Guadalupe, a young woman, clasping her thin arms before her and repeating her vow, crawled on her knees toward the sanctuary. Her small thin father placed a jacket under her knees, then after she crossed the length of the jacket, picked it up and placed the jacket in front of her again. The father and daughter slowly approached the church. The daughter's high cheekbones lifted like Lucy's. If Lucy were on her knees, he would take the coat, kiss it, and place it before her.

In the old cathedral a small crowd attended some mysterious rite, at the center of which was a small child wearing a gold miter. The stone walls of the cathedral's long corridors were hung with gold, silver, and tin ex-votos. So many people desperate for a cure.

He walked back to the botanical garden of Chapultepec Park to note the names of the trees he liked, but ended up watching an old man buying ice cream for his two little granddaughters, so fat and funny. Michael thought, *I am old, I have no children, no grandchildren, no lovely little piglets like these.*

When he went to the meeting place at last, he feared that Lucy wouldn't be there. That somehow he would have missed her, failed her again. He stood in a gallery above the restaurant waiting for her, yet when she came in, he didn't immediately run down to her. He stood watching her, noting all the old familiar details. Those high cheekbones, the long slim fingers, the pointed nose with its little nub like a potato on the end, the hair pulled back so severely. When she smiled at him, he knew that mouth, so compressed with tension, would relax, become full, those eyes small with fatigue and fear would turn a gaze so full of love upon him. He was about to receive from her the living water he thirsted for. He had to hurry, hurry, why watch when he could go touch her, fold her against himself.

When at last he held her, he confessed, "I was watching you from upstairs, I tortured myself, I wanted to rush to you, but I wanted to watch you, too, feast my eyes on you. You are more beautiful than ever before. I kept thinking you can't be as beautiful as I remembered you, but you are."

Lucy was crying. Michael got them a table so they could talk and eat something. Over the most banal of tourist dinners, flaccid shrimp in ketchup cocktail sauce, stuffed peppers in pools of congealed cheese, they talked and never minded the food. By the time they headed for the hotel Michael had found, they didn't have anything left to say. They were happy to be walking through the large pools of darkness, the few streetlights illuminating the old buildings so that it was like a dream street or a ballet stage. Then Lucy stopped, grabbed Michael's arms to hold him, to look at him and say, "The weather report is: sudden wind shears of happiness."

In the hotel room, Lucy went to the bathroom and left the door open. They had fallen immediately back into their so familiar and peculiar mingling of the domestic and the erotic. Michael watched as, a little drunk from the beer at dinner, Lucy looked at herself in the bathroom mirror and grinned. In the mirror, he, too, saw the face of a happy woman. For two weeks, he would try to make her as happy as he could. After she washed her face, he watched her fish out her diaphragm and the tube of spermicide gel. She sat down on the edge of the bathtub, spread her legs, and was about to insert the diaphragm. "I've never really noticed how ugly these little things are. They're that beige color of baby dolls and of mannequins in department store windows." The springy circle suddenly flipped from her fingers and into the toilet. She laughed and glanced at Michael. "Maybe it's a sign. I'm never going to make love to anyone else, so let's just flush it away, do you mind?"

"No, I don't mind at all."

She flushed the toilet, dropped the tube of spermicide gel in the wastebasket, and began to sing, "La la la." Sitting on the bed next to him, she asked, "You really don't mind?"

Michael pinched off his reading spectacles, closed his eyes, and reached for her. Lucy put out both her hands to stop him. "I haven't inspected you properly," she said most severely, like a headmistress.

Michael recognized the command, he stood up, held perfectly still, his eyes closed with pleasure.

Lucy lifted first one of Michael's arms, then the other, smelled under each one. "Yes, it is you, only you have this musky smell of lavender, I'd know you if I were blind."

She spread out one of his hands with her hands, spread out the broad palm, fanned out the strong fingers. She held his hips lightly but surely, gauging their power with a proprietary eye, taking her time. She made him spread his legs and weighed his testicles in the palm of her hand. His keglets of love, he once called them, filled with love wine—she laughed. "How can it be—you here with me from halfway across the world? A miracle!"

The real miracle, Michael thought, was that love could be so incarnate. That it could have such fixity as one body and one body only.

"Turn. Turn, slowly. Stop," Lucy commanded.

Even though he knew he was too fat, looked unhealthy, gray, still as she touched him, he felt he was the most beautiful man in the world. Lucy kissed the small of his back, her hands holding his hips. "Do you love me a little?"

"*Más que un poco!*" He trembled though trying to stand perfectly still.

Now Lucy seemed as if she could not bear not to have Michael in her arms, and she pulled him to her and held him fast with her arms and legs, pulled him to her with such need. He at last loosed the ferocity of his feeling, crushing his largeness into her, so open, so receptive, the largeness of all the things in the world that he loved and wanted to give her, show her, out of all that delight make a child with her. He could think of nothing but that and was sure she could think of nothing but that. Afterward, as they were falling asleep, Lucy told him about a salt marsh north of Boston and how beyond it lay the silver sea—how she had stood at the margin of the vast sea.

So the trip was now launched like all the other trips they took together. They were Michael and Lucy, together again, he said to himself. Miguel y Luz, Luz y Miguel, in Mexico. For two weeks, a short time, a long time. Let them make a world and a lifetime out of those weeks.

The first few days they visited museums: the archaeology museum, the modern art museum, the museum at the Templo Mayor, so that whenever Michael felt the coming rush of his bowels, he and Montezuma's revenge could lord it up in the marble bathrooms, while upstairs Lucy kept looking at the immense basalt boulders shaped into eagles, into a stone conch shell. When he was at last plugged up with medicine, they traveled around the outskirts of the city. At Xochimilco they were poled through the maze of old Aztec canals, in a flat yellow boat bedecked with plastic flowers and named *Almita*. Michael called her attention to the rats preening before them and then diving perfectly into the water like Esther Williams. Above, the silver and gold cones of volcanoes shone like two moons. At dusk they stopped in the ghostly white church of the small town near the canals. With its delicate finials and toothy merlons, prim pilasters, it was pure Renaissance. The church front was in shadow, inside was a wedding with hundreds of candles.

Every night they would make love until they were so sweaty, they slid across each other's flesh or made delightful squelching sounds. And though they didn't say anything, they both thought of a child, a child born at the last minute.

After five days, a restlessness overtook them. They could not stay too long in one place, for then a hotel felt like home, and they would have to ask themselves why didn't they have a home together? They had to move on. Where to go? They had been south to Oaxaca on their earlier trip, why not go east toward Veracruz? They consulted the guidebook and decided to go to Xalapa, a town of mist and flowers the guidebook gushed, in the eastern mountains near Veracruz. They went to the bus terminal early to be the first to buy tickets so they could sit up front, see everything. Success! Seats one and two! Miguel clapped his hands, kissed the tickets, and capered. Once the bus started, he crowed, he snapped his fingers and called out, *"Adelante coche!"*

On the bus were couples and families and a lonesome Japanese tourist. Lucy sat with Michael's arm around her as the bus turned east and headed up into the very high mountains, where the narrow roads ran along ridges so at one moment the drop-off was to the left, then around a curve to the right. Both drop-offs sheer down to green slopes and rivers far away. Near the top of the divide, they drove through clouds. A fan of pine needles, a gnarled branch, the tall ancient trunk loomed near and was gone. Michael put his hand behind Lucy's head and pulled it onto his shoulder. Up in the clouds at the top of the world, he whispered into her ear, "I can never let you go, because between you and me is the love contract. You believe in my existence, and I believe in yours. No one else has ever believed in me like you believe in me—even if I am no longer able to believe in my own existence, I believe in you more than you know." No one, not that experimental man David, could love Lucy, hold her as he held her, of that Michael was certain. And no one would love her child more—Michael could almost feel the tiny head in his hands.

Luz and Miguel held hands, Luz's head on Miguel's shoulder. Michael dozed off and on, he felt Lucy dab at his drool. They were quiet and at peace.

Close to Xalapa, Michael saw the high clouds part, and there was the immense volcano cone of the Pico de Orizaba, so high up in the sky. The jagged crater of black rock showed through the ice cap. It was so dangerous looking, so rough, so towering. Michael felt afraid, something pent up, inevitably explosive waited there. The next moment clouds swept over the crater again, and he was relieved.

The hotel they picked from the guidebooks, Las Golondrinas, "The Swallows," was inexpensive, tucked inside high walls, simple rooms gathered around a court of oleanders, geraniums, a tiled fountain. The nice young men at the desk laughed when Michael talked to them in Spanish with his exaggerated Castilian lisp and said he hoped they didn't hold his French ancestry, of which he informed them, against him, he was sure that the Mexicans had never forgiven the French for Maximilian and the invasion of 1863. In their room, the first thing they did was push the two single beds together. By this time they had both taken so much antidiarrheal medicine, they longed to be flushed out and at dinner broke all the rules and ate salad, had drinks with ice cubes, courted intestinal disaster willingly.

That evening, back in their room, they looked down from their window on the roof gardens and terraces of the pink and blue and green houses built on the slope below, so peaceful. Yet always above them, Michael thought, though hidden in the mist, was the volcano, that indisputable black jagged eruption.

In the next few days, they again quickly established a routine, for both of them were lovers of small routines in compensation for the larger erratic movements in their lives. They ate breakfast at the Café de la Parrochia, where the professors from the local university read their papers and women came in twos and threes to talk. They learned to summon the waiter with the kettles of steaming milk and hot coffee by tapping a spoon against their glass, *ding de ding de ding ding ding*. Then they explored the town, noting for each other all its details, which was the pleasure of and reason for travel to a new place, the surface of things was so new and detailed that one's attention was preoccupied by it, one could forget everything else for a while. In the Parque Juárez, among tall plane and pine trees, roses, gardenias, and bird-of-paradise, university students underlined information in their textbooks, couples locked themselves in long embraces, kids played tag, and impeccably dressed government officials got their shoes shined before hurrying off to work under the large arches of the confectionery-pink colonial governor's *palacio*. The streets were lined with shop fronts of pastel yellow, blue, and green, spruce yet crumbling a little, bougainvillea and roses spilled over the walls from hidden gardens. Showing up so vividly in this prosperous pastel world were the very handsome Xalapeños, with thick black hair and good haircuts, strong-boned open faces, polished red brown. Only at moments, as Lucy and Michael walked along back streets, did they see the poor, thin children and their mothers carrying laundry or setting up a plank to sell their vegetables. The black crater came and went in the sky.

Late in the afternoon of their third day, Lucy and Michael spotted a child pulled along by the leash of a dog wearing a pink net tutu. Behind him, walking in the same direction, was an old woman with bright red lips and cheeks, pink hennaed hair under a green gauze scarf, and out of the basket on her arm popped up the heads of two cats in harlequin ruffs. Miguel and Luz followed and soon arrived at a parish church, La Merced, which for the day had cast off its sober elegance to celebrate the fiesta of the Blessing of the Animals. Stalls selling corn on the cob, crepes dripping with honey, and all sorts of candies and drinks crowded the terrace in front of the church. An electrified band on a bandstand blasted out song after song—a local favorite seemed to be a song called *"Hay Xalapeños."*

From every direction came more people with their animals. On the shoulders of a dignified man with a white mustache rode two parrots, green like living plants and wearing bowler hats. Turtles had sporty beach umbrellas and lizards sequined collars. A beagle had dressed casually, in a pair of cutoff jeans and a T-shirt with a notepad in the back pocket. Two Doberman pinschers were dressed as a bride and groom, white veil and tuxedo. Now the band gave a rousing blare, and the priest appeared in the doorway of the church. The crowd moved forward, and the priest in his golden vestments—with an Indian-pattern-woven stole and glasses taped together—blessed a container of water. His acolyte holding up the container, the priest dipped a plastic pink rose in the water and shook it at the crowd and their animals, blessing each one. The crowd pressed forward, holding up the cats and dogs and birds and lizards. Lucy pressed forward in delight. Michael heard her laughter spilling over the crowd, and he thought, yes, she's like that, joy breaking out unexpectedly. Then she turned to look at him with such joy. He pulled her to him, fiercely.

She shouted over the loud music and the feedback of the speakers, "It's wonderful, isn't it? I feel blessed by the animals, I'm going to get a cat as soon as I get home."

"No, let me be your cat, you can doze with me, listen to music, read books." Michael for the moment let himself conjure up a vision of another life. In this heady company, this late sun so gold and warm, how could he help himself?

Lucy said, "Did you see the boy with the chicken? He's my favorite. There he is—see the boy with the chicken?" The boy, dark, barefoot, had under his arm a most handsome red-brown chicken, with feathery pantalets, one foot tied with a straggling red ribbon, their presence the lone testimony to a bygone day when the fiesta was to bless the farm animals, the real wealth of the people. The boy and his chicken inched forward to be sprinkled with the blessed water, then he turned and walked on a road out of town.

In the middle of the night, Michael awoke and could not get back to sleep. He turned over and put his arm around Lucy, listened to her breathe. He knew how lovely her skin was when she slept, rosy and clear. He began to worry as usual about how badly he was treating her. He felt guilty about his part, whatever it may have been, in the end of her relationship with David. And the thought of his wife angry and sad and alone was terrible. Wait, wait, he still had to tell Lucy, so that he could keep speaking to his wife and try to work this all out. If he and Lucy had a child, there would be the child, too, not only to delight in but to worry about, to add immeasurable depth to his guilt.

Lucy in her sleep spoke softly, indistinctly, in a kind of soft protest. He touched her hair, he tightened his arm around her, fiercely to protect and comfort her. What good was he, though, a living corpse, to her, to his wife.

CHAPTER 13

Three days left. Lucy silently counted them on her fingers. She looked over her shoulder and saw sadness gaining on her. In two days, Michael would return to Japan and his wife. Early on the fourth day, she would go on to Denver and be with her family, yet even in their midst alone, so alone and exhausted without Michael. The world of Michael and Lucy, like a suspension bridge of marvelously strung lacy cable architecture, without its necessary tension, would spring apart and collapse into the sadness it had spanned.

Michael felt it, too. "I should try to be cheerful, but the signs of landfall are all around us, the driftwood, the sea birds, the mist in the distance." After lunch he lay down on his bed in the darkened hotel room for, he said, "a gloombath," so overcome with despair was he, embarrassing himself even as he spoke, she saw, by his melancholic, melodramatic tone. She sat on the bed next to him, her hand on his hip to comfort him and herself by touching him. He reached out his arm and murmured, "Lie down next to me." She did, and he began to talk, talking to distract himself, telling her how often he had been struck on this trip by the resemblance between the Japanese and the Mexicans, physically, the same head, the same body, and now Mexico began to make him think about Japan: did places one loved come to resemble each other, or did they recall the love of the other, because they truly resembled each other?

Lucy stood up suddenly. She couldn't lie there with him. She had to go practice loneliness now, in order to survive imminent loneliness. "I can't sleep. I think I'll go for a walk."

"I'll wait for you here." Michael's slight frown told Lucy that he understood her panic—she could never surprise him. Kissing his forehead, she slipped on her sandals, picked up her purse, and left the room quickly.

Outside in the bright sun, she blinked and breathed shallowly. Sitting with her coffee on the terrace of a café, she avoided looking up at the terrifying big volcano and concentrated on the little green-furred volcanoes rising on the outskirts of Xalapa. Odd how the volcano shape could become so funny and lovely in these small domesticated volcanoes. Opening her guidebook, she read that their green was that of coffee plantations and they were located outside a little town called Xico, not far away at all. The town sounded pretty. She caught a cab and went to Xico. She walked along its sidewalks under the large carved and weathered eaves that kept the houses and shop fronts in shadow. The buildings were plastered and painted cream, white, and red, while the doors were usually two doors wide and of a powdery blue, or of cracked leather and nail studded. Window shutters stood open behind grills, and Lucy saw a bird in a large cage, jute sacks bulging with coffee beans, a wooden chair with its prim, straight back, a courtyard giving on a patch of weeds, all the rooms empty of people. Lucy kept looking in the windows, she wanted to be inside a house, cool and silent and shadowy, inside some ordinary room, quiet. At the Xico market she found all the people who had left their windows open. The market sold the stuff of everyday life. There were stalls for shoes, purses, clothes, appliances, cooking utensils, fabric, and oilcloth decorated with roses. Stalls whose vendors were peasant women, with their long braids, sitting next to bouquets of gardenias, baskets of dried beans and seeds, rows of Prell shampoo bottles filled with golden honey, vats of mole, bowls of light and dark red chili powder, trays of brown dried ants. She bought a charm, a cardboard rectangle decorated with a saint's picture, herbs, and a spangled plastic horseshoe.

Lucy became nostalgic for everyday life, an everyday life with Michael, in which all the exquisite domesticities they managed to achieve even on this trip, the talking to him while he lay submerged in the bath, the lying in bed talking and talking, the teasing him about his thatchy thinning hair and his attempts to make it grow with applications of some sticky cream, the comfort and majesty of his flesh—if only she had these every day of the year. All she had were several days of hotel life with Michael, and then Michael would be gone, and she would be back to the old everyday life she kept trying to transform and failing to transform. Lucy sat on a bench and looked at the green cones surrounding the town, she looked up, and there was still the Pico volcano, with its silvery snows and black crater high above the clouds. Perhaps the volcano would never erupt again, that compression of geological feeling would be trapped forever.

Back at the hotel, Michael was reading a newspaper and waiting for her. He came over to her to hold her. Yet she couldn't give in to his touch, instead she struggled free and announced that she was hungry and they should go eat. When they couldn't find the restaurant they had decided to eat at, she became angry. Michael kept walking back and forth, sure that the right street should be here somewhere, and she said to herself, how can he be so inept? When he suggested they eat at a local small restaurant they knew, she grew angrier, she wanted something more than the same little tacos, again. They finally sat down in a huge restaurant, the only customers, and ate bad food in mutual gloom while the manager, who doubled as a waiter, hovered over them. Lucy was even more depressed. Michael, too, had become irritable, and when they paid the check, he said the service had been so bad, they shouldn't leave a tip, it was against his principles. Lucy knew this would cause trouble, and she said it would be his fault. Michael made her hurry away, while the manager was in the kitchen, but he saw them leave, saw there was no tip, and chased them to the front door of the restaurant. Lucy walked out to the street as if she didn't know Michael. Embarrassed and ashamed, Michael stuffed several bills into the man's hand and caught up with Lucy, who said, "I told you so," in triumph and in misery. Then they began to laugh, but still they were sad. In the middle of the night Lucy awoke in a panic. With only a day left, she regretted the hours she had been angry with him.

They moved one more time, to Veracruz and the Hotel Colonial, with a balcony opening right on Veracruz's central plaza. At lunch they drank too much, slept heavily in the afternoon, and sat in the plaza for hours in the evening. They watched the white plastered plaza fill with women in sleeveless dresses and men in tight short-sleeved shirts, formal in their own way. They listened to the marimba bands and laughed at the local dance competitions held on temporary stages, blindingly lit up and loud with the masters of ceremonies and their microphones. There were sailors from all over the world, and prostitutes. Lucy saw a prostitute in a very short flowered dress who looked like a child. She and Michael should take that child away, take her home, someone so small, so helpless. That would be simple. A child they could hold tightly, cherish, love the world through. Michael struck up a conversation with two Mexican couples sitting next to them at the restaurant who turned out to live in the United States. Both the men were well-off businessmen, in colorful vacation shirts that stretched over prosperous American stomachs. Their wives were dressed in pink shorts sets, gold sandals.

Michael got them to talk about themselves, to talk about why they lived in the States and why they wanted to retire in Mexico. Then they asked him about his house in the States, and he told them about his Shaker house, his garden. Lucy felt that Michael's life without her was beginning to reassert itself, so that before they even parted, he was married again.

The next day they took a cab to the airport. Michael insisted she take it back to the hotel immediately and not come in. He said he could not bear to have to turn away from her at the gate. So they embraced on the sidewalk. Lucy tried to laugh, but the pain was so simple and direct, she could not hide it. Her face against his jacket, she knew she should say something about the future, but she didn't know what to say.

Michael kissed the crooked parting of her hair, fingered her earlobes, held her neck, pushed her hair from her face to kiss her cheekbones, her temples. "I won't promise anything until I know I can do what I promise. I can only say wait, wait. I'm a coward, a horrible coward, but leaving her without her agreeing is too violent for me."

Once again Lucy was losing Michael, and she had known precisely and clearly that the trip would come to this, and that nothing would ever come of her love for him. What if she were pregnant? It seemed so unlikely that she had almost forgotten it might be a possibility. She dismissed the thought again, before it could swell into some false hope. All she could say now was, "I love you, even more than before, if that is possible. I always think when I see you I'll love you less, my love will turn out not to have been so objective a fact." At the same time, Lucy knew this love had exhausted her one more time. She could never do this again.

He bundled her back into the cab. As the cab took off, Lucy turned and watched Michael out the window. She waved and waved. Michael walked down the street waving at her, then he began running alongside the taxi, his white shirt pulling from his pants, flapping. The cab pulled ahead, turned the corner, and it was as if Michael had died.

Maybe she would go back to Xalapa, stay in Xalapa for a while where she had been happy. Stay in the presence of volcanoes large and small, instead of going to Denver. Stay until she knew whether she was pregnant or not, until she had the force to return home alone. Maybe in Xalapa, she thought, she could become Arthur Wall's Buddhist nun, wandering lady traveler, and begin to strip herself down of all attachments.

She called her mother to tell her she was thinking of a change in plan. Her mother's voice quavered on the telephone. "I'm so glad you called, I wanted to reach you but didn't know how. I have something I need to tell you—I've told everyone else." Her mother had found out early in June that she had cancer, throat cancer. "All I know is that they wished they had caught it sooner. I'm going to start treatment soon. Your father and I agreed not to tell you or Caroline until we knew exactly what the treatment would be and when it would start."

Holding the receiver in the hotel lobby, Lucy looked at the water in a fountain, flowing so slowly, but flowing still. Her mother's trembling voice broke her heart, sounding as fragile as a young girl's voice trembling with the failure of a first love. Lucy wanted to turn away, frightened and embarrassed at something so intimate that she could hardly offer her pity. She would, of course, go to Denver immediately.

Lucy waited for her flight to Denver in the hot breezy airport outside Veracruz. Families waited with her, with little girls in pink ruffled dresses and hair ribbons, boys in soft sweatsuit outfits, red and black and blue. Shopping bags surrounded each family, an archipelago of package islands stretched across the waiting room. The mothers administered commands and crackers. The fathers, wearing sunglasses, walked up to the window and looked at the runway, walked back, stopped, said two words to the mothers, checked the tickets, checked their watches, walked back to the window.

Lucy sat by herself, with her one bag. At the end of the runway, the Gulf of Mexico led to the ocean, but she would be flying in the opposite direction, back toward the mountains.

A small boy fell in front of her, she reached out instinctively to help him up. His mother smiled at her, the boy began running again.

The small boy falling through the ice, Lucy falling through the ice, Lucy saved, the child lost. Michael lost, her mother lost.

The shadow of her plane from Veracruz to Denver rippled over the mountains, stretched flat again over plateaus and fluttered again over more mountains. Now at last to the east the plane shadowed one continuous flat plain, with the thinnest tracery of streams. Denver, she always forgot, was a city that sprawled on the Great Plains. The great wall of the Rocky Mountains stood behind it.

As the plane prepared to land, Lucy broke into a sweat, afraid of every noise, alert to every movement of the stewardesses. This fear of dying in a plane crash became the fear her mother might be dying. What must her mother's fear be like? Her mother's voice breaking on the telephone, so girlish and pure, how could she comfort that voice?

A rush of golden hay fields, and then the white tented peaks of the airport terminal like a miniature mountain range of melting ice cream cones. In the distance were real mountains with jagged peaks like saw teeth. Lucy breathed slowly, deliberately. All the bustle of her trip, packing, unpacking, the hurried escape from town to town, would give way to holding still. The noise of grinding bus gears, of tinkling marimbas would give way to silence. Small gestures, small talk would count as all turned to vigil.

CHAPTER 14

A s Lucy stepped into the busy terminal, Evan yelled, "Lucy!" and ran to hug her. "Feel how strong I am, I've got lots of muscles." Caroline hugged her, lanky Caroline, leggier than ever in her shorts, her hair even blonder in the summer, making her eyes a bluer blue and with as always a look—not unfriendly—that said she couldn't wait to be alone and get on with whatever project—a quilt, a sofa to reupholster, a deck to build—was at hand. They made their way back to the main terminal, Caroline's older boys materializing along the way from the little strip of snack bars and gift shops, showing each other surreptitiously the candy bar or car magazine they had bought. Tall mountains, tall family. The two older boys, Ben and Dan, were taller than Lucy had imagined possible. Evan let go of Lucy's hand and dogged their heels. Next to his older brothers, he seemed so small, but with his deliberate tread, his body inclined forward with the seriousness of his deliberation, he looked like a little man.

Caroline asked about her trip and listened eagerly to all the details. "I'm so jealous. When Dan and Ben go off to college, Evan and I are going to be on a plane somewhere so fast, it'll make everybody's head swim." She inquired cautiously about Michael. "Was it good to see him?"

"It was wonderful to see him. It was horrible to let him go again. That's all there is to say."

Caroline nodded in sympathy. "At least you have that. I don't even have someone to think about. But I've gotten so used to it, I'm so busy that I hardly miss it."

Lucy said, "That sounds pretty good to me." Finally, she asked, "How's Mom?"

"She's at the doctor's now. The treatment has started."

"Maybe I can help by driving her to the treatment."

"She won't let anyone drive her, even Dad. You know how she is, she wants to get there on her own and to believe that at the end of her two hours she can get herself home."

"You'd do the same."

Caroline laughed. "You would, too. You know, too, she's so ashamed of being ill, of being a nuisance, that driving herself saves her from having to impose on anyone. So we treat it as if she were going to the grocery store."

Everyone in her family was proud like this, with so innocent and futile a pride, Lucy suddenly thought to herself.

Caroline continued. "Dad waits at home in case she calls and says she's too tired to drive home. So that's why he didn't come to the airport."

"How long have you known about the cancer?"

"Just a week. They've known since the beginning of June. You know how they are. They sat on the secret until I'd have to know anyway once she started the treatment. Mom thinks she was doing me a favor. 'We didn't want to get you all worried during those last few weeks of teaching.' I think she wanted to get through her big Fourth of July blowout before she told anyone."

"Someday I'll call home and I'll ask how's everything doing, and Mom will say, 'Oh, fine, the funeral for your father went off nicely.'"

Ben appeared, wheeling Dan in a wheelchair they had picked up along the way. Evan stomped after them yelling, "Let me push! Let me push."

"Let's pretend we don't know them."

"And Dad?"

"I always forget that Dad's the best person to have around at moments like this. He's practical, calm, and ready to do whatever she wants."

"So, tell me what you know. I know I'll find out more from you than I will from her. Or from Dad, too, he's so closemouthed."

"What I know is that it's a throat cancer. Which is unusual, since Mom's not a smoker. She'd been complaining about this dry mouth. Then her dentist saw something in the back of her throat and told her to get it checked. The tumor had been there for a while. I can see it now, this whitish lump with veins running over it. Horrible."

Lucy looked down at her hands gripping the black rail of the moving sidewalk. Her poor mother, who always kept herself so neat and pretty from head to toe, had this horrible thing caught in her throat.

"Mom, of course, wants them to cut it out right now. But that won't help."

"She's got a good doctor?"

"Think so. He's the one specialist in throat cancer in town, and he's in touch with her cardiologist. Apparently, they can't do chemotherapy because of her heart problems. Only radiation. They zap the tumor to shrink it. She's got these tiny tattooed dots for them to line up the beams. The boys think it's pretty neat to have a tattooed grandma. They also call her 'Grandma Nightlight,' because they hope she'll glow in the dark with all the radiation."

Evan ran up to his mother. "Dan and Ben are going to get in trouble playing with those darn wheelchairs, aren't they?"

"They better not."

Evan ran back to his brothers and shouted, "Mom says you guys better not get into trouble!"

Caroline continued. "After the treatment's over, they'll operate. They'll go in, and for a whole day she'll have to sit with her throat open and tubes of isotopes placed next to what's left of the tumor to burn it away."

Lucy shivered—she could not bear even the sight of herself getting a shot, as if the fragility of this thin sack of flesh were too exposed. She remembered something. "Did I ever tell you this? After her heart surgery, she told me that if she died, she was sure Dad would remarry, which was all right with her, as long as the other woman didn't spend her money. Then she turned to me and said, 'If your father died—I'd take a lover, but I wouldn't remarry. Men have too much control over your money.'"

Caroline cut in, "Do you ever wonder why neither of us is married?"

Lucy laughed and continued, "She was trying to get him to make a will with her, and he kept resisting, shying away from the thought of death. What's funny is that when I reminded her of this conversation one time, a couple of years ago, she got all flustered, said she didn't remember saying that, and if she did say anything like that, it was probably that if Dad died, she wouldn't take a lover, because she had too many scars on her body from all these operations."

"You know, I'm not sure that she changed the story—she probably thinks both of those things."

"Oh, yes, our two-brain mom," Lucy said, falling back on the explanation she and her sister had worked out in order to account for how their mother could think two entirely different things about the same event at almost the same moment.

At the doors to the little train that would take them to the big terminal, Caroline looked around. "Dan! Ben! Evan! Come on!"

Evan yelled, "Dan! Ben! Get your butts over here!"

"Evan! Stop that, right now, today. I don't want to hear that from you ever." Caroline turned to Lucy. "I can always tell when he's been playing with the kids down the street."

"If Mom died, where'll she go? That old graveyard where Grandpa Carpenter is?"

"Good question. What about Dad? Do we have to box him up and send him back to Alabama?"

Lucy started laughing. "Let's cremate him. We can keep him in a box on the mantel, and if we ever discover that we have a childhood trauma to exorcise, we can shake the box and yell, 'All your fault.' It'll be cheap therapy."

"But I don't have a mantel," Caroline said, then burst out laughing. "I've got a better idea. Mix his ashes with some catnip and make a catnip ball. Let the cat bat it around. Then I could say to Evan, 'Where's Grandpa? Under the sofa again?' Serve him right for his old joke, 'The only good cat is a flat cat.'" Caroline was laughing so hard, she could hardly talk.

"A student told me her mother cremated all her cats and kept their ashes in her cupboard. When she moved, she had to 'consolidate space,' so she poured all the cat ashes into a big pickle jar."

"We could consolidate Mom and Dad together for eternity in a jar."

They laughed and felt guilty. Their mother could be dying. Yet laughing about death was a comfort, it meant she was still alive.

Off the train and to the baggage claim. The boys grabbed Lucy's suitcase from the moving belt. "Those boys are good for something." In Caroline's car, Lucy sat up front with the suitcase wedged between her and the door, for the trunk was full of quilting material and paint cans. Her knees were under her chin, and her feet rested on a pile of magazines, clothes, newspapers, cassette tapes, and paper coffee cups. "I see nothing's changed. How many years back do you think the bottom layer dates?"

"Maybe I'll meet a gardener someday, attracted to me by my mobile compost heap."

"Car composting, there's a money-maker."

"Dad's on my case, too. I had a flat tire, called him, of course, and he couldn't get to the jack in the trunk."

"His truck still full of trash?"

"Of course. He's got no room to talk—literally."

"Mom told me once she was afraid to go and leave him for any length of time. When she got back, there'd be cars parked on the lawn—"

"Oh, yeah, the shade tree mechanic at work—"

"—clothes everywhere, dishes piled up, newspapers, the grass three feet high if it wasn't all dead."

The prospect of their mother not coming back home struck them both for a moment.

The boys began hitting each other at first in fun, then too hard, and Ben yelled, "Stop it, Dan!" and Caroline yelled, "Okay, you two, cut it out right now." Evan yelled, "Cut it out, Dan and Ben!" in exactly Caroline's voice, so that they all laughed. When she yelled at the boys, Caroline's voice was so like her mother's voice, and Lucy wondered: if she, too, had a child, would she be possessed by that voice?

Her mother's powder-blue car was parked in front. She was home from the clinic.

When her mother had the heart surgery, fifteen years before, Lucy had been in Italy, and when she saw her mother again was shocked to find this big woman had become so thin, girlishly thin, and oddly young looking, with her tinted blond hair, her high cheekbones. Even now, at sixty-eight, as she came out the front door in her slim pants, her turtleneck, smiling, her blue eyes without a cloud, she still seemed so young. She didn't look ill at all.

"Hi, hi, hi. So good to see you." She hugged Lucy, and Lucy could feel the bones of her shoulders through the knit shirt. She was too thin.

Lucy took her bag to the bedroom downstairs—"her room," her mother always called it, although Lucy had never lived in this house to which her parents had moved long after she had left home. When she came back up to the kitchen, her mother was stirring something on the stove, Caroline had set up her quilting, Dan had turned on the living room TV, Ben had opened a bag of chips, Evan was in the back rooms of the house calling for the cat. The old Siamese was sitting at Caroline's feet, curled up in his bed, an aluminum roaster pan with a dish towel in it on the kitchen floor.

Lucy looked down at Pasha. "Are you sure Pasha's still alive? Maybe he's just dried up."

Caroline said, "Hard to tell sometimes. But when he hears Evan's voice, then you see he's alive and he's fast."

On cue Evan yelled from the hall, "Pasha, Pasha come here," and the cat's rheumy eyes opened, head lifted, and in a second, he had trotted off to the living room and hidden himself behind the heavy sofa.

When Evan came into the kitchen, Caroline winked at Lucy and her mother, "He's probably hiding from you—outside. Go on out and find him."

"Your bicycle's out there, too," her mother said. "Grandpa fixed it for you."

"Where's Grandpa?"

"Pulling weeds in his garden, or in the canoe. Go out and see." Evan ran out—Grandpa was a big attraction.

Lucy tried to help her mother fix dinner but bumped into her and stepped on Pasha, out of hiding now and lurking around their feet, giving his strange yowl. She decided to set the table. Caroline knew better than to get in her mother's way and kept sewing. They didn't speak about the illness, for their mother didn't bring it up.

Her father came in. He was even taller than the boys, and Lucy had to go up on her toes to kiss him, he would never bend over. When he sat down, her mother called the boys to the table, and dinner was served. Skinless pale chicken breasts, with paprika freckles, limp green beans, good lettuce from her father's garden, instant mashed potatoes, and ice cream with chocolate syrup and stale cookies. Iced tea to drink. This was home.

Everyone talked, except her father. Because he was hard of hearing and refused to get a hearing aid, he couldn't keep track of the conversation. He often said he didn't feel he missed much. But then he would suddenly interrupt, as he did now, asking Lucy, "How's your word-stringing coming along?"

Her parents were very proud of her books, had them out on the coffee table, and reported on their appearance at the public library. Lucy said, "Think I've got all the words, I can't find the string." She felt guilty for taking the trip to Mexico, imagining her father would believe that she was goofing off on this next book—what a vestigial thought, she told herself—still, she could not help herself saying, "Soon as I get home, it's back to work." She hoped.

Evan had been twisting around in his chair while everyone talked, with Caroline poking him now and again to sit up and eat. He started humming, and then he announced, "Grandpa, my mom and Lucy are going to put you and some catnip under the sofa!"

Caroline and Lucy burst out laughing. Her mother looked puzzled, but her father didn't hear it and helped himself to two more cookies. Ben said, "Evan, you're so stupid—what are you talking about?" and Evan yelled back, "YOU are STUPID, fat boy!" and hit Ben, who hit him back, and that was the end of dinner.

While Caroline cleaned up the kitchen, Lucy and her mother sat on the back porch to watch the sun set over the little lake behind the house and over the dark mountains in the distance. The older boys played basketball, while Evan careened on his bicycle between them.

Around the lake appeared small figures, single or in pairs, some walking briskly, arms pumping, while others stood holding a child by the hand. The cottonwood trees were shedding, their fluffy cotton wool flew on the breeze—the lightest thing in the world, Lucy thought. "It's good to be home," she said.

"So good to have you here," her mother said. "I love this time of night, except it's getting cool. I always say that right after the Fourth of July, you can feel autumn coming. The TV showed that up in the mountains, some aspen are already turning yellow."

Lucy shivered. "That's a long fall into fall."

Caroline and the boys went home. Her mother and father settled down to their evening occupations. In his study, her father sat at his desk reading a book on Istanbul. Books on Islamic history columned up around him. The last time she was home, he had been plunged into Russian history. Her mother watched television and read a memoir by a German war bride about her hard life in the Wyoming desert. Lucy sat down with a book on the sofa. At ten her father came up, stretched, and said as always, "I guess I'm going to shower and take it to bed. See y'all tomorrow morning."

Her mother, a half hour later, closed her book. "I guess I'll say goodnight, too, dear." Lucy followed her into the kitchen and watched her put on the burglar alarm, punching in the code number, the year of her marriage.

Downstairs in her bedroom, right under her parents' room, Lucy unpacked. She listened for her father's shower to stop and took her own. Then she climbed into the old poster bed and read a bit. No more footsteps from upstairs. They must both be in bed.

How tired Lucy was. Tired for such a long time. How exhausting it had been to make herself try to love David, to convince herself that she could live with him. Then the trip to Mexico, that violent and tender hurtling around the country, to end up in Xalapa, with that huge volcano appearing like a vision of enormity and then disappearing into nothingness. Now she was "home"—of course not her own home—but a good temporary home, where there was bustle, flesh to touch, laughter, the nice silence of several people sleeping in the house, and despair.

Lucy looked up at the ceiling. Her parents slept right above her in their king-size bed. They had stayed married and were, despite some hard years, for the most part happily married. Did her mother wonder why one daughter couldn't get married and the other couldn't stay married? There must have been a time when Lucy herself would have thought it worthwhile to analyze why she didn't get married and try to relate it to or blame it on some flaw she had perceived in her parents' marriage, the casual tyranny of her father, usually unexpressed but felt, the way her mother had had to work out her teaching career around her father's career and the raising of children. But to Lucy now, these reasons seemed so minor, the need for analysis must be gone. All that was left, on her part, was a sense that her life was so different from theirs, she couldn't explain it to them or seek their advice.

It struck her that her mother had not asked about her trip. Caroline would have told her that Lucy was traveling with Michael. Her mother knew that Michael was married and so had probably thought the less said about that the better. Maybe after Lucy's breakup with David, too, she had given up trying to track Lucy's love life, it had taken too complicated a course. The reason could also be, Lucy realized, that her mother was waiting for Lucy to bring it up. She was too polite to introduce the subject herself. But Lucy didn't want to explain anymore to her mother or herself. What was there to say? He was married, she loved him, she had to see him, and she had seen him, and now he was gone. All that remained was the too-vivid feel of his flesh, a too-painful sense still of what it was like to have her face ache from laughing, her lips sore from kissing, and the possibility that she was pregnant. This was the last thread connecting them. The last thread holding back her complete surrender to the loss of him. All that, however, she had to put away for a while and think about her mother.

Lucy awoke several times during the night, the last time right after daybreak, the gray light edging through the blinds, and then went back to sleep. She dreamed that her mother lay dead in her coffin, and Lucy stood next to the coffin. Then her mother's head lifted, her head wavering on a lifting long serpentine neck, the face sweet and unknowing, her eyes closed in a dreamy fashion. Her mother kept murmuring, trying to say something, trying hard, pitifully hard to articulate something, but the words seemed stuck in her long throat. The head swayed back and forth. Lucy, in terror and sadness, cried for her mother and for herself.

Two hours later, hearing her father's steps right above her head, probably shaving, she got up and dressed. Upstairs she turned off the burglar alarm and went outside. The sky was dark blue, the mountains a lighter blue as the rising sun illuminated them. The cottonwood and Russian olive turned up the silvery sides of their leaves as a slight wind blew. The air smelled sweet, like sage and wet lawns from the sprinklers that went on automatically very early in the morning. Denver always smelled like this, such a particular smell. Every place had its smell, Xalapa had smelled like coffee, Hunnewell had a sweet lake smell, Somerville on certain windy days smelled of the ocean. In a week, Lucy knew, she would no longer be able to smell Denver, as she became a part of Denver herself.

The next morning, right after breakfast, Caroline and Lucy were walking around the lake. A blue heron, like a thin blade of blue and gray, stood on a dock on one side of the lake and, as the sisters approached, took wing and flew low over the water in swooping beats of his wings to a dock on the other side of the pond. As they walked around to the other side, he seemed not to be watching them, but the bead of his eye turned slightly, and again he flapped his long, long wings and, with his legs trailing, thin, limp as thread, flew back to his perch across the lake. When they had gone all the way around and were back to their parents' yard, they bent over to weed the rock garden they had planted several years ago for their mother. The weaker perennials had died away, but a few were tough and had spread along the lakeshore.

Lucy said to Caroline, "I know you said Mom doesn't want anyone to drive her to the clinic, but I think it's important to see what she has to go through. Otherwise it will all be invisible to us."

"Let's ask her. You would think she, too, would like someone to see what's happening."

"Out of politeness, she would never ask us to go." Lucy was thinking about her dream last night. "Do you think Mom and Dad are simply as formal, as detached in some deep way, as they seem? Sometimes I think of them as statues carved out of a rocky cliff by the wind, tall, naturally formed, deeply silent. But I wonder if, after all, maybe they want to say things, but can't say them? And now that I'm forty, it's not as if I feel it's too late to talk—it's that I feel there's not much to say. I love them, they are kind and funny, I have no quarrel anymore, if I ever really did."

Caroline laughed. "That's because you live far away! Living here means we talk to each other and see each other every day, and so there are these little irritations and collisions. You're right, though, in a way it doesn't matter anymore, they're just themselves."

"Do they feel that way toward us?"

"Let's hope so."

They told their mother that they were curious to see how the treatment worked. Curiosity, not pity, seemed permitted. She was happy to have them come along. That afternoon her mother drove them to the clinic. Chrysanthemums, big balls of dark red, yellow, and white, were stuffed into planters in the parking lot of the clinic, which didn't look like a clinic at all. This Victorian house was built, Denver style, of red sandstone blocks softened with time and weather. The red set off the lacy white gingerbread trim of the porch, which was loaded with more chrysanthemums. Lucy would always from now on think of cancer and chrysanthemums. In the small waiting room, several people sat quietly, nodding when her mother came in. Clearly they knew each other, their appointments always scheduled for the same block of time. Lucy and Caroline were introduced to Matt, Betty, and Irma. Her mother, Lucy noticed, used her nice formal voice, one that could be absolutely sincere but not intimate or chatty. Yet these waiting room companions were her intimates here in the waiting room. When the other three had been called for their treatment, her mother said in a low voice, "Everyone pretends not to look, but every day we check to see who looks good, who looks worse."

Lucy was surprised by the direct statement. It was as if here her mother could speak out loud about being ill, with a kind of casualness she would never display at home.

The nurse came for their mother. Chatting and picking lint off her pale blue smock and pants, she escorted them down a pastel-pink hall. Inside a small room, with a large glass window, was a high bed. Her mother, without prompting, went in and lay down on the bed. Sally and a technician, out in the hall with the machines, spent the next ten minutes lining up several beams of light with the tattoos on her mother's face and neck. Her mother wriggled to Sally's requests: "Move a little to the right, now the left a very little bit, tilt your head." Then Sally, from a closet, got out her mother's mask and mouthpiece. "Hold still, that's good, dear," and Sally inserted the mouthpiece—her mother helpfully baring her gums—and placed the mask, made of some sort of plaster, over her mother's face. The mask was then screwed tightly to the table to hold her mother motionless during the radiation. Finally, Sally draped the lead vest over her mother's chest, so only her bare throat and chin were exposed. Shooing Lucy and Caroline back out into the hall, Sally introduced them to Barry, the technician. Lucy suddenly thought, what if I'm pregnant? Will the radiation hurt the baby? But looking at her mother beyond the glass, arrayed with the trappings of a medieval torture chamber painted light lavender—what crime or sin or secret must be confessed?—how could she worry about anything else?

"Ready?" Barry asked. After her mother murmured something, he pushed the button and her mother was burned most exquisitely and precisely right in front of her. Lucy heard a faint sound of Mozart from inside the radiation room.

"All over." Sally opened the doors, lifted the lead blanket, unscrewed the mask, removed the mouthpiece. Her mother, released, sat up. Caroline and Lucy and her mother went back to the waiting room. Irma was waiting for the receptionist to get off the telephone. She looked up at Lucy's mother. "Three weeks down, four to go?" Lucy realized that Irma wore a wig. Her mother's hair would not fall out, that was the effect of chemotherapy, not of radiation. No wonder she kept looking so un-ill, untouched, compared with the others.

Her mother checked out with the receptionist, and they left.

On the way home, her mother said, "That redbrick clinic always makes me think of my grandparents' house."

"I think it's sandstone." Lucy instantly regretted her own precision.

"Oh, you are so smart," her mother said quite sincerely. "Your Great-Aunt Dora's house, too, was built of that red—sandstone, did you say?"

Lucy wished she hadn't said anything. Her mother's attempt to be precise for her was like a reproach.

Caroline prompted, "That house down on Galapagos?"

Lucy pictured large lizards in the sun, Darwin's finches, huge tortoises, islands of rock and shrubby vegetation. The Galapagos islands in Denver. In a way, her mother's Denver was as small and as far away as those islands from this sprawling city. Her mother's Denver had good schools and cheap streetcars that went everywhere, and an extended family that got together all the time and ate big dinners together.

"That house—"

"Which house, excuse me?"

"Our first house—on the next block from Aunt Dora's—was so big. I was spoiled, the oldest by four years. I had a room to myself, a big poster bed. My grandmother made me a quilt with bunches of violets. When I was eleven, I tried to get everyone to call me Violet."

"That's funny." Lucy had never heard this before and smiled. She could still see in her mother the romantic young girl.

"I hated my name, Bessie. Sounded like a milk cow. And Grandma sewed clothes for me, with elaborate tucks and set-in lace and ruffles. I was like a princess, an only child. My uncles took me out for ice cream sodas, they were so tall—you think it's only your father's side of the family that's tall. This was all during the Depression, but I hardly ever felt any pinch. Your father's family suffered like so many families and was one step from the relief lines. My dad worked for Western Union, my mother's brothers worked for the railroads, so we ate well, big roasts, hams, pies. My dad was generous, though. I remember we took heavy baskets of food to people he knew were, you know, having a hard time."

Lucy thought of two childhood pictures of her parents in the family album. Her father with his scowling black eyebrows perched on rough unpainted wooden steps. Her mother lolled in lace on a velvet chair.

Her mother liked to dwell upon her idyllic memories. Yet Lucy knew that although her mother seemed not to accumulate sorrow on the surface, there had been enough for her. It hid underneath and erupted in moments of anger and strain, then disappeared, seeming to leave no trace. Her mother's mother had died of cancer, and it had been a long-drawn-out death at home, with her grandfather nursing her. They had moved to another house, a smaller house, a house her mother told Lucy she hated. And after her mother died, her grandmother cooled toward her. The princess became a goose girl who worked full time while putting herself through college and, at the same time, mothered her younger sisters, took care of the house. Once she told Lucy that then she only slept three hours a night and stuck pins in her arms to wake herself up when she dozed over her books. Or, Lucy thought, maybe to make herself feel something. A half century later, the goose girl remembered only her life as a princess.

Back at the house, Lucy made tea, but her mother couldn't drink any, her throat hurt her so.

CHAPTER 15

Every weekday, her mother went to the clinic. Lucy had been in Denver three weeks, and there was no need for her to stay any longer. Even though she tried to help with the shopping, cooking, and housecleaning, her mother stubbornly insisted on doing almost everything herself. There was no point in waiting for the end of the treatment. After the radiation treatments were over, it would be two more months before the doctors operated to remove what was left of the tumor. By that time, Lucy had to be back in Boston to teach her seminar. However, the thought of returning to her empty apartment and working on a stalled project made Lucy feel very tired. Perhaps, she told herself, the fatigue was a showing of physical sympathy with her mother, a sharing of her exhaustion. Or, and Lucy hardly dared think it, as the day approached when her period should come—but didn't—she could be pregnant. In that thought lay too much joy, too much fear. She would feel as foolish, as incredulous as old Sarah in the Bible when the angels foretold the birth of her son, Isaac. A pregnancy test would tell her yes or no as efficiently as any angel, but Lucy didn't buy one. She would know soon enough. She had become expert in finding pleasure in suspended moments, which in the end turned out to be strung from the most fragile of supports.

Were cells clustering, those grains of rice as Hana had called them, to make Michael's baby? A baby with Michael's jowls, Michael's hair, Michael's big body, Michael's flesh. What a world of delight she had in conjuring up Michael's child. What if the baby looked like Lucy's family? With her mother's high cheekbones and large mouth, or her father's thick black eyebrows set in the mildest and sweetest of baby faces. Would the baby, like Lucy, have her eyes tilted and so very slightly crossed? Lucy had never given much thought to these things, not in such detail. The joy of these living details had been saved up for her.

She wished she could tell someone. Would she tell Michael immediately—at least call his voice mail and leave the news? She would wait until she knew something to call him, she decided. When she was certain, she would tell Caroline. But her mother? Her mother had enough on her mind. Or could it be that her mother—so enamored of babies and having babies—would find this baby a lively distraction, something alive? What if she lost the child? At forty, the possibility of miscarriage was high. What if she lost her mother?

On a Sunday, her mother said, "Let's go to the mountains. It's been so long since I've been up in the mountains."

Lucy wanted to go, too. In Denver she had stranded herself on the high plains, looking up at the mountains. When she was a girl, her family had driven to Denver several times to visit her mother's family. They would drive often a whole day and night, and the next morning. After looking for hours at flat prairie, the mountain peaks with their snow caps shining would appear at last above the highway signs. How big they were. How excited she had been.

Her mother, her father, Lucy, Caroline, and the kids drove up to the mountains, though not too far up. With her heart trouble, her mother could not breathe at the higher elevations. Her mother suggested El Dorado Springs, an old mountain resort town, folded in a narrow canyon of high red rocks. "When I was a kid, people from Denver, not rich people, just plain people like my folks, used to come up to the Springs in the summer to cool off."

"It won't be like your mother remembers it," Lucy's father muttered to her on his way out to the garage, carrying the cooler with the picnic lunch in it. They drove up in two cars: Caroline and the two older boys in her car; Lucy, Evan, and her parents in her father's truck.

El Dorado Springs, her mother declared in triumph, had not changed. "It's exactly as I remembered, only a little older." The summer cabins that lined the winding red canyon road were still there, but the paint had peeled off, the screens on the sleeping porches were torn and curling up. Aging hippies puttered around the front yards where ancient Volkswagen minivans rusted on blocks.

"Evan, when I was a little girl and came up here," her mother sighed, " I loved to lie in my bed and see stars through chinks in the roof."

Her father glanced at the cabins. "Those chinks are big holes now."

Lucy envied her mother her chance to live in the place where she had grown up, to have all her memories attached so firmly to rocks and cabins and sandstone houses.

They drove beyond the little town of El Dorado Springs, farther up the canyon, where the orange, red, purple vertical wall faces were dusted with the white powder that rock climbers used to mark footholds, footholds from which every year two or three climbers fell to their death. Along the road, parked cars and trucks spilled climbing equipment. Men and women in special pointy shoes and nylon clothes were coiling ropes and gathering metal pins. They drove past a man trying to get his five-year-old, all suited up, to climb a boulder. The child wailed.

The road ended at a picnic ground. They tucked the cans of soda behind rocks in the rushing stream so they would be ice cold by lunchtime. Her father held a transistor radio to his ear to listen to a talk show, and the boys took off to climb the pile of rocks the stream rushed over and to skip stones where the stream fanned out to a rippling pool. Her mother, after all her efforts to launch this outing, was too fatigued to do much of anything. She sat down next to the stream. "I'll be just fine sitting here. I could sit forever listening to a mountain stream." Caroline stayed with her and quilted. Now that she had reached the mountains, Lucy was eager to climb higher and higher, "to see something," she said. She took off for a short hike.

The trail was steep, and soon her chest and legs hurt, but the pain felt good, like a color as brilliant as those of the deep blue sky, the red and pink rock outcropping, the yellow brown-eyed Susan, and purple penstemon. The park trail climbed up and up, turned rocky. She caught at the twig branches of scrub oak or its roots, still she slid and fell several times. There would be big bruises by evening.

Her legs were getting tired, but she pushed herself to keep going, to get up out of this canyon, above its walls that channeled her vision so narrowly, to see everything laid out before her: the Plains below, the rows of steeper mountains behind, even the Continental Divide.

A glance at her watch told her it was lunchtime. She should head down, but now she was getting closer to what at least looked like a ridge top. Sweat dripping from her face and evaporating instantly in this dry air, she began to climb again. She had to finish what she had set out to do, to go up there, sit quietly for a moment, try to see everything, try to think about everything.

Then sharp cramps nearly bent her double. She stopped for several minutes. When she tried to start walking again, she stumbled and hit her knee sharply on a rock. She started crying in pain and fear. The cramping in her lower back and abdomen doubled her again, and biting her lip, she tasted blood. She gasped, it hurt so much, and then she felt the wet warmth between her legs. Lucy reached for the little green scarf she used to tie her hair back and pushed it between her legs. She kept crying from pure physical pain and now from grief. After a long while, the cramping stopped. Something was over. Lucy curled up like an animal, smelling the smell of her own blood, how hot was the blood between her legs. She lay so quietly, insects began to sing in the brush as if she weren't there.

She roused herself and sat up. She had to return to the picnic ground. Heavily she pulled herself to her feet and stiffly started back down again, stumbling, dislodging rocks that rolled down the mountainside.

A little above the picnic ground, where she rejoined the stream, Lucy pulled out her scarf, a soggy red mass, and washed it in the water that rushed through the canyon, that had carved it so deeply. Then she took a long look at the red ridge above her, the stand of black pines to her left, the sandy pink larger boulders to her right. She had to fix this place in her mind, so she could come find it again, if not in actuality, at least in her heart, for here was where those few grains of rice that perhaps had clustered in her had rushed back to join the world. Or at least the possibility of those grains. She stuffed the scarf back in.

Back at the campsite, she surreptitiously pushed paper napkins between her legs. Then everyone came back for lunch, and they ate their sandwiches, fished the sodas from the stream. All this had happened in the short time it took for the sodas to get cold—nothing dramatic. Wasps immediately swarmed over the food, the chipmunks raced down the tree trunks, and bluejays dove into the nearest brush, fixing their beady eyes in expectation. The boys threw potato chips to the bluejays, and they came even closer. Lucy tried to fix her attention on their fantastic blue and black. Then the sadness of missing Michael began to well up, now there was nothing to protect her from the absolute loss of him. It spilled over into the sadness and fear about her mother, about the baby. Death was so like love— nothing in one's powers could be done to reverse it, both meant inevitable loss. Loss that could happen so quickly, quietly.

Lucy looked at her mother. She might die of cancer despite the treatment. But her mother would die anyway, and her father, too, not immediately, but rather soon, though they looked so young. She looked at Caroline and the boys. Caroline might die young, or one of the boys. She herself might die tomorrow. Sooner or later they all would die, as perhaps the little bit of a baby had died today. Lucy looked at the canyon's red cliffs, the cold rushing water, and remembered her vision of the ravening maw feeding upon children. Children die, adults die, everyone dies, drifting down a slow river or hurtled along by a rushing mountain stream, everyone was carried off to die, while someone, like herself, stood listening to the water flowing.

Lucy took a deep breath. She looked hard at a bluejay. The crested head, the loud squawk, the neat catch of the chip. Clever bird.

That night she dreamed that she stood inside a circle, inside were gathered flowers and trees and dogs and lions and monkeys and white rabbits. Inside the circle all were safe and at peace. Lucy knew the circle had something to do with Michael, the circle was Michael. She awoke and wept for herself, for all the animals and the flowers. Michael was not there, would never be.

Lucy decided it was time to go back to Boston.

The day before she left, she ate lunch alone with her mother, her father had gone off to do some repairs at their church, and Caroline and her kids were at their own house. When Lucy came into the kitchen, she saw her mother seated at the kitchen table, staring out in front of her, preoccupied, brooding over something, her hands folded over a magazine. For the first time, her mother seemed old.

Lucy wanted to rush and hug her, but not too hard, for her mother was so brittle, she might crush her.

Instead, she bent down and kissed the cheek as soft and dry as tissue paper. She turned away to put on the kettle for tea.

"Oh, you're back. I was waiting for you. Now, there was something I wanted to tell you before you went back home, what—" Her mother stared at her, puzzled. Moments like this had happened more and more often these last two weeks. Lucy and Caroline joked that their mother was having a brownout, a temporary loss of power. Then her mother's eyes flickered around the room, over the table, and she startled Lucy by talking for a moment like her old self—she pointed to a photograph in the magazine of the latest fashions and declared she didn't think "you girls"—Lucy and Caroline—would look good in that. Then she broke off and stared out into space.

"But that wasn't it. Wasn't what I wanted to talk to you about." Again she looked around. At last, under the sugar bowl she found a slip of her lavender stationery with the blue flowers on it, familiar to Lucy from a thousand notes detailing the family news. She waved it at Lucy. "Yes. I want you to take this piece of paper and write down all the things you want when I, you know, am gone."

"Oh, no . . ."

"No, no, listen to me. Go through the china closet, my jewelry box, too, take a look at all the furniture, and anything you think you'd like, put on the list. Hold on." She took a long drink of water, her face tightened a bit with the pain of swallowing. "There. Now, I can't guarantee that you'll get what you want, but I'll try my best to give you at least something you put on your list."

Lucy sat down at the kitchen table and took the paper. "Maybe it'd be better if you picked out things for us, the things you think we'd each like? That way it's like a gift from you."

"Oh, you know, you're both a mystery to me. I can't guess what you'd like. I'd get it wrong."

"I'll do it."

Her distracted mother was bearable, touching. This requisitioner of lists terrifying. The teakettle whistled. Lucy busied herself by making a cup of tea and a sandwich. She put a dish of rice pudding in front of her mother, whose throat was so sore she could eat only the softest food. Sitting down at the table, but not directly across from her mother, Lucy vowed to herself she would never make the list. Her mother would have to choose for her. What would she have wanted anyway? The most precious items were her mother's possessions, and their powers couldn't be transferred. Lucy didn't want to accumulate more things, she wanted to clear out her life, throw off the weight of things in her life.

Her mother sipped her water. Lucy had noticed that now when her mother drank from a cup or a glass, some small muscular failure made her lower lip quiver as if she were about to break out in tears. This quiver moved Lucy with an almost unbearable anguish, her own lip trembled, her eyes filled.

Her mother stared out the window a moment and then turned to Lucy. "I've been thinking about you. I was thinking that—if you didn't want to get married, that's your business, and I can see why someone might not. But look, you've taken care of yourself, you have a good job. Why didn't I tell you to have a baby? Your father would have disowned us both, but I've thought a lot about it, and my life would have been nothing without you girls. I could have come to live with you and taken care of it. I could have gotten back the crib from Caroline—she's still got it, I think."

The old woman reached her thin, thin arm across the table and grabbed Lucy's hand tight. "I should have told you that. So you wouldn't have to be sorry when it's too late. Maybe you still have time. I've read about these new medical miracles. Go ahead, don't worry about us. Now you just think about that, all right? Let me know and I'll come running." Then she sat back, took a sip of water, the lower lip quivering.

Lucy thought of the rice clusters swept away by the stream, or even if she weren't pregnant, another chance to be had been lost. Lucy nodded her head twice, not knowing what else to do. Then pulling her hand away, she picked up the slip of lavender paper, which in her room she tore up.

CHAPTER 16

Upon her return to Somerville, every morning when Lucy woke up, she was possessed by a most unfamiliar, faint, yet certain sense that her life would not get better, ever again. This came to her as a sensation rather than a thought, a sensation like a slightly bitter taste or acrid smell. For Lucy, even the worst years of her life had been governed by the conviction that life would get better. High spirits, a willful enthusiasm could conquer all. But too many losses had piled up this year. Now she could not recognize herself as the person she once had been.

The month of August, she decided not even to try to work. She would wait until school started and moved her along with its necessary tasks.

On the second of August, as she was walking home from a bookstore, she saw Arthur Wall sitting in a coffee shop next to the window. Her first instinct was to not go in. She had no conversation in her, only sadness, and he was in an even sadder state, what was there to say. Yet he looked so exhausted and pinched, she changed her mind. The few times they had spoken, he had been funny and kind to her. Let her be kind to him, let her help him if he needed help.

She tapped on the glass. He looked up and smiled a little. She went in, got a cup of coffee, and sat down.

"I hope I'm not disturbing you."

"No, please. Bonnie, Meryl's nurse, insists that I go out for an hour or two every day. Otherwise, I would never leave the house. I feel I have to stay close to Meryl. But it is nice to see you."

Lucy didn't know whether to inquire how Meryl was, for she had understood the disease was irrevocably progressive. Instead she said, "I'm sure it helps her to know you are close by."

"I don't know that," Arthur said sharply. By way of apology, he changed the subject and asked about David.

"We're not seeing each other anymore."

"I'm sorry."

"It's all right. I have other things to worry about." She told him about her mother's illness. "I find even though I'm not in Denver anymore, I have to keep myself in some suspended state until I find out whether the treatment is going to work or not. I can't think about anything else right now. I've been hiding out from my friends, because I don't have anything to say."

"But you stopped to see me."

"Because you know what that's like."

He saw a bookstore bag lying on her lap. "What book did you buy?"

Lucy pulled out a slim book, slightly embarrassed. "I find myself reading books about renouncing the world. That's the state I'm in. This one's by a medieval Japanese author. He's writing about the hut he lives in, after he runs away from the civil wars and plagues that are destroying the capital."

Arthur nodded—he knew the famous essay, of course. "You once told me that you might buy a pretty little house if you had some money. You're giving that up for a rough hut?"

"The hut is the barest of houses and right at the moment seems the most attractive to me." She stopped, then laughed. "In fact, I think I've always been attracted by huts. Sounds funny to say, *I've always been attracted by—HUTS!*—by shacks, ice-fishing huts in photos, see-through houses—"

"See-through houses?"

"I saw a house in Italy once, on a lake. Well, it wasn't quite a hut, in fact it was a lovely villa—"

Arthur smiled. "A villa hut?"

"I mean that the house had this emptiness, lightness. With the glass door and glass window on the other side, I could see through it to the lake. So hutness, to me, I guess is a combination of emptiness and plainness. Funny, now that I start to think of it, I see how long this small house theme has been with me. When I was a child, we used to go to Denver and the mountains on vacations, and I'd draw over and over again pictures of small mountain cabins, with streams by their sides and in the background huge black and purple mountains, snowcapped." She stopped. "I can tell I haven't been talking much recently. Lots of words backed up. Forgive me."

He said, "Please, I love it. All there is at home is silence."

They both were silent. Then Lucy made an effort and, pointing to his notebook, asked, "How's your lady?"

"My lady's left the court. She's dressed in nun's traveling clothes, dark gray, and she's walking from temple to temple. For the first time we see people outside the court, a group of travelers sitting under a cherry tree, eating, resting. No more long descriptions of layered gowns, of poetry contests, of the tangle of ambition. She seems free, rather happy. And your Lucy?"

"Ah, she's still at home waiting for me to send her on her travels."

Arthur looked at his watch. "Excuse me, but I told Bonnie I'd be back at five. I'll let you read about the hut in peace and quiet."

Lucy was reluctant to let him go or perhaps to be alone again.

"Are you walking home? I'll walk with you, if you don't mind—I'm on your way."

"I know. It'd be a pleasure to have some company."

They passed from Cambridge, with its tall houses complete with Victorian furbelows and slate walks and red-brick sidewalks, to Somerville, where the sidewalks turned concrete and cracked and weedy, and the houses were of clapboard or siding, plainer than plain. Cambridge boutiques with suits of chic chenille gave way to bridal shops of glittering wedding dresses and flouncy pink bridesmaid dresses. Saints sprang up here and there in Somerville yards, their hair and faces and robes thick with chalky paint. A Virgin and Child still huddled underneath their burlap swaddling, even though winter was over, Easter died and risen from the dead, and summer full blown.

"The Virgin Mary—under wraps." Lucy laughed. "How would I explain to Mrs. Yu what *under wraps* means?"

Arthur said, "Ever since you talked about how Somerville is the city of saints, I've noticed them everywhere. It's like some sacred but ordinary world filled with local deities, upon which one could call. If you knew their name. If this were your home."

When they reached his house, Arthur in turn seemed reluctant to let Lucy go. He pulled out a recording of Rossini's opera *La Donna del Lago,* from the bag he was carrying. "Would you like to hear it? We can at least listen to the first act."

Lucy said yes.

Inside, in the hall, Lucy looked at the mail piled up on the table by the door and a dusty wheelchair leaning against the wall. The few pieces of furniture in the room on the right—a bed, a chair, a small table with books piled on it—stood placed at the odd angles where the movers had left them. The walls were bare. This must be Arthur's bedroom. The room on the other side with the closed door must be Meryl's room. He took Lucy upstairs to where he had set up his study. Here the books piled up on the floor, the papers stacked on the desk gave some sign of life. He told her to sit down in the old overstuffed chair, and he would be right back after checking in with Bonnie. He came quickly back to Lucy—Meryl was still asleep—opened the opera and put it on. He then removed some books from a chair and sat down across from her.

After the overture, hunting horns sounded, and Arthur said, "Here's the lady of the lake singing her sunrise song to the dip of her oars."

They were silent again for the rest of the act. Then Arthur turned off the music. "We'll have to hear the rest another time. I've got to get dinner ready." He paused a moment. "It's so odd to listen to music with someone. I feel a bit like the tenor, a lady comes out of the mist with a boat and rows him away to safety." He paused. "I mean, maybe it's not so safe to spend so much time alone."

Lucy nodded, she had felt for the first time in a long time at peace sitting there with him, saying nothing. She stood up to go.

Then he said, "Would you like to stay to dinner? I don't really cook, and I don't like Bonnie to feel she's obligated to do that, too, so I order out."

Lucy immediately suggested, "Why don't you let me cook? I'll go to the store and get a few things and come back and put something together."

"You don't have to do that."

"Please, like you said, it's not safe to spend so much time alone." He agreed.

Lucy cooked for them that night, and for almost every night over the next three weeks. She could do nothing for her mother, but she could help Arthur. She cooked, she shopped, she even helped with Meryl when Bonnie and Arthur needed her. The sight of Meryl, so silent and sheeted in that white room, moved her. The few times Bonnie and Arthur needed her help, she tended Meryl as if she were her sister, her mother. Most of the time, she spent alone with Arthur. While he worked, she would sit in the big chair and read, or sometimes they would listen to music. She even transplanted a few things from her garden to his garden. She told him, "So many things died in my garden while I was away, I don't have the heart to bring it back. Over here I feel like the survivors may have a chance." She pointed out to him the different flowers and told him what they would look like when they bloomed next year. "These are carnations—next summer you'll see the petals do have the feeling of flesh their name promises. This is thrift—there will be little pink balls high up on stems above the grassy mound. The sage will have purple spikes. In the back is a black blue columbine, the flowers have a curled-up spur. It's the Colorado state flower—I knew that before I was ten. This is cupid's dart, it's a light blue with rosy markings at the center. These are all perennials, but these"—she pointed to some pink and white petals floating in a head on long stalks—"are cleomes, just some annuals I bought yesterday, but I can't resist how they leap out from a garden, and they bloom this late in the summer."

The days passed so slowly, it seemed like a dream as Lucy and Arthur waited together for something to happen. Sometimes Lucy was embarrassed about the time she spent at Arthur's, the planting, all her talking. She was happy to not be always alone at home, she was happy to be with someone she didn't have to talk to unless she wanted to, but she might be imposing on him. Once she asked him if he minded. He said simply how much he, too, liked having her there.

They would often sit on the porch in the evening. Arthur didn't talk very much, he made Lucy talk. As he listened to her talk about her nephews in Denver, Arthur asked her if she wanted a child. Lucy flushed. Arthur persisted. "If you had a little boy or girl, what would you name the child?"

Lucy deflected the question. "What about you?"

"Meryl didn't have any children with her first husband, and she didn't seem eager to have one when we got together." Arthur thought for a moment. "I have two Chinese names, *Lo-tzu,* or Summer Dress, and *A-kuei,* Tortoise."

Lucy cried softly. "Let's not, if I start thinking about names—"

"They are from a Chinese poem, about an old man who suddenly finds himself with two young children. He says,

> *'All the world is bound by love's ties;*
> *Why did I think that I alone should escape?'"*

"Summer Dress." Lucy repeated the name to herself. "Summer Dress, the most perfect name. A name light and bright and clean and eternally so, even though at the same time it makes me think of the melancholy of fleeting summers, how fast summers go."

When Lucy stood up to go that evening, Arthur kept her awhile on the porch steps. "It helps having you here. Makes things seem less desperate."

As she walked home, Lucy had a feeling that Arthur had come almost too close to her this evening. Their conversation had been more like the conversation of potential lovers than friends. Then she told herself that his need, as well as her own, to get through these hard moments had nothing to do with love or sex, it was much more grave than that.

In the last week of August, Meryl's condition grew much worse. Arthur had no time to work or to talk. Lucy shopped and brought over food she had cooked but saw him only for moments at a time. That same week, her mother's doctors decided to move up the operation on her mother's throat, the radiation had been so successful. After the operation, Caroline called to say that the surgeon thought that they had gotten all of the cancer out. Her mother would have to go in for monthly checkups but everything looked good. Lucy cried, for the pain her mother had to endure and for the relief the news brought. She didn't immediately tell Arthur. She felt guilty that her vigil was over and his growing more desperate.

CHAPTER 17

Until Lucy had come upon him in the coffee shop, Arthur had not known the extent to which, spending so much time with Meryl, he, too, had become paralyzed. He hardly moved except when he worked on his translation and when he attended to Meryl. Paralyzed and mute. After the long days of silence at home, he seemed to have forgotten how to say things to anyone. When he had looked up and seen Lucy through the window of the coffee shop, he realized how much she had made him feel alive before. As they talked, at first she seemed so tired and sad, but he could make her come alive again, even return her for moments to her old volubility. Then as they stood on the sidewalk in front of his house, Arthur had a terrible impulse to touch her hair, her face, put his arm around her shoulders.

So he had invited Lucy into his house to listen to the opera, and all during the first act, he could not keep himself from imagining what it would be like to reach over to take her hand, then pull her close, hold her head between his hands, smooth her hair against her temples. Her eyes would open wide, a bit frightened, yet she would hold still, lean in slightly, and he would kiss her face, lightly,

lightly her eyes, her forehead, her cheeks, her mouth, so lightly it nearly broke his heart. Then he pulled her very close, tilted her head, and kissed her deeply. He touched her with a hunger, and he began to kiss her and hold her breasts, then they were on the bed, and he kissed her hungrily all over, and then came into her with all his need.

The power of his imagination was so strong that he had had to stop the music and send her home. Yet he couldn't, he was greedy for her presence. So she had made him and Bonnie dinner, and he let her get into the habit of coming by in the evenings. So now every day was the same as before, except he had Lucy. Meryl woke up at three or four in the morning. Arthur woke up to sit with her. The early hours seemed the most wakeful and painful for her. When Meryl dropped off at seven, he went down to eat breakfast, to shower and shave. Bonnie came and fed Meryl through the feeding tube. He worked for a while. Sometimes he was so tired, he put his head down at his desk for a half hour, the ink on his notes transferred to his forehead—later he would see the words printed there in the mirror. He went for his walk. Then Lucy came over, and he had a respite before Bonnie left and he put Meryl to bed, read to her or played cards.

Although he worried that Meryl might be upset that someone else was in the house, he could not give Lucy up. He could not stop thinking about Lucy, he bought good things to eat—for a long time he hadn't cared at all what he ate—and music that might please her, planned questions to engage her in easy conversation. Sometimes he even found himself wishing he had a sofa, so they could at least sit on it together as they both read and listened to music. She would sit with her legs curled up, a barrier between them, but her legs would be almost touching him. He encouraged her to plant her plants in his garden, even insisted upon it when she asked if she was imposing on him, with an insistence that felt furtive, like lust.

He had seen that she was very preoccupied by her mother's illness. He had talked to her about that—out of sympathy at first, but then to bind her to him, with shared sorrow. He even began to imagine having a child with her, as he talked about children with her. Meryl had never pressed him for a child. He was too busy with work, with the constant moving around. He let himself imagine having a child with Lucy—maybe she imagined it, too? Some evenings he wanted so desperately to ask her to stay, to put Meryl to bed and then come to her in his bed. He would hold her so close, go into her, drive their deadness away, who knows, make a child?

If he made love to Lucy, would Meryl be able to tell? How could he tell if Meryl could tell he had made love to Lucy?

At the end of August, Meryl began to sink swiftly. At night she would slip too far into sleep, a light coma, the doctors said, from which she could hardly be roused. Even her terrible muscle cramps could not bring her out of this sleep. It had to do with the increased difficulty she had in breathing. The next step was a face mask ventilator, which was acquired and installed in her room. After this ventilator failed to do the breathing, they would have to insert a breathing tube into her throat. This last step was for a patient with the will to live. Meryl seemed to have less and less. The doctor recommended a hospice worker to come over every day to help Arthur and Bonnie in this last stage.

Arthur saw less of Lucy, though she stopped by almost every day to drop off groceries or some prepared dish. That, however, only increased the force of his thoughts about her.

One morning, as the early sun beat in the window, the hospice nurse sat with Meryl and Arthur. She told them quietly about the orchids she raised in a greenhouse behind her house, a greenhouse she had fashioned from old window glass scavenged from dumps and curbsides on garbage collection days. The hospice worker said that in Mexico they enclosed orchids in cages, like birds.

Bonnie had most ingeniously wedged in the corner of the window an open red umbrella to protect Meryl against the sun yet still let it shine in the room. The color, cast on her gray face, turned it a horrible caricature of a healthy pink. Nothing could disguise or relieve the tedious horror of the long days in which an even more complete stillness, if that were possible, had overtaken Meryl. She could not move a finger, could not make a noise, until it seemed as if she were already dead, only the machine of the ventilator was alive. Yet she could still defecate, she could still blink, she could still stare at him, in a communication perhaps so full, it seemed flat, beyond meaning.

He willfully thought of Lucy. Lucy was life, Arthur said to himself. What did that mean? Simply that if he thought of her, he felt alive. The times he had spoken or watched her came back to him so vividly, in such detail. Lucy in the garden, her head pulled down like a turtle, then the direct look at him, that laugh, so open, so exposed, the smell of sage as she stripped it with her hands and crushed a leaf to smell it. Lucy skating clumsily, but skating with joy. Lucy in his yard, planting the flowers from her house. Then he would see himself lowering himself onto her, see her pulling him close.

Earlier in the month, Lucy had brought over one evening a rose cane. Her neighbor had pruned the rosebush that climbed his fence too promiscuously, sending reckless bright green canes on expeditions into the air. Arthur stuck the thick cane, completely covered with dark pink summer roses, into a metal wastebasket he found in the house and weighted it with heavy stone to keep it from toppling over. The next morning he had put the cane in Meryl's room, it fell in a big arch over the table of medicines by the window. Now as he sat with Meryl that day, he began to concentrate on the roses, Lucy's roses on their cane, like the curve of her arm, a pure curve. Meryl lay there knotted up, and Arthur made himself think of Lucy, that arching rose cane.

His one worry became that Bonnie or the hospice nurses would throw out the rose cane while he was out of the house for a moment. He told them again and again to keep changing its water. The roses kept on blooming.

The first of September, as Arthur sat with Meryl, her breathing grew ragged. Was she, at last, ready to die? The breathing became more even, though thick and dark. That went on for hours. He woke up in the middle of the night, with a book on his lap, the light on. He heard Meryl breathe so very slowly. A breath, a huge pause, another breath. The hospice nurse had told him that at the end the dying breathed like this. He looked under the sheet and saw, as the nurse had said, too, her legs turning purple, as the blood pooled there. The breathing was gasping, juicy, he squirted morphine into her mouth with the syringe to ease that gasping, as the hospice worker taught him. He should call one of the nurses, but he couldn't break his concentration by leaving her alone for a moment. Finally he was so afraid of not being able to help her in this extreme moment that he called Bonnie. And as he broke down, Meryl gave way. By the time Bonnie arrived, Meryl had stopped breathing. It was dawn, and the room smelled of roses and excrement.

He looked at the flowers. Now they meant only Meryl to him. He was suddenly disgusted at his thoughts of Lucy.

A week later, he had Meryl cremated. He flew to California to scatter her ashes in a ceremony held with her few friends. In California, where fall would not show itself, winter hardly at all, he felt a return to his old self, as he had been with Meryl, lighter, transient. In California while visiting his old department, he had impulsively asked for his job back. When the dean notified him that he had it, he called the Institute to get out of his contract there.

On the plane back to Boston, Arthur wrote in his journal:

September 10. This week I will finish the translation. My lady is on the road somewhere between temples. As she gets older, she begins to brood about the pain she might be giving her father as he wanders in the afterworld, about the fate of her children being raised by other women, the deaths of her former lovers. In the final scene, after hearing that the ex-Emperor has died, she runs barefoot behind his cortege as his body is carried to the cremation ground. When I picture this scene, I see myself chasing after Meryl. I betrayed her, so easy it was to betray the dragonfly in heavy glasses. Now she's not alive, and I find I can't betray her. It is as if I am not exactly alive either. Why should I be alive when she is not alive? And not being alive—why should I act as if I am, how can I stand that? The sudden and sharp fragments of memory I have of her— these are the bits and pieces that I must review, catalog, and catechize myself with. Is this at last a kind of love—loving a shadow, when you are a shadow yourself?

In his bag he carried Meryl's glasses, her ceramic dog, the pink glass clock.

All that was left was to rid himself of the house in Somerville.

That afternoon, Arthur climbed out of a taxi, stood in his little driveway, and watched Lucy weeding the backyard of his house. She had kept up her work on the garden. He had never done anything in the yard. Over on the side of the house, he saw the arching green cane that someone, the nurses or Lucy, had planted there. Next year it would bloom with those pink flat faces.

Lucy tossed the weeds onto the driveway, each weed weighted with its own clod of dirt clinging to the clod, exploding on the cement. Lucy made more work for herself, Arthur thought, as he waited for her to see him. For the first time, he noticed that the house had once been painted a creamy white. As the sun set, the house glowed with a coat of rosy opalescence. Without blinds or curtains at the windows, and at this angle he couldn't see the furniture inside, the house seemed empty, but in a living way, with an odd reflected light filling it like the watery light reflected up onto the arch of a bridge. That was simply because Lucy took care of the house, he knew. It seemed disloyal, to have the house look like it was alive.

Lucy saw him. "You're back." She peeled off her garden gloves and pushed up the old straw hat she had on her head. She came closer, and he saw that face coming too close to him. He hardened his face. His manner became formal. Meryl would be his guide in this, her face in death after he had closed her mouth, stern, commanding.

Sensing his sudden coolness, Lucy seemed to hesitate.

Arthur saw Lucy's head arched back on the pillow, felt his hands pressing down on her shoulders, pulling himself up on her, hungrily.

Then he saw Meryl's head flung back in her dreadful, final paroxysm.

They sat down on the porch. Lucy offered him her sympathy, and when he asked about her mother, she finally reported that her mother's operation had been a success.

"So what now?"

"Well, school will start, so that will give me something to do. I also feel as if I've somehow gotten a good rest, that I can start doing things again. I'll try to work on my book, and I think I will really look into moving."

Arthur looked at the flowers she had planted. "The mountain hut?"

"I think I'll pass on the mountains. I'm back to dreaming about my grandmother's house, small, with a garden, a woman living alone, animals, gladioli, and tomatoes in the garden."

"Maybe out in Hunnewell?"

"No, I looked at a house near the Institute, but out there reigns the tyranny of lawns. I've come to be sick of lawns, when I'm out at work and pass by a thick lawn, I feel ill. It's like a wall-to-wall carpet, and bare floors are nicer, with funny pieces of furniture. The little town is dreary with wealthy young couples and wealthy retirees, who seem to loiter in the coffee shops like the homeless on their grates. So I think if I ever move, I'll stay in Somerville. I like the people in the neighborhood, I like the small yards. I find myself looking at houses with 'for sale' signs, and I've started studying the photos of houses in realtors' windows. The photos, usually Polaroids, are overlit, bleached like an Icelandic house in winter reflecting Icelandic snow. I study the captions. Captions are a cheap architectural education, you learn the names for all the different styles of houses around here."

"What would they call this house?"

She turned her head and looked up at Arthur's house. "The caption for your house would probably read, 'Turn-of-the-century mansard roof cottage'—you know, that big-hipped roof like a too-big cap pulled down over the ears of the first floor—'with original period details, needs some work and love.'"

Arthur, leaning back, watched Lucy as she talked. He said abruptly, "Why don't you live here?" He realized she might think he was asking her to live with him, so he added, "I've accepted an offer to go back to my old job in California. The Institute was kind enough to let me go without any notice."

Lucy didn't say anything for a moment. Then she said with her usual warmth, "Congratulations. I'm sorry you're leaving. I hope you know how much I'll miss you." She laughed a little. "Oh, no. Now I'll have to go back to eating by myself all the time."

Once, as he held out his hand to receive a famous translation prize, he spotted Meryl talking and talking at her table in the crowded banquet room oblivious to what was taking place on the podium. This did not make him angry. In fact, it kept him from taking the award and all subsequent awards seriously. In the future, he would give his talks, be taken out to dinner, and be praised, and she would not be there in the room talking on and on. Arthur felt exposed. She had served as some sort of protective skin between himself and others. He would get back her protection by a constant practice of invoking her, daily, hourly, by the minute. He heard Lucy speaking and made himself listen.

Lucy offered, "If you only need someone to watch the house until it's sold, I can do that. I talk about a house all the time, but I don't need a whole house."

Arthur insisted that she take the house. He grew almost angry at her hesitation. Finally, she gave in. After she left, he went into the house, ashamed and glad that it was over. He would move as soon as he could get his few things packed.

By the end of the week, Arthur had signed over to Lucy the title of the house.

Two days before he left, Lucy and Arthur sat on the porch once more, after an afternoon of packing up his books to send back to California. Now that he knew he was leaving, now that he was secure in his relation to the memory of Meryl, he found it possible to be easy in her presence.

"Maybe I'll get a cat," Lucy announced.

Arthur said, "'Everything human is Saigyō's cat,' the Japanese poet Saigyō himself said."

"What does that mean?"

"Make up an answer that suits you."

Lucy laughed. "All right, I would like it to mean that despite all our human complicated thoughts and cares, we are as single-mindedly alive, and as marvelous as a cat. What does the saying really mean?"

"When Saigyō called on the shōgun, the shōgun was so impressed by the poet-monk that he gave him a pure silver image of a cat. On the way out of town, Saigyō gave the silver cat to a child he passed in the street. Everything human can be given away, without attachment."

"I prefer my version, in which Saigyō's cat is a real cat."

"I think your version and the legend's version are not so different."

Lucy made a face. "I can't think that hard. I picture my cat—my version of Saigyō's cat—shading in and out of the shrubs."

"And a child, in a summer dress?"

"Let's see, yes, crouching on her heels, arms hugging her knees, in a yellow sundress"—Lucy smiled—"and looking at the cat. I would teach her how to scratch the cat at the very base of its spine so that it stretches and twists to offer all its glorious surface. You'll have to tell me where I can get a copy of the poem about Summer Dress and Miss Tortoise."

Arthur thought about the poem. All the time he lived with Meryl, he believed he had avoided the bond of love. How curious, now that she was dead, he found himself bound more and more to dwell on, ponder her presence. Before she was ill, she had seemed such a curious being, with that otherness of an insect. The paralysis had made her seem a woman at last, requiring a human passion. For the first time in his life, he was bound by the bonds of love and affection and by sorrow and care.

The day he left, he stood outside the house and looked at the rose cane. The little roots—Meryl must have seen them first. She did notice details. Maybe when Arthur had finally seen them and said, "Oh, there are roots," she had laughed to herself, she had already known. As she lay there, her eyes on the rose branch, did she start to think of herself as this green cane of roses, with these new roots? Did she live as the rose branch for whole moments, the long graceful arcing cane of the rose branch, the little root-feelers, the thorns, the tight buds?

CHAPTER 18

Toward the end of September, Lucy stood in her yard, Arthur's yard now her yard, looking at the rose branch, that bright green against the black wall of rock. Then her vision shifted and she saw that black wall clearly for the first time, the black eruption into her world from below.

She was forty-one. A year of so much heartache and weariness had stripped her to the bone. That abrupt wall of black rock, rising, dark and powerful, with its jagged face, with the infinite glittering layers of rock pressed together, that black rock was her bone showing. To her surprise, she discovered bone a comfort.

Lucy had spent September working on the house to make it enough hers by the time school started. She had painted inside and put a big table in the kitchen, which extended along the entire back of the house. She hadn't put up any curtains, and once winter scattered the leaves of the trees around her house, anyone would be able to spy upon her, but she had nothing to hide. Her garden was already under way when Arthur was here, and now the pink and purple heads of the cleomes she planted sprang fiercely at whoever passed along the sidewalk. From outside, the house still looked a bit forlorn. It needed paint, and the roof looked ragged with missing shingles. But that bone laid bare in the backyard, there was something solid there, elemental, a foundation.

This last year, only one thing had stayed constant—the thought of a child. Her folder on abandoned children, the worldwide massacre of innocents, was fat now with articles torn from the paper, from magazines. She wouldn't cry over those articles anymore. She would act. She called several adoption agencies and had them send information to her. School started, but Lucy refused to let herself become simply carried away by work with all its endless distractions.

The next weeks went by quickly as Lucy pored over brochures and notebooks full of photos and little histories of so many children. She didn't tell any of her friends or anyone in her family what she was doing. She kept hesitating, yet at the same time she felt urgently that she had to act. When she received a notice of an adoption party run by the state department of social services, she decided to throw herself into the flesh and blood reality of this world. On a warm, bright, blue-sky day, a Saturday morning, with not much traffic on the highway, with coffee and a doughnut, with the radio on, she drove down the highway. The trip seemed like so many of the long car trips she had taken in her life, but erupting into this familiar pleasure was the certain knowledge of the enormous step that she had taken into what would be the rest of her life. She held the wheel too hard and couldn't hear the radio because she could only think about her destination. She kept picking up and reading over the steering wheel the slip of yellow paper with its faint Xeroxed instructions. Anxious to get the exit right, she would check the number and then check it again. Still she missed the exit, and when she found the right one, she missed the next turn. Almost weeping with frustration, she finally stopped to ask for directions to the Monsignor Cavallo Center. At last she saw a sign and minutes later turned into a vast parking lot. Did the Catholic center hope the pope would come preach here someday? Lucy parked in the huddle of cars, old small cars, old trucks, older model vans near the enormous flat-topped center, like a whitewashed warehouse topped with a cross. Next to the hall was a grove lined with white plaster statues of very healthy-looking Christs manning their stations of the cross.

Under an overhanging roof, kids sat at picnic tables finger painting, weaving pot holders, led by energetic young women dressed in shorts and T-shirts, their blond hair in ponytails, voices sweet and cheerful. Three boys in wheelchairs, strapped to sit up, heads banded to not wobble, were parked near the picnic tables, their eyes rolling as if to get at the paint, or perhaps simply rolling.

The huge room inside was split in two. On one side swarmed adults and children and tables and tables of food. On the other side were empty tables. A priest with his white collar appeared from time to time to check out the setup of the lectern for some other event that would happen later in the day, Lucy guessed. Why didn't the room tip, she wondered, with this nervous crowd weighed against that dusty solitary priest?

At the long table inside the door sat the older versions of those young girls outside, wearing shapeless pantsuits, glasses, hair dyed black or champagne, bright kooky necklaces and red lipstick and smiles well disciplined, below eyes heavily made up and weary. Lucy got her name checked off by Elaine, her name tag read, who smiled, asked Lucy where she was in *the adoption process,* had she started her home study yet? Lucy confessed, "No, sorry, I haven't started yet, I'm—"

"Just looking," the social worker said, and regarded her with the look of an experienced saleswoman in a department store. Her eyes shifted to the couple behind her, yet she said kindly to Lucy, "Well, it's a good thing to come to these events. You can see the kids, get a feel for the system, learn to talk to social workers—that's a big part of it, let me tell you. That's a skill to master."

She asked the couple their names, checked them off her list, and said, "Where are you in *the adoption process?*"

Lucy took her bag of chicken wings over to the groaning tables of food. Everyone had been asked to bring something to this potluck lunch. Lucy thought chicken drumsticks would be light and easy for the kids. She had made them herself, but they suddenly seemed so plain compared with the Jell-O salads with faces picked out in raisins and carrots, cupcakes with elaborate piped-blue frosting, yards of sheet cakes shaped like rabbits and dogs. As she wandered through the hall, she noticed that the two most concerned parties at the party—the children to be adopted, identified by a yellow badge, and the couples who might adopt them—moved in different orbits. At the round tables crowded with folding chairs, couples sat hunched over the big binders of children's photos with write-ups. *Slap, slap, slap* went the heavy plastic pages. Sometimes the wife would stop and say something to the husband, who would pause then pick up the pages and start turning them again. Hovering around the tables, but not sitting down, were other couples, waiting to get their turn at the albums. Meanwhile the children pictured in the binders raced around and between the tables.

Elaine was floating around and came up to Lucy. "Why don't you go talk to that couple there? They adopted through social services and came here to talk about it to people like you. So grab yourself a plate of goodies and go on over, talk to them. That's probably the best thing you could do, to get a picture of what it is really like." She smiled and turned away as someone called, "Elaine, Elaine."

Lucy looked over at the table. A short round ball of a woman sat there in a flowered T-shirt and dark pants. She wore big glasses and had permanented her faded brown hair. Her husband, thin and short, with grizzled ginger hair, tapped an unlit cigarette on the table, at which he sat askew, ready to take off for his smoke outside. This couple sat apart from the crowd. The man looked nervous and bored. The woman sat expectantly, nervous, too, her hands pressed together into a double fist on top of a white photo album.

Soon Lucy was looking through the album with Pat and Richard, as much for Pat's sake, she felt, as for her own. She saw the photos of Cindy, a child they had wanted desperately, and though Cindy was not free for adoption, they had taken the chance. In the end, her mother took Cindy back. "Even tho' the mother was a drunk," Pat said, and looked at the photograph of a little girl in shorts and T-shirt. On her head was a plastic headband mounted with a large plastic star. "It was on July Fourth, at a picnic." She looked up at Lucy. "Be real careful, the social workers will tell you to take a chance, that it will probably work out. But then they get kind of cold, and you know something's happening. Then they call up and say, they have to come take your kid away."

Richard stopped tapping his cigarette, "The mother was a drunk."

Pat took a breath. "Well, it took a while to get back into *the adoption process* again. We wanted Cindy, and losing her, well it was like she died, except we knew she was out there with that bad mother. But I kept going. We ended up again with boys not yet free for adoption—Richard was against it, he said we couldn't go through it again. But you can. Once I met the boys, I couldn't back out—you have to watch yourself, you get attached, and you get yourself into things that you should have seen coming. Like I told you, you have to be real careful with the social workers that they don't force the wrong child on you. Sometimes you get the feeling they're working against you, not with you. They keep back the ones you're interested in and keep showing you the ones you aren't."

Richard cut in. "It's like going to a used car lot. They're trying to sell the lemons."

Children as "lemons," children as "good deals": Lucy was certainly getting the picture. A cruel picture, but at the same time so ridiculous she couldn't help but laugh when she could have as easily cried. "Well, you never know even if it's your own whether the child will be a schoolteacher or a psychopath."

A tall, older boy stopped at the table, in a long flapping T-shirt and shorts, short hair. "This here's Frank," Pat said. Frank was a shy teenager, a few pimples, dark circles under his eyes.

"Did you eat lunch, Frank?"

Richard grunted, "Probably started with cake and finished with cake."

Frank protested. "I ate some other stuff. Can I go out and play baseball?"

Pat watched Frank leave. "He's thirteen, but he's only in fifth grade. Makes it kind of hard, because he's so big. Lead poisoning, both the boys got it. Frank got it worse, cause he was older, had more of it. Billy's doing fine in school, right at grade level."

Her husband excused himself to go smoke and look for Billy.

Pat barked, "Try the soccer game." She turned back to Lucy and relentlessly kept talking. "You have to do your research. In public libraries, they have the listings of who's available, and you can plow through those on your own. Now when the kids come, at first they don't trust you, and then there's their grandmother or somebody coming around, taking them for a while, stirring them up, and they don't know what's going on. And they get mad at you, because who else is there to get mad at? And then one day they ask you if you are going to leave them, ever. Then they start calling you Mom and Dad. It's rough." Pat turned over another page, and there was the whole family, a group portrait taken at a local studio. Lucy looked through pages and pages of birthday parties, fishing trips, vacations, Fourth of July sparklers held by Frank, with dark, dark circles under his eyes, and Billy, with fainter and fainter circles. And Pat growing even rounder and more and more tired. "In the end, you've got them, and they are yours for good. You do what you can. You love them."

Richard came back with both boys, all of them eating doughnuts. He jingled his keys.

"Guess we got to go." Pat gave Lucy her address. Her skin was downy, and soft with fine creases. She might be the same age as Lucy. Lucy thanked Pat, warmly. The crowd was thinning out, and a social worker called for everyone to take some of the food home, not let all this great food go to waste.

The priests and now some nuns were busy at a table over at the other side of the room.

Lucy walked to the door. There on a large sheet of orange poster board, which she had missed on her way in, was listed the *Adoption Party Specials!* photos of five children and typed-up captions. There was "Jaquie, seven, some trauma from abuse and possible fetal alcoholism, seeing a counselor, making progress, likes rabbits and birds, legally free for adoption to a family with older children. Will need counseling to continue indefinitely." Jaquie smiled in the fashion of any child portrait photo, except the background wasn't the drape of studio cloth but a dark brown Naugahyde sofa, on which she sat holding a wilting paper plate on her lap. There was "Keith, severe disabilities, special needs, legally free for adoption, for a family who has the time and the care to give. Keith smiles a lot, and his smiles are priceless." Lucy looked and recognized one of the children outside strapped in a wheelchair, sitting alone now except for two of the young social workers in training, who talked with each other. Lucy could hear Keith grunt and the girl say, "It's all right, it's all right," and Keith grunted again and then wailed. There was "Kitty, thirteen, making progress with her therapist, been with several foster families, looking for a family of her own. Because of a long history of abuse, Kitty needs a lot of one-on-one attention. Couple without young children preferable." Kitty, in her photo, looked younger than thirteen, with a small opaque face and short tomboyish hair.

She squinted off to the left from the eye of the camera. Lucy recognized her as the stone-faced girl who kept weaving her way up one row of empty tables and down another, a pattern of sorts to her weaving.

Lucy suddenly remembered years and years ago in New York City, late in the evening, coming back from dinner to a nice hotel. In a doorway crouched a girl the same age as Kitty—her hair long, though, and hanging over her face. She was so young, and Lucy felt she should do something, call the police to come get this child. But her lover hurried her along, and although she did leave the girl twenty dollars, she had been ashamed of herself for years for not taking that girl home with her. She was in graduate school and broke, but still she could have helped her. So many years ago, yet how clear that night was to Lucy right now. The last "specials" were two little girls, sisters, bright-eyed and polished up so they shone, in identical Easter dresses and eager to show them off to the camera. One lifted up her skirt like she was a princess going down a palace's grand staircase. "Kerri and Sherri are not yet legally free for adoption but need a family to take them home. Sweet and bright, these sisters have a lot to give, but they need each other. For a family able to take them both in, big rewards."

Lucy turned away, her face flushed and her eyes brimmed. As she headed for her car, she looked at the trees of the grove, so carefully planted, and the vast parking lot, the blue sky, and her car, a few other cars. Something broke inside Lucy. In the last year, she had entered a new world, in which at every moment she became more and more aware of its awful contingency. That was the way the world worked—one was so protected, one forgot that chance played its hand at every moment. If not this child, this other child. So close to home, Lucy had at last come upon her local version of the river of children feeding some huge hellish mouth. She stood on its bank, wanting to fish them all out, but she couldn't do it today. All she could do was watch them go by and promise them that soon she would rescue another in their name.

Driving home, Lucy cried over her steering wheel. And that night she dreamed she had a baby, thin and rigid like a pencil and with a full set of teeth, and a strangely adult face. This little pencil with teeth was bound to a board that Lucy carried awkwardly to the airport. During the flight, the baby became a real baby, but she couldn't seem to feed it. In fact, she kept forgetting to feed it. The child seemed wistful for its mother, some mother. Lucy worried, too, about her traveling companion, a younger handsome man who was simply there to help her but confessed, as they went into a Japanese beer place, that he used to have a drinking problem.

Lucy awoke full of the horror of that image of the pencil baby, yet also with the strong, very real sense of having at last to take care of someone other than herself. How many more of these child dreams would there be?

CHAPTER 19

Lucy was terrified to stop acting on the adoption. Her fear was not that if she stopped, she would never come back to it, but rather that without pursuing it, her life would be the most horrible nothing beyond the most basic functions: working, eating, sleeping. She threw herself into the lap of a local adoption agency and soon was busy filling out the application and gathering the documents—birth certificates, information for a large bank loan, an account of her family. It was like having her life flash before her eyes, but she was not going to die. Her life simply was going to change forever, which she saw now was the whole point, she had to change her life or die.

For the first month, she was afraid that for some reason she would be rejected. Her heart would beat so hard, she had to stand still. She became so preoccupied with this fear, she often forgot what she was doing. She locked herself out of the house three times. Sometimes she would be holding a bag, and then suddenly drop it. She got a speeding ticket on a familiar road she knew was heavily patrolled. Yet she didn't mind being pulled over. She could have hit a child. After that she did not drive to the adoption agency, for on those days she came the most undone. Luckily, a commuter train stopped near the agency.

At last one day, as she got off the train and climbed the steep wooden stairs to reach the street above, Lucy saw those stairs as beach stairs, and the stairs framed against the sky made her feel absurdly that the sea, the infinite sea, was visible at the top of the stairs, and suddenly she was extraordinarily happy, for she was convinced she would have a child. She kept seeing herself stopping and picking up a child, carrying the child on her back.

Several weeks later, the agency had several photographs to show Lucy of a child who was available for adoption. In the end, adopting a Romanian child was at that moment the most uncomplicated, the surest, and the quickest way to adopt for someone single and over forty. In the photos, the child was round-faced, her expression stoic. Her hands clasped the rings of the little walker in which she sat. Her hair was dark, her eyes dark. Two days later, Lucy signed a contract for the child. She wrote the largest check she had ever written in her life to pay the agency's fee, the Romanian fees, the translator's fees. She told Hana, Caroline, and her mother about the child.

Somewhere, at this very moment, thousands of miles away, Lucy's baby was waiting for her to come. Every day, all day long, Lucy thought about the child waiting for her. This was what her sister Caroline must have meant when she said that in the last months, the desire to see the child, to have the child in hand, is so strong, almost unbearable. The difference, of course, was that Lucy didn't have the baby safe inside her, she was literally out of reach. Every day, too, she would cry a little for the baby that perhaps had been inside her, the small grains of rice.

Michael's child, too. She had schooled herself to not think about Michael. But at moments she couldn't help it. Once, just as she had come to the conclusion that the baby would probably be too big to use the old white wicker bassinet with its arched hood that her mother had kept all these years in the basement, she remembered a trip with Michael, long ago. Driving in France, she had seen pollarded trees in a row along a small river and was struck by the stumpy thick trunks, the wild shooting canes of wicker soon to be harvested. Although she didn't want to tell Michael about the child she might have lost, she wanted obscurely to comfort him for the loss. And to tell him that her love for him had not died but was flowing from her to him to the child. She wrote him three postcards, with a serial message: "I had a dream that I was with a man who had a child. I took the child in my lap to read to her and impress her attractive father. But he saw what I was doing and went into a house. I was embarrassed. Then a cat jumped into my lap behind the child. I looked into the child's eyes and the cat and the child opened their mouths to two perfect Os and began singing, not with words but a lovely vocalizing pure and sweet and unearthly. I opened my mouth and began to sing this music of the spheres with them. I quite literally could see the black-blue night with stars." She mailed the cards and forgot about them.

Unexpectedly on a Saturday, a day when she didn't usually work, she pulled out her notes for her book, turned on the computer, and wrote several pages. For the next two weeks, she was very excited, writing more pages, taking long notes. While walking, she carried a small notebook to write down ideas, phrases. All the words spilling through her kept her from sleeping at night.

Two weeks later, the flood of words was over. But Lucy Baldrich and her companion, Eileen Riley, were on their way. Now she would have to work to mine, day in day out, the ideas given her. Although she was exhausted, she kept working. Once the child was here, she would not have much time, she kept telling herself—she had to get as much done as possible.

She started to see more of her friends again, dropping in often as she had in the old days before David. On a Sunday afternoon, Lucy drove to Hana's house. The children played outside with Howard, so the two women could talk. Taro, the cat, slunk into the room and, seeing Lucy, jumped up into her lap, turning over a basket of small carved gourds on the coffee table that fell to the floor with a pleasant hollow clatter. He stretched, curled up, and closed his eyes under her caresses. Lucy murmured to him, "You're just a cat. Congratulations." Wasn't cat fur deliciously silky, the little bones of their shapely legs so fragile?

Hana came in with the tea. She put it on the coffee table, picked up the gourds, righted the basket, lay back down on the sofa, and turned her head to watch Lucy and the cat. "You should get a cat."

"That's true, the baby needs a totem animal, an animal companion. I'll get a cat as soon as the baby is settled."

"Why not get one now?"

Lucy laughed. "I want a human pet first!" She drank her tea. "You know what's funny about having a 'home study'—where the social worker checks you out to see if you have a criminal record, if you have running water in your house? It makes me feel for the first time that I have a home. It's not just having a house—one can feel equally at home in an apartment, I know now. When I'm walking home from the store and see the house, I feel as proud as any homesteading pioneer who has built her cabin of logs or sod for her family. Eastward ho!" She stopped. "Maybe at last I won't always be outside a house, looking at the windows lit up, where families live."

Hana said, "I always liked the old pictures of those sod houses in the history books at school. Families burrowing underground. Becoming part of the prairie."

Lucy said, "Remember last year when you told me the children fragmented you? I think of it as giving my body up, becoming a rotting body of loam, decomposed in the sweetest of corruptions. The child will sink its roots and spring up from my earth, as if I were a sacrifice buried in the field to make the crop grow."

Hana nodded. "Yes, that's another kind of fragmentation. I see your rot gleaming with phosphorescence, foxfire." She smiled. "Yes, the child will come, root herself, and prosper. You'll finally be grown up."

Howard had walked in. "She's over forty. Of course she's grown up."

Hana protested, "No, no. I don't know how to say it, but now you've changed, grown up. Your antennae are finally reaching out to feel someone else. I can see these large feathery antennae, like big moths have, that are reaching out to other people to feel them all over."

Howard and Lucy laughed. After Howard left again, Hana said, "Oh, I meant to tell you that I saw David at the airport as I was picking up Howard. He was on a trip to some conference in China. I told him all about you, that you were adopting, how great you were looking, about your house. I wanted to make him feel like you went on and did very well without him."

Lucy was silent for a moment. "I think he's probably feeling he's lucky to have escaped from me. I think of him sometimes, for I did love him in a way, but strangely it never became in a family way and not even in a friendly way. That's what I really wanted. The thing I liked so much about Michael was that he was like a part of my family, a best friend, and a lover, too."

"Have you told Michael you're adopting?"

"No, I'm not in touch. I can't think of him. Everything is in the past now, over, put away. Now that I'm an adult, as you say, I've put away childish things."

"I'm not quite sure that's what I meant. You'll see that a child can't be everything to you. A little adult love is very nice. I want you to find someone."

"I suppose that would be nice, but I think I'll be too busy to worry about it for a while."

Hana persisted. "What was Arthur Wall like? Did you get to know him? I know I shouldn't have been thinking of this while his wife was dying, but I wondered if he might be interested in you."

Lucy blushed. Those evenings at Arthur's in August, had he wanted something more from her? Had she, unconsciously, been hoping for something from him? "I think, honestly, that we were keeping each other company in a desperate moment. It helped me, and I hope it helped him, I'm not sure." She remembered those moments on the porch when he seemed to be coming closer to her and then turned away. "I haven't heard from him." Perhaps his memory of her would always be marked by its association with Meryl's death and he would not be able to talk to her. She could understand that. "Anyway, I'm so tired of love. I'm getting so old. It'd be nice to be with someone forever in a vague way, like I was with Arthur. That would be enough. I don't know if I'd want to make love to someone again. I remember that I used to think about sex a lot, but that was before the continental divide of the adoption. All I remember, for example, at this moment is that I liked to look at men's forearms."

Hana sat up straight and laughed. "Yes, it's so unfair. They say women dress sexy, unbuttoning the top buttons of their dresses, but when men roll up their sleeves in front of you—you know they know."

"Between the wrist and the elbow is the best. Above the elbow it's a bit too much. Yes, I remember that I used to look at forearms. A long time ago, it seems."

Hana said, "What about Arthur's forearms?"

One day Lucy had seen Arthur without his shirt as he passed the kitchen on the way to his room. His chest was childish, white, and angular. The handsome head, she saw, perched like an almost-too-heavy bloom upon the reedy thinness of his body. The white skin of his shoulders was not as fine as his face, but rough, irritated with a slight rash. His arms seemed suddenly very thin—and where the ribs should have swelled out, they caved in, caved in from the collarbone down, as if some giant fist had delivered a silent, terrible blow when the bones were still baby-soft. She had had a sense of his fragility at that moment. He seemed so vulnerable that she had made herself forget it the next instant. "Diffident forearms, I guess. A little thin."

"Diffident forearms?" Hana joked. "If he had fallen in love with you and pursued you, you might not have found them so diffident."

"Maybe."

Before Lucy left, she invited Hana and her family to a tree-planting party in two weeks. Martin was giving her a ginkgo tree as a garden-warming gift. It would be in the afternoon, so all the children could come.

CHAPTER 20

Two days before the conference in China ended, David decided to do something impulsive, be a Lucy-like traveler. Instead of spending the long weekend in hot, polluted, and crowded China, he would go to Japan, go to Nagasaki, the city of martyred crypto-Christians. Soon he was in Tokyo and leaving on the bullet train for western Japan. In Nagasaki he headed for the Glover Gardens, where in the nineteenth century the consulates of Europe and the United States and the foreign merchants' houses were located. There he rode the escalator encased in a glass tube up the hill, deafened by Mozart Muzak and sandwiched between two tour groups of middle-aged Japanese women and men. At the top of the hill, the tour guides, young Japanese women, raised their flags as if to signal a charge and the tourists followed the flags and the tap of their low heels. David visited the Ouray Catholic Church, a small church like any other church at home, white plaster, wood trim, narrow wooden benches, stained glass with blond Christs. The only Japanese figures were being crucified in a large painting on one wall. This was too easy. He wanted a little adventure, something Lucy-like. He took out his guidebook and found a small entry on the

Gotō Islands, off the coast, where many of the persecuted Christians had fled in the sixteenth century. Now the islands were famous for their resort beaches, but there was the Dōzaki Tenshudō church, built in 1874 on a lovely inlet, the book said, and housing a collection of crypto-Christian artifacts. David rose the next morning and caught the hydrofoil for Fukue, the main port of the Gotō Islands, seventy-five kilometers from Nagasaki, of rolling rough sea, black like volcanic glass.

All his maps were bad. They showed the church off to the right of the port, but at what distance? David wandered on the outskirts of Fukue until he ran into a signpost that pointed down a road, *Dōzaki Church, 7.5 kilometers.* David calculated that was about four to five miles. He would walk.

He left behind the new houses that clustered on the edge of the town and was soon surrounded by fields. Cars passed him and people stared. One young man stopped and asked him where he was going.

"Dōzaki."

"Far," the young man said abruptly, then smiled, it was the right word.

"Yes, I know," David replied.

"Far." The young man grinned again.

"I know. I want to walk." David waved at the man and kept walking. A matronly woman stopped her car and rolled down her window. "Far," she said, and then in very fast Japanese explained, probably, that the church was very far away.

David smiled, nodded his head, but he was annoyed, partly because he began to realize that the church was far away. Still he had committed himself. He kept walking. Soon he was over a hill, and it was all weathered Shinto shrines, farms, and rice paddies, and on concrete aprons by the drainage ditches, seaweed was spread to dry in the sun. The town of Fukue was out of sight.

On top of a hill, he saw a cemetery where against the light stood the black shapes of Buddhist gravestones and one cross. He walked and walked.

He was overtaken by a large bus, playing loudly a tune both saccharine and jaunty. At first David was cheerful, it might be a bus he could take on the way back. Then he got a good look at the back window and saw it piled with toilet paper and cardboard boxes. It was a grocery bus making the rounds of these hamlets. Old women bent horizontal came scurrying down to the bus stop with their grocery carts. They counted out the money, fumbling through their change purses and craning their heads up, twisting them up sideways, expectantly. All old women, and so horribly bent over. David stood as straight as possible. These women were much older than he was. That's who lived here on the island, the old people, their children having escaped to the city. David was pleased at his observation; this was what Lucy liked to do as she traveled, look at things, notice things like this. But as time wore on, he grew irritated. Where was the church? He should be close, shouldn't he? Foolish to come to the islands, foolish to walk. The yellow flowers in some fields nodded in the breeze. He grew tired of only yellow, yellow, yellow flowers. If only someone would stop now, he would take a lift. He wiped his forehead with a handkerchief—it was hot in the full sun.

He came upon a town on the side of a hill. A large white statue of the Virgin Mary and crosses cluttered up the skyline. The Jewish side of him protested. All his life the clutter of Christianity had filled the air of every town he had ever lived in, and look, here it was true, too. What was he doing here? He had come to see the subtle dissolution of the Christian in the Japanese.

The Dōzaki church must be close. On an inlet, the guidebook said, and now a stream next to the highway widened into a tidal plain, where old women dug for shellfish in the mud flats, their white cotton head scarves flapping in the sea breeze.

When he was about to give up, at last he saw the red-brick church perched right on the mouth of the inlet, looking out to sea, looking for ships coming from far away, as if it were ready to leap on these ships, leave the land on which it had been founded. In the church's little garden was erected an ugly modern bas-relief commemorating a massacre of Japanese Christians. Next to it were humble stones once belonging, a placard said, to a Buddhist temple. There were rough crosses carved into them. He bought his ticket and went in.

The inside was mercifully cool. He walked up and down the church looking at the exhibits. He saw a pair of scrolls, one of a Japanese-looking heaven with an ascended Christ who resembled Confucius, Japanese garments turned into priestly vestments with Christian insignia on the neckbands. He found a collection of Kannons turned into Virgin Marys, each Kannon with her slightly tilted and inclined mild face, her flowing robes, standing in box shrines with open doors, all very Kannon-like, except that the Christian Kannon held a baby in her arms. So many Kannons. In jade, in bronze, in soapstone. The goddess smiled gently, a smile that haunted him.

In the last row of exhibits, he stopped before a tiny Kannon of white porcelain, tinged with blue like the milkiest white skin, a Kannon standing on a Buddhist lotus blossom, holding the Christ child and, unlike any other Kannon, her robe undone to the waist. David stared at her voluptuous breasts, full breasts about to spurt with milk, and he thought of Lucy's breasts. He had come to the ends of the earth, and here were Lucy's breasts, Lucy with a child.

When he returned home, David was still thinking about Lucy and the child. Hana had told him the child was Romanian. Too bad Lucy hadn't adopted a Chinese girl—he spoke Chinese, who else would have had more to offer Lucy and Lucy's child? It gratified him to know Lucy had a house. He found himself thinking that would keep things equal. They could move slowly. Often he would say to himself, once she had the child, she would realize that she needed a man, too. She would be very happy for some adult company, for dinners, for sex in the afternoon. She would have her house and child, he could have his house and his work and his solitude. They would both be happy.

On a Saturday morning, after a good week's work—incredible how much research and writing he had done in the last year, David dropped by Lucy's new house. Lucy always did the unexpected thing, now he would do the unexpected thing.

Her house was small but looked solid, although it was like Lucy to live in a house that needed to be painted. She had a garden, and he recognized several of the plants she had had in her old garden.

When Lucy opened the door and looked so surprised, he quickly explained, "I wanted to drop by and congratulate you." He cleared his throat. "New house and soon a new baby!" Lucy looked different, softer and sweeter.

Lucy invited him in and, at his request, gave him a tour of the house. Inside he saw it was freshly painted, and all the rooms were alive with her things from the old house and with some sort of empty space left for new things, which gave the rooms a fertile spareness. As they looked at the house, he asked her questions about the adoption, and she, in her old excited fashion, started telling him the story. Even when he said to her, "You'll never start your book now," and she snapped, "I've started writing," he felt they were having some of their old exchanges again, but in a friendly way. She asked him about Olivia and Maureen, Maureen's baby, which was due soon, about his work. He told her all the details of his adventure in the Gotō Islands. It was as if he were in love with her, telling her the best things he thought about his work, and even more, he was offering a picture of himself traveling as she said she traveled—a sign, he thought, to her, of what life could be like with him now.

He stood close to her, kept smiling at her, and waited for her to start, as she had once before, to look at him with a heightened attention, with love. As they talked, the more relaxed she became, and the more attractive. Yet something was different.

When they reached the kitchen, he understood the change in her. He saw she had been cooking, and that there were a stack of paper plates and cups piled on the table. She was getting ready for a party. Lucy had a rich life going on without him. She was talking to him in a friendly yet formal way. There was no invitation on her part—he kept waiting, but she would not make a gesture. Then he became afraid that she might, if she talked about the past, say something like, it was for the best they had split up. He couldn't bear that.

They went to the backyard. David was immediately alarmed by the glittering black violent eruption of rock into the yard, this wall of rock breaking through the green grass, as if a stony behemoth had lifted its back. As Lucy was telling him about the glacial history of Somerville and how the rock had been formed, David recognized the rock as the rock in his dream of Lucy's face, so long ago now— he could almost see the lizard. He frowned and looked down at his hands. "Well, I've got to go."

In the front, he stopped on the sidewalk and made an effort to end the visit on an easy, friendly note. He meant to say it lightly, but it came out not quite right, "Maybe after the child arrives, you'll find your 'Genius of Affection.'"

Lucy blushed and laughed. "'The Genius of Affection,' what ridiculous things I say sometimes. Now I think I'm more interested in 'The Genius of the Place,' and the place is anywhere, as the lines from the church service say, 'when two or three are gathered together.' Funny, I still remember those lines from the prayer service—I guess I'll be Episcopalian until I die, no matter what." She stopped and then said, "I'm having a garden party this afternoon.

Martin's going to plant a ginkgo tree for me. Would you like to come by? The Yus will be here, Cappy, Hana, and their families." Here was her gesture, but it was not of love, of excitement, only a gesture of for-old-times'-sake friendliness. He thanked her, but he had other engagements that afternoon, waved, got into his car, and drove away.

As David turned into his driveway, his house was lit up with the same sun that shone at Lucy's, only a bit lower in the sky, even more golden. The simple happiness of sunlight. Who would love him now? He felt very sorry for himself. As he stood in his backyard, he thought that three years ago he would have been calling for Venus, the old old cat. She would appear black as night except for one white toe, that drip of cream on her paw. Silent, slim, tiny like a kitten though she was old. Her ghost there in the shadows, standing near her grave by the pine tree. If he had lived with Lucy, he would have had to have a cat again. Good thing they split up. No cat. He was too old for another cat. He should fix up this house of his, get the trim painted, the side porch redone, the bathroom tile repaired— even better, retiled. Make the whole house brighter. Yes. Less gloomy. Monday morning he would call a contractor.

CHAPTER 21

When Michael returned to Japan from Mexico, he had delayed his arrival by taking side trips to famous gardens in Nara and Osaka. When he finally got to Kyoto station, he took, instead of a taxi, even though he was exhausted, the lovely slow bus, which crawled northeast, with stops near the temples in his neighborhood, the recorded voice announcing in Japanese and in a plummy English, "This stop is convenient for Nanzen-ji temple, for Ginkaku-ji temple, for the Shisen-dō temple." He and his wife lived in temple land like a monk and a nun. He thought of Lucy, sleeping with Lucy, holding her close. He could not bear ever to hold her again, knowing he would have to let her go. He hardly let himself think that she might be pregnant. The odds were against it—he was such a failure that he couldn't even give her this gift.

As he walked up the hill from the bus stop, Michael wondered, would his wife be there when he got home? If she wasn't there, he would be so worried. If she was there, then despair would begin all over again. The street was dark. He could hear the mountain water rushing through the culverts.

The gate was unlocked, but then it always was. As he slid it open, low barking began inside the house. Michael stopped. Had she gotten a dog? If she were there, certainly she would tell the dog to stop barking or she would come to the door. The dog barked and barked. She wouldn't leave a poor dog locked up in the house?

He came closer. As if he were a thief, the dog barked frantically, and still no low voice quieted the dog. The pitch of the dog's yelp rose and rose, until at last a voice said something. She had taken pity on the dog, and the dog calmed down. Michael felt suddenly happy. She had a dog that was hers alone. She had begun to live her own life alone.

He entered the garden. Here was her revenge. The garden had been neglected. Weeds raised their heads above the moss. Stalks of flowers had fallen over, she hadn't staked them but had let them go blooming on and on until their heavy heads fell over. The dog had dug a few holes—that was all right, he was a dog. The abandonment by her, however, was a direct blow. He was angry and he was guilty, for he knew he deserved it.

As he entered the house, the dog barked again, once, for show.

Inside he found her cooking dinner, her scissors snipping at the greens, the rice cooker ending its cycle, the fish ready to be steamed. She was home, and he was home. Nothing seemed to have changed. Yet there was the dog. It growled, licked her hand, and lay back down. A young dog, the kind of dog he saw everywhere in Japan, a foxy yellow and white dog with sleek short fur and pointed ears and a brush of a tail curled up in a circle. She said, "His name is Yoshi-tune. He was abandoned, and I had to take him. Dinner will be ready in about ten minutes."

Michael suddenly felt a terror—like Persephone, if he ate the food, he had to stay in the land of the dead. Still, as always, he sat down and ate.

They talked politely to each other, about the dog, about how her students were doing, the new friends, mostly American and British, she had made. Every time before when he had returned, she had acted as if nothing had happened. This time it was again as if nothing had happened but in a different way, as if nothing had ever happened between them, except that they had been merely friends and, for a while, shared a house.

At the end of the meal, she said simply, "I'm not going back to the States in October. There's nothing at home for me."

She would stay in Japan and teach English. She had found a position in a local school. He looked at her. After not seeing her for several weeks, he thought that she seemed to have grown more solid, as if she were attracting gravity. And she had become eerily more Japanese. She had perfected the bow, in all its infinite forms. She could sit with her feet tucked nicely under her rear end. She held her rice bowl properly, her thumb hooked over its side, and her tea bowl with both hands, fingers wrapped around it for warmth.

He said quietly, "So at last we can sell the house? You'll need money—I, of course, will send you half. Do you think that will be enough? Japan is so expensive. What will you do until I sell it? I'd be happy to send you money."

"I'll have enough. I've already found an apartment. Karin's moving."

He knew that apartment of Karin's, an art historian they had met together but who had become friends with his wife. The apartment was a tiny, tidy place. Karin had already introduced his wife to the neighborhood. She had visited the local baths, *onsen*, with Karin, gone around to the local shops with Karin. So this lichen had attached herself to a new rock.

"I can live there on what I'm earning. When the house is sold, maybe I'll look for another place." She stood up and delivered herself of a parting shot. "I'm moving next week. From now on, you'll have to pay your own bills. Cook your own food. Iron your own clothes. You'll have to come home every night to an empty house."

He was a little scared and even lonely in advance. Yet the relief was immense—he foresaw a day when he would not have to feel guilty every day, not to bear every day the weight of her unhappiness.

The following week, Michael helped his wife move. The dog went with her, so he felt assured she would not be too alone. She shut the new door in his face, as he lingered on the doorstep, and he could not be angry.

He would go back to Boston, he would sell the house and send her the money—there would be lots of money, he hoped, for the Shaker house. At last he could tell Lucy that waiting was at an end. He could keep his promise to her, as he had always said he would. For the moment, though, until all was a little more settled, he would not talk to Lucy. It would be crude to say baldly that his wife had left him. And he had to get used to the idea that now he owned his own death, that his wife would not be there waiting with the coins to press his eyelids down.

Let him wait a bit, get back home, sell the house, then go to Lucy, ready to offer himself.

At the end of October, Michael found it so strange to drive to his house, along the small country road through the ancient apple trees on Orchard Road, through the shadows of the black green firs. He stopped to piss in the woods beyond the Shaker graveyard, where the two companies of white iron markers faced each other in an eternal dance, the brothers on one side, the sisters on the other. What was it about a graveyard that always made him want to exercise a bodily function? He thought of how he had watched Lucy pissing once as they stopped along the Maine seashore, crouching, with a leaf in her hand ready to wipe herself, and looking around her as if wondering, amused, how she had come to be on this strange planet. It was one of his favorite memories of her.

Michael parked, and soon he sat in his own living room talking to the young couple who had stayed in the house. When he was a young assistant professor, poor and transient, had he and his wife been like these two, so drab and pale? The child, too, was pale and thin like tallow and ill mannered. He had thrown rocks at Michael when he came up the walk. The mother called, "Cedric, I'll make you go to your room, if you don't stop that," which did not stop Cedric at all. Was this wan family happy?

He followed the wife down to the kitchen to get a cup of coffee, reassuring her when she apologized that this plant, that plant, and that plant—she could never remember their names—had died, that she hadn't been able to weed the garden quite as much as she would have liked. An understatement, for Michael had already seen that the garden looked as if an advance team of thicket from the forest had taken it over. In the kitchen, brown grocery bags stood on end, turning a bit in the draft from the open windows. She was packing the cans of food and half bags of flour and sugar. He bumped into one of the bags. It skittered and tottered but righted itself. The coffee was very bad.

This family had not enjoyed the house, he sensed. At first he felt indignant, then he felt they were right. The house seemed at first wonderful, built by the people who had written the song that made everyone sit up straight when they heard it: "'Tis a gift to be simple, 'tis a gift to be free." Yet soon the young couple, the child, must have felt this house, with its six floors, too big, too gloomy, too far from town.

After the family drove away, Michael went to the kitchen for a drink of water. He saw several of those brown bags still standing in the kitchen listing lightly. Long ago, before they were married, he and his wife had stayed with his mother, a good Catholic, who had assigned them rooms at opposite ends of the house. His wife had whispered to him, "I'll come to you in the middle of the night." He had gathered up paper bags and set them up in the small hall leading to his room and right inside his room, then turned off the lights. She meant to come so quietly, but he laughed in the dark as he heard the hollow bump of the bags, her gasp of surprise and then her hesitation. More skittering as she bumped her way into the room. How loud paper bags sounded, bang, bang, but hollow bangs.

Even then he had wanted to warn her off, erect barriers. And in the long run, they had ended up sleeping in separate rooms.

Over the next several days, Michael saw that if he were not careful, he would find himself starting to settle into a version of his old life. He spent his time rescuing what was left of his garden and offering the most abject of apologies to his cats, which were grudgingly accepted. The difference was the heavy silence in the house, as he went about the daily business of making and eating dinner, the quick cleaning up.

This solitude—at last literal, as opposed to the solitude of marriage—he assured himself was the fate he deserved for failing his wife and Lucy. Even the foxes and deer that he used to see didn't come near, he told himself, working it up until now it seemed to him the entire animal kingdom avoided him for his spinelessness—even as his cats stared at him from the windows where they lay, propped up against the screen. He deserved the loneliness of the few years remaining to him, they seemed a garden so desiccated, a bone garden, a Buddhist cemetery, full of stone obelisks, bristling and crowded, no lawn, a boneyard of his animals that had deserted him in the end through death and been buried one after another under the trees. He deserved only the most severe of gardens for himself, a garden that exacted extreme austerities. Yes, he would become even more monkish, wilder, removed from life, a wild monk in retreat in the black forest of Massachusetts.

It would be better, of course, if he had an abbess in retreat with him—Lucy as abbess, they would live together in cold chastity. Or rather, since his carnal love for her was chaste in its way, like brother and sister, they could get along quite nicely with a chaste incestuousness. Certainly not cold. No, when the wrestling began, she was hot and sweaty, and yet her skin stayed so dry, the cool color of quince blossom, a creamy rose.

He went to his office to pick up his mail. Among the requests for recommendations, the announcements of the various committee meetings, were three postcards from Lucy.

The postcards came like a rain dream in the desert. Although they were postmarked in Somerville, the pictures on the reverse were the same, of a highway in Colorado, a gray ribbon threading through a green tundra landscape eleven thousand feet high. Her handwriting was the usual Arabic calligraphy, almost impossible to decipher.

Michael hunched over the cards. Lucy was only relating the dream of a child. She must not be pregnant—she would have told him if she was. Yet this brief note, so full of a general love, could be a knife threatening to cut away all dead tissue.

The next morning, Michael woke up with an unfamiliar determination to act. He would go see Lucy. He would see a realtor about selling the house. After he split the money with his wife, he might still have quite a bit of money, enough to retire on, if he lived frugally, and write his books. And he would live somewhere in the light, not in these gloomy forests. Somewhere near the sea, the sea he had loved so much as a child. He looked at the hosta catalog—there were some hostas that could tolerate seaside conditions.

CHAPTER 22

L ucy's tree-planting party took place on the Saturday night before daylight saving time would end. That, in Lucy's mind, was the beginning of winter, when all of a sudden it was dark at six, then five, then four. Before the first people arrived, as she cleaned up the kitchen, she thought about David's visit. She had talked too much, and maybe it had been the wrong thing to invite him to the party at the last minute there at the curb, but she had wanted somehow to be kind, include him. Or was it to make up for the wrong she felt she had done him? She should never have forced herself into his life. Wrong for her and wrong for him. It had laid waste to them both.

Then her mother called to say hello. Everyone in Denver was fine, she was fine, the doctor gave her a clean bill the last checkup. Her throat still hurt and it was so dry, her salivary glands had been burned out, but otherwise she was fine, fine, and everyone else was good, the boys bigger than ever—Lucy was moved to hear her mother returning to the old familiar litany of family news reports. She wondered, would there be a time when they all forgot about the cancer, not completely, of course, but would the memory of those terrible months fade? Then she forgot that thought as she listened to her mother offer to accompany her to Romania if Caroline, for some reason, could not go.

When Lucy hung up, she didn't have that feeling she used to have of being left alone. Her East Coast family, as she had begun to think of them all, were arriving shortly. There were Mr. and Mrs. Yu, Hana, Howard, Sachiko and Tak, Martin, Match and Fergus, Cappy and Bill, and their oldest son, Mark, aspiring tree maniac and a disciple of Martin's. She who had thought she had nothing, had everything. It was as if she had turned the least little bit, and they had all appeared waiting to welcome her home.

Her karmic change of destiny. Now she believed she could trace its path. It had begun with falling in love with Michael. That had been real—for the first time in her life, she had truly loved someone. That love was now ready to be at home with the child. She still missed Michael, but he had his own life to lead with his wife, she wished them well. It was enough that she had loved him.

In the backyard, Lucy had set up two long folding tables. One of her earliest memories was of the trestle tables outside her great-grandfather's house on Memorial Day, laden with biscuits, corn, banana cream pie, iced tea, and lemonade, where all her father's family ate and ate after visiting the graveyard. An hour later, her tables were loaded with dishes: a casserole of Martin's vegetables, Hana's sushi, the Yus' soup, Cappy's roast. They ate, talked, and laughed. As Lucy joined them, Match was telling Sachiko and Tak about her cannibal ancestors, and she smiled, showing off her brilliant white teeth. A moment of silence, and then the children ran away and started chasing one another, and soon they were pulling off their jackets and throwing them—pink, purple, and blue—onto the grass.

Martin looked around the yard and said to Lucy, "It's the urban pastoral."

"These shepherds and shepherdesses and gardeners—in exile from what corrupt court?"

"The rest of life. For the moment."

Cappy took offense. She lived in a huge house in the suburbs near the Institute. "Wait a minute. I have the rights to the pastoral."

"Just the suburban pastoral."

Martin dug the hole in the yard. He and Mark rolled the ginkgo tree over and positioned in the hole, then filled the hole with Martin's secret mixture of soil and fertilizer and compost. "You know ginkgoes are one of what they call grandfather-grandson trees. The grandfather plants it, the grandson enjoys it."

Match instantly said, "A *grandmother-granddaughter* tree!"

Cappy laughed. "We're already expecting Lucy's grandchild?"

Martin bragged, "I'm giving this baby a fifty-dollar hole—there's so much good stuff in there, it can skip a generation."

Lucy said, "Wait a minute, I want time to slow down, not hurry up."

"Wait until you have to spend all day with the baby, then you'll see how slow time can go!" Cappy said.

Hana said, "I love how ginkgo leaves turn into golden fans in the fall." She saw Tak had his jacket off again. "Tak, come here and let me put that jacket on. I don't want the colds to start so soon." After she had snapped Tak back up, she said to Lucy, "Now that the children are older and you have a baby I can get my hands on whenever I want, I'll sink back into my work. The poems began to rise up in my head again, I feel myself growing lighter, thinner. Maybe I'm just getting older. But if so, I have to say I find it very interesting. I'm going to let myself go. Doesn't that sound wonderful? All my life I've been waiting to let myself go."

Lucy laughed and looked forward to the future conversations she would have with Hana on letting themselves go.

The afternoon grew dark, the breeze turned chilly. People began to leave. As Lucy stood in front of her house watching Hana and Howard try to shoo the two children toward their car, Michael drove up. He hurried across the street from where he parked, carrying a big cardboard box, constantly looking down into the box. There were scuffling noises, the box's lid popped open, and two white plump paws appeared, two ears black and white and pink, two huge golden eyes with black pupils, round, so round. In the backyard, Michael put down the box and pulled out a fat cat and held her in his big hands next to his chest, stroking her, calming her. Sachiko and Tak started yelling, "A cat! A cat!"

Michael came up to Lucy, who was looking worried, almost in a panic, and at the same time so relieved, it was comical. "I stopped by your apartment, and the garden was gone, completely cemented over. There was a different name on the mailbox, and I was so afraid you had moved away. Then someone came out of the house and said they thought you had moved up to this street, and I saw Hana and stopped. I was so afraid I'd lost you."

He looked down at the cat and the children's hands stroking the fur. "This stray cat has been showing up at my door. If you don't like her, I'll take her back, but she's very sweet, this cat."

"Oh, yes, trees need cats to climb them." Hana nodded wisely and smiled. "Tak, now, pet the cat gently, gently, gently."

Lucy watched Michael and Tak and Sachiko. Michael's large hands had calmed the cat, so she seemed not too unhappy having the children touch her. She had thought to get a kitten, but this cat was so funny, with huge plump white furry thighs, a sleek black cloak draped over her plump white shoulders.

Hana whispered to Lucy, "Oh, Michael's still the same. He's like a big mattress," and laughed. "Have you told him about the adoption?"

Lucy whispered back, "No, I haven't been in touch since June. What am I going to do? What should I say?"

Hana said instantly and firmly, "You don't have to say anything, you don't have to do anything. Just go on with your life and see what happens, but don't you do anything." After letting Tak pet the cat for several minutes, Hana said, "Now Tak, we have to go," and carried Tak off to the car.

Match and Fergus stayed a bit longer to admire the cat. Match said, "Put butter on her paws to make her stay at home. That's what my mother always told us." Then she took Fergus home, crying, after they pried him away from the cat. Michael and Martin resumed the gardening conversation that had gone off and on over the last several years, in which each exercised the pleasure of plant pedantry in perfect freedom. Michael recounted tales of the groves of cryptomeria he had seen in Japan—"Cryptomeria, *crypto*—'hidden,' *mera*—'fruit.' You push aside the fronds for the little fruits hidden in the green boughs, like the clitoris in a woman's fleecy venerean folds."

Martin countered with an account of his latest acquisition: "a bamboo, a chousquea coxlea, fluffy and shaggy like a flock of sheep sticking together."

"Did you know that when the Earl of Arundale opened the door to his garden for Francis Bacon, Bacon stepped in and cried out, 'Resurrection! Resurrection!'? Did you know that the first people to greet Christ when he rose from the dead were a woman and a gardener?"

"I thought the legend was that the people visiting Christ's tomb mistook him for a gardener."

When everyone had left, Michael inspected where Martin had put the tree. "I was worried that he would place it too near the house. He likes to live dangerously. As I remember, he's put his own trees so close to his house that eventually they'll uproot it." He then inspected all the other plants in her yard and started to tell her that she should turn the backyard into a moss garden, "In two years, you'll hardly have to weed at all, and then you can be like the monk gardeners in Japan, with their tiny baskets, plucking the few blades of grass so gently, ruthlessly."

Then Michael helped Lucy clear up, take down the tables and put them away, bring the chairs back in, and do the dishes. He washed and splashed water everywhere, yet never completely rinsed the suds off the clean dishes. As Lucy discreetly wiped them clean, Michael sat down and took the cat up onto his broad lap. "You can see someone took good care of her, she's so fat and silky." He laughed. "This fat cat has certainly led a different life from that of the cat in Bashō's poem:

> *Between boiled barley*
> *and romance, the female cat*
> *has grown thin."*

Lucy laughed, "That's one way to diet." She stroked the cat. "But she looks resigned to a comfortable retirement from the field. Maybe she enjoys a contemplative calm."

Michael said, "We will take good care of her now."

Lucy sat down. This "we" she heard most distinctly, but was wary. He would leave in a moment, go back home, what could that "we" mean? She discovered, at that moment, too, that she had spent so much time planning for this child alone that she didn't know if she could think about sharing the child with him.

Michael seemed embarrassed by her silence. "Perhaps you won't need some old broken-down carcass weighing you down. Just say so, and I won't intrude on your life. I'll drag myself back to my hermit crab shell."

"That you share with your wife?" Lucy forced herself to say this and found that, instead of saying it with anger or hurt or even embarrassment, she said it easily, lightly. He had his life, she had hers, the past didn't matter. She had only a future.

He said immediately, "I'm selling the Shaker house. You can't believe what I might get for it. Only half of it is mine, of course, I'll send the rest to my wife. She likes Japan. She's staying there for the time being."

Lucy held still. "I'm sorry for both of you." She asked, "But where are *you* going to live, then?"

He paused a moment, too. "I think I'll finally move next to the sea."

"You always talked about doing that." This was the comfortable tone to strike, of old friendship, of memories of conversations and intimacies in the past. Yet at the same time, the information hurt her. He would move from one big house to another house, in which he would be caught up in renovations and garden planning.

Michael's next words confirmed her thought. "I'm looking at houses down on Cape Cod. In East Sandwich, not the rich Cape or the literary Cape, but the very plain Cape, of the little gray and white houses lining the beach between salt marsh and cranberry bog and sea. I can't have the garden I used to because of the soil, so I'll have to plan carefully what plants to have, but the bogs with their reddish color and the marshes with their winding streams are like gardens. It'll be like when I was a kid, in Narbonne, watching the ships coming in and going out, real ships, working ships, because of the Cape Cod Canal. At night they're lit up, and from my bed I'll be able to see them, moving so slowly, coming in and going out."

So Michael, too, was caught up in a new life, a life without her. Still, Lucy enjoyed the picture he conjured up for her. Cranberry bogs, salt marsh, the sea! She saw the dull dark red of the berries, the green-gold hay, the green-black sea, the white sand, the lights bobbing in the distance. "I bet you'll find a way to have a large garden. I know you."

"No, no, I'm going to practice simplicity from now on, don't encourage me!" Michael laughed. "Although I have started to think about using the sea as 'borrowed scenery' to bring the sea into the garden. It means I'll have to give up my walled garden, but gardens are beautiful that fade into a desert or a woods, or an ocean, desolate and sublimely beautiful." He glanced at his watch. "It is so late. Sorry to have kept you up. Where do you want the cat to sleep?"

He was behaving with such formal courtesy that Lucy could not think of anything except his immediate question. "On my bed, eventually, I hope. But tonight let's make her a little bed near her water and rig up a temporary litter box, too." She pulled out an old sweater from the hall closet and folded it up and put it in a low wide wicker laundry basket. Michael gently laid the cat down. He began to look around for his jacket. "Well, I'm glad you stayed in Somerville. It's a lovely, funny town. Remember, on the lamppost near your old house, we once saw a sign asking about an erring parrot taped above signs for lost cats, found cats, kittens with six toes." He had his jacket in hand. He waited. Then he asked, "Oh, can I use the toilet before I go? It's a long drive home." Out of habit, he looked around the kitchen for something to read and rooted through the several magazines there until he saw a newspaper, then headed off for the bathroom. Lucy laughed, it was so like him. Then she thought, what wasn't like him was to shut the door. That shut door meant they were strangers again. Lucy sat in the kitchen looking at the new cat. She crouched down and with the tips of her fingers stroked the cat's fur, so lightly as not to disturb her. The household divinity was at last installed, Lucy said to herself, this was what the house was lacking. Was the cat still alive? Yes, yes, her round belly rose and fell, and Lucy heard these little high-pitched sighs, ladylike snores. Lucy whispered to herself, "I am old and I shall die, and the cat will die, but I won't forget until I die the touch of this fur."

Lucy stood up and went to the shelf where she kept her adoption papers. She took out the photograph of the little girl, Mariana. The white face, the high arched eyebrows, the curly cap of hair. The look that seemed to be wary of but curious about the photographer. That was the look that made Lucy love her.

What if something happened between now and the date of the trip? What if the Romanians refused to let her have the baby at the last moment, because of some bureaucratic squabble, and she and the child had to take the consequences? All over the world were people waiting, in futility, for their lives to change, for a chance to live. Lucy made herself very afraid.

She reminded herself that there were so many people she had met who had gone to China, to Russia, to Texas, and brought their girls and boys home safely. And then she remembered the child-singing dream and wanted to believe it a prophecy. That child sitting in her lap had become the child in the photo. The cat was here sleeping in the basket. She saw again their mouths rounding in perfect Os, and the celestial singing that lifted in the air, and her own voice, too, singing in perfect pitch.

Something unpleasant about that dream, yes, the man in the dream had gone cold, turned away, gone away. Lucy picked up the photo and went to the bathroom door, knocking on it hard and turning the knob.

As she turned it, Michael opened the door, and she nearly fell in on him, there with his belt unbuckled, unzipped, in one hand his newspaper. He looked at her in surprise, then put his arms around her and held her closely to him. And for a moment, it was as if the time in between when Michael had lived with her and now had never been. And yet that time had brought her this child. She pulled back a little and grinned. "I'm expecting a child."

Michael stared and then breathed out, "I didn't dare ask. When is it due?"

"Sometime in the next several months, I'm waiting for a call." Lucy laughed, then explained it all, showed him the photo. They pored over the papers, all the very few details they had about the little girl, her weight at birth, at six months, at a year, her height, that she could sit up. There was so little information, they had to trust in the photo: in those raised eyebrows, the determination of the little hands grasping so firmly the handles of her chair.

It was very late, time to go to bed. They went upstairs together. Yet as she took her clothes off and was ready to slip under the covers, Lucy said, "Oh, I forgot to lock my door." She ran downstairs through her house naked—what if the neighbors saw her running naked through the lighted house, she didn't care—locking the kitchen door, turning out the lights, the outside light still on, shining on the new ginkgo leaves fluttering in the light night wind. She locked the front door and turned off the front porch light, turned off the hall light—quickly, quickly she went through her mental list, yes, stove off, iron off—she hadn't been ironing today—lights off, everything put away, tidy—except for her study, well, it never was—and she ran lightly up the stairs. She knew her way in her own house in the dark, she knew her way to Michael in the dark.

She almost got in bed again, but "I forgot the cat." Downstairs she ran again, gathered up the sleepy cat, ran upstairs and deposited the cat on the foot of the bed, got into bed, reached over to stroke the cat, and then at last lay back down.

Michael laughed and pulled her close to warm her, pulled her close, and it was Michael, she was home, everything so familiar and yet exciting. She took a big sniff of him, lavender and musk, and began to feel him all over, his shoulders, his arms, his knees, his thighs, his ears, his balls, his long long flute, ready to be played, and with her teeth still chattering, she started talking: "It's like home, like when you come back from a long trip, things seem old and new, and you discover them all over again."

Michael reached up and gripped her shoulder, pulled her down. She resisted for a moment, just for fun, then let herself be pulled down into his arms and held so closely.

Then Michael released her a bit and with his fingers circled her breast and kissed her neck.

Lucy, dreamy, running her nails across his back, eyes half closed, said, "This makes me want to start playing the piano again."

Michael laughed, pushed apart her thighs, and lowered himself onto her. "I don't crush you, do I?" he whispered. He went into her and began to rock inside of her.

Lucy gasped—it had been so long, her cunt hurt at first—but soon it would all turn so sweet. "No, it's a good kind of crushing. I don't even care if you live somewhere else like Cape Cod. I give up, I love you." She locked her arms at his waist and pulled him deeper into her.

"No, I'm not leaving you, if you don't want me to. If I go to the Cape, you'll go if you want to go, the baby will go, the cat and my cats will go, or we'll all be here, we'll be here together, if you want me to be here. But I wanted you to know that I kept my promise. I'm sorry it took such a long time, a waste of time for all of us, it's all my fault."

Lucy lifted her head to kiss him, then said, "I'm too old to worry about it. It took the time it took, and now there is the baby, so be quiet, let's—" She opened her legs wider and pulled him to her, oh he was heaven to touch, to bear up under. Even if he went away, she was beyond worrying about it—he could come and go and come again. She was settled in one place with the baby. But she hoped he would stay and love them both.

CHAPTER 23

In March, Lucy and Caroline went to Romania to get the baby. After all the months of thinking about the baby, looking at the picture of her a hundred times a day, gathering clothes and furniture for the child, a child not with her in her womb, but a child alive, somewhere out in the world, Lucy was wheeling an empty stroller through the airports of Boston, Zurich, Bucharest. The stroller was so weirdly lightweight compared with the satisfying heaviness of a stroller with a child in it. Caroline kept telling people who looked askance at the vacant stroller that they had "checked" the baby by mistake.

The day after arriving, Lucy sat huddled together with the other adoptive parents on a couch at the orphanage, waiting while the children, in a ceremony both practical and ritual, were divested of their orphanage clothing and dressed in the clothes their new parents had brought. The children were carried out, and the pinched faces of both child and parent looked at the camera. Later, back in the apartment in Bucharest, Caroline told Lucy that her mother had studied a copy of the photo of Mariana from the orphanage and said, "Don't you think one leg is shorter than the other?" In

Bucharest, with the baby nicely weighing down that stroller and her arms, Lucy could laugh out loud. And so what if one leg had turned out to be shorter than the other? She was Lucy's child.

The baby was marked by her time in the orphanage in both difficult and wonderful ways. At fourteen months, she could not even crawl. When Lucy tried to put her down on her feet, she would hold them out straight in front of her. Yet the orphanage had kept the baby alive and had kept her soul alive. As they drove away from the orphanage, the driver turned on the radio, and loud pop music blared out. The baby pulled herself up on Lucy's lap—no car seats in Romania—and began to waggle her bottom and shake her head back and forth. She was dancing! Laughing!

Four months later, the baby could walk and sing "row, row, row your boat." Lucy bragged about her as everyone brags about their child, and she did have a lovely child, a child with fantastic golden-brown curly hair springing from her head, whose first word in English had been *cat*—the cat was almost as big as the baby when she got home, so she figured rather prominently on Mariana's horizon—which pleased Lucy to no end.

On Sunday, Michael with the baby on his shoulders and Lucy carrying Dinah the cat in her basket, walked to a local church, St. Catherine's, for a Blessing of the Pets. Lucy had tied a red bow on Dinah. They met Martin, Match, and Fergus, who had brought their goldfish in a small bowl, "our own little Caribbean." Inside the church, crowded into the pews, were dogs barking at each other, children holding their guinea pigs next to their chests, rabbits held by their parents, parakeets in cages. Some of the children brought their stuffed animals. The priest held a short service, with a brief sermon about an embassy from a church in Pittsburgh who wanted to know if St. Catherine's *really* let the animals into the church for the blessings service? Then the offertory hymn was sung, the barking became a chorus of howls, the plate was quickly passed, and at last the animals and their owners processed up the aisle to where the priest and his lay appointees stood. One of them, a local politician, smiled and scratched dogs, cats, ferrets, rabbits, and gerbils under their chins, in the Somerville equivalent of baby-kissing for votes. Each child, each adult was talked to, the animal blessed.

After the service, Michael sat under the ginkgo tree. Lucy was on the telephone with Caroline, her laughter rang out the back door. He held the baby on his lap. He had held children before, nieces and nephews, and he had always felt this violent tenderness for them, but he had restrained himself, he had told himself they weren't his children, he had to be careful, he couldn't let himself fall in love. He laughed at that—he could have let himself love them, he probably had anyway. Now, late in life, he could let himself love this child sleeping on his lap, a slight moisture on her upper lip.

He looked at the rock wall. The Shaker house was about to be sold. He had sent divorce papers to his wife. She said she would sign them. He hoped she had made her own life there, it must be easier to live life without constantly watching over a prisoner. This spring he had laid mosses next to the rock wall, laying down different kinds of mosses, some like the finest velvet in their nap, some with little green starry tufts. It would be an education in mosses, he explained to Lucy, dark black-green moss, brownish-green moss, and bright emerald-green moss, moss soft thick and silent and green, staying green, when next winter came and everything else turned brown and black or faded to pale gold.

Dinah, the cat, rolled over to air out the fur on her belly. She arched her back, and there were her many little pink teats, so pink next to the white fur. Those pink teats, that soft flap of belly—had Dinah had kittens before she came to live with them? Dinah, Michael judged, must be about three or four, she had many good years left. Still Dinah would go the way of all cats, get old and die. He and Mariana and Lucy would bury Dinah under the moss, make a Dinah shrine. He himself was old—how many years did he have left? Now that he had kept his promise, how many years could he manage to stay alive. Long enough?

Grateful acknowledgment is made to the following for permission to reprint previously published material:

Alfred A. Knopf, Inc.: excerpt from *Translations from the Chinese* by Arthur Waley. Copyright © 1947 and renewed 1969 by Alfred A. Knopf, Inc. Reprinted by permission of Alfred A. Knopf, Inc.

Laurel Rasphica Rodd: excerpt from *Kokinshū: A Collection of Poems Ancient and Modern,* by Laurel Rasphica Rodd with Catherine Henkenius. (Princeton University Press, 1984. Paperback edition: Cheng & Tsui, 1996, p. 58.) Reprinted by permission of the author.

Weatherhill, Inc.: excerpt from *A Haiku Menagerie: Living Creatures in Poems and Prints* by Stephen Addis with Fumiko and Akira Yamamoto. Reprinted by permission of the publisher, Weatherhill, Inc.

Marilyn Sides's first published short story, "The Island of the Mapmaker's Wife," was chosen by William Abrahams for the *1990 O. Henry Prize Stories*. *The Kenyon Review* honored her with an award for Best Emerging Fiction Writer in 1991. Her collection of short fiction, *The Island of the Mapmaker's Wife & Other Tales* appeared in 1996. Sides teaches literature and creative writing at Wellesley College. This is her first novel.